She slid her arms around his middle and kissed him softly on his back. "Hey lover." Her voice was barely audible over the noise of the shower and she ran her hands down the length of his back. His body was slick with water.

Tyler turned around to face her and she had to step back. His shaft was fully erect and it closed the distance between their bodies.

"Hey you." His voice was sensuous and his tone was laced with desire. He pulled her towards him. Their bodies melted together under the spray of water and Tyler ran his hands down the length of Desiree's body as if he were a blind man using Braille.

She wound her body around his before stepping back. "Let me bathe you." Her voice was husky with desire.

NEVER SAY NEVER

MICHELE CAMERON

4/5/08

Michele Cameron (signature)

Genesis Press, Inc.

INDIGO LOVE SPECTRUM

An imprint of Genesis Press, Inc.
Publishing Company

Genesis Press, Inc.
P.O. Box 101
Columbus, MS 39703

ISBN: 13 DIGIT : 978-1-58571-269-4
ISBN: 10 DIGIT : 1-58571-269-8
Manufactured in the United States of America

First Edition

Visit us at www.genesis-press.com
or call at 1-888-Indigo-1-4-0

DEDICATION

I dedicate this novel to my parents, Martha and Philip, because they taught me to reach for the stars.

ACKNOWLEDGMENTS

I want to give special thanks to my senior editor, Deborah Schumaker, and to my line editor, Sidney Rickman, for being so professional, patient, and helpful. Also, many thanks to my copyeditor, Brian Jones.

The Omega and the Alpha

CHAPTER ONE

How in the world am I going to break the news to my family? Desiree looked forward to, and at the same time dreaded, seeing them. Her fingers nervously tapped the steering wheel as she thought about how she would survive the questions she knew she would have to answer before the day was done.

Driving the familiar route of Interstate 84 from Danbury to Brewster on Labor Day weekend was not a problem. It was a trip she could accomplish without diligent attention. She manipulated the radio dial until she found 98Q, her favorite station. It played the best hits of old and new.

Chewing absently on her bottom lip, her thoughts returned to the emotional drama she had suffered during the week, which had led to the breakup of her three-year engagement to Travis.

The reality of the situation was that it did not matter that she had been the one to set the wheels in motion. What mattered was the expiration of a six-year friendship, a subsequent engagement, and the deep, cutting hurt she'd felt at the look of unconcern in Travis's eyes when she said with finality, "We're through."

She inwardly groaned at the thought of being alone again. What did women without boyfriends do for fun? As it was, Desiree had only a small group of friends, and from now on they would see her in a new light. No longer would she be considered safe. Her single friends would now view her as potential competition at social events and would watch her closely to see if she found their significant other attractive.

Did she dance too closely with their man? Did she swing her hips too provocatively when she walked across the room? Did she make an excuse to visit the ladies room at the same time that their men left the room so that they could rendezvous? She knew this would be the case, because there had been times when she could have been found guilty of the same thoughts.

The invitations to her married friends' functions would lessen now that she didn't have Travis to drag along with her. How many times over the years had she heard her sister Dominique utter the words, "Keep single women away from your man. I know that I do. It makes life so much less complicated!"

Immediately thoughts of Dominique made Desiree feel a little queasy. Dominique had never been crazy about Travis, but she had accepted the fact that Desiree loved him and wanted to marry him. Desiree had grown accustomed to the seemingly innocent remarks at family gatherings when Dominique would, a little too casually, ask her if she and Travis had set a date for the wedding. Whenever Travis was present at these times his face always remained impassive as he let Desiree do the explaining. She was always prepared ahead of time with a nonchalant reply. "First, we're trying to get established in our careers," or "Travis's job makes him travel too much," or "We're waiting until we're more financially secure."

Though breaking up with Travis had been a spur-of-the-moment decision, it was the result of past slights and small insults that she had closed her eyes to for far too long, such as the times he forgot her birthday and showed up with a card and a bottle of perfume from the drugstore later in the evening only after she had reminded him what day it was.

She couldn't forget the hurt she felt at finding out that he'd sent his mother and sister flowers on Valentine's Day when all she got was a phone call. She felt a wrench in her insides remembering how what had begun as a perfectly normal Tuesday had ended with a life-changing night.

Travis had been surprisingly candid and almost brutal in his responses to her questions when she confronted him Tuesday night. It was painfully obvious to her that he would have been content for them to meander along the way they had been: spending every Tuesday and Saturday night eating the dinner that she prepared for them at her apartment, watching BET, and then going to bed. Desiree knew the drill and automatically set her alarm clock for Travis to get up at 5:00 a.m. She would sleepily watch him dress for work, and then he would give her a quick peck on the cheek and leave. Yes, he was comfortable with their relationship; a little too comfortable, according to Desiree's best friend Natalie. She again felt queasy when she thought of Natalie. *I can get through this*, she mentally encouraged herself. She would focus on her career.

Desiree worked as a paralegal at Buchanan & Buchanan Law Firm, which was located in Danbury, Connecticut. The firm was in the process of restructuring and broadening its legal team in order to compete with the larger law firms in the area. Consequently, it was aggressively recruiting lawyers with reputations for winning big cases. Several months ago the firm was buzzing with news of the coup it had managed to pull off by adding Tyler Banks to its staff.

Tyler Banks was an example of a new breed of lawyers who rarely had to try a case. Their opponents would rather settle than let them have their day in court. From the first day he had entered the halls of Buchanan & Buchanan, the firm had been riddled with gossip.

The word was that he was divorced, but he still wore a wedding ring. Desiree had passed him several times in the hallway during the few months he had been employed at Buchanan & Buchanan and had nodded her head politely in response to his nod. If they happened to arrive at the coffee pot or water cooler at the same time, he always stepped aside and let her proceed ahead of him.

The members of Buchanan & Buchanan started their mornings with a weekly staff meeting. Usually, the presence of the firm's paralegal department was not required, but upon checking her voice mail when she got to work on that terrible Tuesday, Desiree had received a message from Arthur Buchanan, the president of the law firm, that she was expected to attend.

During her three years at the law firm, Desiree had occasionally attended other staff meetings at the request of the lawyer she was supporting; however, this was the first time she had ever received a direct request from the head honcho himself. She didn't even realize that he knew she existed.

Desiree had sat nervously at the conference table and listened as Arthur Buchanan methodically asked questions and quizzed each lawyer one by one. A few of the lawyers fidgeted when asked questions, and some of the others sat stiffly in their chairs.

Desiree was the only female in the room. Seated at the last seat of the long cherry wood conference table, a frightening thought entered her mind. Was Mr. Buchanan going to fire her? She couldn't afford to be out of work. Then she pushed those thoughts aside. *Girlfriend, you are whacked!* she thought. *You aren't so important that the big man himself would bring you here to fire you. He would just write that on some little sticky note and have the custodian leave it on the monitor of your computer.*

She inwardly chuckled at her own thoughts, and then forced herself to turn her attention back to what was being said. She thought wryly, *There might be a pop quiz on this material later.*

Tyler Banks was fielding the questions asked by Arthur Buchanan with ease. He spoke in a low, confident voice that was soothing to the ear. This was the first opportunity Desiree had had to study him in detail without appearing rude. She already knew that he stood

5

about six feet, three inches. He had a little meat on him, but not too much. Scrutinizing him now she could see that his nose looked as if at one time it had been broken, leaving a small bump on the bridge. His jet-black hair with its shock of gray at the temples brushed the nape of his neck. Wide emerald green eyes and a small cleft in his chin lent interest to his face.

Feeling Desiree's eyes on him, Tyler Banks shifted his eyes to her and held her gaze. She was embarrassed to be caught staring and dropped her eyes. *I bet he's wearing contacts.* She then quickly switched her attention to Arthur Buchanan, who was now speaking.

"I have asked Ms. Diamond to attend our staff meeting because, starting today, she is going to be Tyler Banks's personal girl Friday."

Desiree's body froze in surprise at his words. Once again, Tyler Banks's eyes met hers across the expanse of the table.

Seeing her reaction, Tyler smiled, showing a set of perfect white teeth.

"As some of you may have heard, our law firm has been asked to take on a very controversial case concerning sexual harassment in the workplace," Buchanan said. "Our client, Claire Worthy, alleges CEO Bernard Slaughter of Reynolds and Smythe fired her because she broke off a sexual relationship with him. Ever since the Clarence Thomas-Anita Hill hearings, sexual harassment in the workplace has been a very touchy subject.

"These kinds of lawsuits are rampant, and it is our job to make sure our client is taken seriously, not viewed as a conniving female trying to benefit from her own indiscretions. I have appointed Tyler Banks to handle the case. He will be handling other small cases in the interim, but the Worthy lawsuit can put us on the map with other big-time law firms."

A deafening silence descended on the room as five other lawyers shot stony looks at Tyler Banks, who appeared to be unmoved by the undercurrent of hostility.

Arthur Buchanan cleared his throat. "I feel that Tyler is the best person to represent us because he practiced law there for so many years. He knows all of the ins and outs of the system down there and as we all know, there is a lot more to winning a case than being an excellent lawyer. Winning this case could earn the firm a lot of money and establish us as one of the best law firms in New England." Buchanan coughed slightly and continued, "During the time that Ms. Diamond works with Tyler, please do not call upon her to do any legal work for you. I know how difficult it is for her to say no when it comes to her job." At this comment, Desiree gave a start of surprise. Arthur Buchanan smiled briefly in her direction. "Her workload will be full enough as it is." Closing a folder in front of him, Arthur Buchanan said with finality, "If no one has any more questions, everyone except Ms. Diamond and Mr. Banks is excused."

As all the other members of the legal team silently left the room, Buchanan turned back towards Tyler Banks. "Desiree will set up an initial meeting for you and Mrs. Worthy next week." He mused, "I think it would be a good idea for Mr. Worthy to be there also. Because of the seriousness of the allegations, we need to know how strong his commitment to their marriage is and whether or not he is going to support his wife through this ordeal."

Tyler Banks's only response was to nod his head in affirmation.

"Ms. Diamond will be working closely with you in order to make sure you have a complete history of Mrs. Worthy's social and business activities before and after her employment at Reynolds and Smythe so there won't be any surprises in court. The media will most likely try to turn this into a three-ring circus. Not much else of interest is in the headlines at this time. People are over-saturated with the antics of today's celebrities, and this case will be something the public can really sink their teeth into."

That afternoon Desiree was kneeling on the floor of the firm's library when she heard the operator's voice on the paging system. "Phone call for Ms. Desiree Diamond."

Hastily scrambling up from behind the library stacks, she placed several large law books on the cherry mahogany table before punching in the code for the operator. "This is Desiree Diamond. You have a phone call for me."

"One moment please. I'll connect you," the impersonal voice answered her.

Immediately she heard the voice of her best friend and confidant, Natalie Statum.

"Hey, girlfriend! What's up?" Natalie's warm voice seemed to be in the same room as Desiree instead of Los Angeles, California, and she felt a twinge of loneliness for the daily companionship of a black female friend who shared her hopes, dreams, and desires.

"Nothing much, except I had to go to a staff meeting this morning." Desiree's voice dropped to a conspiratorial whisper as she continued, "Being a black female paralegal seems unimportant until it's meeting time and you look around the table and say to yourself, 'Has no other black person applied for a job here? Am I a token, or am I really just that damn good!' " Natalie chuckled, and Desiree joined in.

"I know what you mean. I felt the same way back home when I went to court and defended my first client. I was the only black person in the room other than the people on trial and the bailiff." She paused. "You need to be here in California with me. After I moved to Los Angeles, I found a whole different social scene. A person of color doesn't have to feel like a nomad in the wilderness. There are all kinds of social functions where minorities can network and socialize." Natalie added, "Things are finally changing for African Americans, and L.A. is at the forefront of the movement. In L.A. people of color are making significant strides and have the opportunity to shape their lives the way they want."

"Oh yeah, tell the L.A.P.D. that!" Desiree retorted.

"Oh well, I don't count them, they're not human!" Natalie replied sarcastically. "Girl, the men, uhh hmm hmm. Last year, I went to a fundraiser for sickle cell anemia, and if I wasn't already married to Martin he might have a little problem getting me to the altar."

Desiree's voice sounded mournful. "For you to make a statement like that, life must indeed be more advantageous for African-Americans in L.A.," Desiree replied.

"Come see for yourself. Black History Month isn't too far away, and there's always a lot to do around that time."

"I might just do that. There are so few professional black men here that I've given up finding a male friend to talk to about the law. Take my firm, for example, they recently added another lawyer to our team of twelve and the only thing black about him is his hair. There isn't one African American male on staff. They won't even hire one for me to look at."

"Seriously, Desiree, come out for a visit. You know that my son hasn't seen his godmother in two years, and flying to Danbury with him is out of the question. The last time I went to visit my parents and put him on a plane Michael pitched such a fit on the plane that I was totally embarrassed. I know that Martin will gladly pay for your plane fare because he's tired of me complaining all of the time that he moved me out here where I have no family or close friends."

Natalie's husband Martin was ten years older than Natalie and a lawyer in Greensboro, where she and Desiree had attended college. Natalie had met him after a man crashed into her and totaled her Camry. Martin won the case, Natalie got a new car out of the deal, and the two had been like peanut butter and jelly on bread ever since.

Natalie had married Martin immediately after she had graduating from college and six months later they moved to California when Martin was offered a partnership in a prestigious law firm. Natalie was now pregnant with their second child.

"I'm going to take some vacation time and visit some after you have the baby. Right now it would be impossible. The firm has a big, controversial case, and I'm the designated paralegal to work on it. You may have heard of it. Claire Worthy is the client. She alleges that Bernard Slaughter, the CEO of Reynolds and Smythe, one of the Fortune 500 top ten stockbroker companies, fired her because she ended their affair."

"He probably did," Natalie dryly retorted. "Believe me, since I've been practicing law I've seen it all. This is a good thing for you, Desiree. This experience will look wonderful on a resumé for law school. Why you are wasting your time doing all the work as a paralegal when you could be the lawyer?"

"You know the reason why," Desiree responded. "The reality is that I have to save money for law school."

"I know, I know, the five year plan. I also know that your parents are more than willing to help you financially."

"They've offered, but they paid for my college and I don't want them to put out any more money for my schooling."

"Yeah, minorities got a tough break when Bush was elected into office. All of the scholarship money for minorities vanished. If I hadn't married Martin, I would be waiting to go to law school."

With a sudden change of subject, Natalie laughed, "Remember all of those fine-looking black men at school? Damn, those were the days."

"Yeah, it sure gave me a false sense of security. I was too busy having fun to realize that after graduation all of those fine good-looking men would scatter all over the country like ripped up pieces of paper. I wonder if there's a central place where they all go. Maybe like a watering hole of some sort." Desiree sighed.

"Speaking of men, how are things going with you and Travis?"

She could sense Natalie was choosing her next words carefully.

Desiree and Travis were from the same hometown. Desiree had run into him at a barbecue the summer after she graduated from A&T and they had been dating ever since.

Travis was actively pursuing a career in photography. He spent a large portion of his time in New York City in hopes of signing on as a photographer with a top-notch modeling agency. In the interim, he spent time either with Desiree at her place in Danbury or his mother's at her house in Brewster. His mother was a widow, and he had a handicapped sister that he took responsibility for.

"Things are going along pretty smoothly, but there's no change." Natalie was the one person Desiree felt she could confide in without hearing "Humph!" or "Wake up and smell the coffee, he's *never* gonna marry you!"

"I'm not trying to stick my nose in your business, Desiree, but I think that you've given the relationship enough time. You say that things are going along smoothly, but you need to be telling me and that there's progress in your relationship, that the two of you are making plans for your future. I hesitate to say this because every man is different, but they say that a man knows after six months whether or not he's going to ask his girlfriend to marry him."

"You're beginning to sound like my sister," Desiree said, a little stung by Natalie's unsolicited advice.

"They say by the third date that a man knows whether or not he wants to marry a woman." Her sister Dominique's words resounded in her head.

"Honey, you're my best friend," Natalie continued, "and I don't want to hurt you. I just don't want to see you waste your time on someone who's not worthy of you or someone who doesn't want to commit."

"Our plan is for me to continue to save money for law school. It's so expensive. Even with me saving ten percent of every paycheck we still would incur quite a bit of debt. The game plan is that we get married after he starts making more money," Desiree said defensively.

"I know all that. I just don't see why all the financial burden of law school should fall on you. Go ahead and borrow the money. If you and Travis do get married he can help you pay it back. After all, he'll be reaping all the financial benefits of you being a lawyer just as much as you will. And remember, when you do the math, two paychecks are always better than one."

Desiree was silent. This was the most advice Natalie had ever given her about her relationship with Travis.

Hoping that she hadn't offended Desiree, Natalie added softly, "I just want you to be happy. Wanting one thing out of a relationship and settling for something else is beneath you. Don't waste any more time on him if he doesn't intend to do right by you. I don't want you to wake up one morning and wonder where all the years have gone."

"I know that you're right, Natalie, but I haven't wanted to pressure Travis because of the responsibilities he has on his shoulders."

"I understand that, Desiree, and I'm not trying to push you to do anything that you don't want to do, but I think that you should find out once and for all where you and Travis stand." Natalie hesitated, then said softly, "I hope I haven't overstepped my boundaries as a friend. I would never deliberately hurt you. You know that you're the sister I never had."

"And you know that I love you as if you are one of my own sisters. I heard what you said, and you've given me a lot to think about, but I have to go now before I get fired. Then I'll have two problems on my hands," Desiree continued, only half jokingly. "You know Travis will never marry me if I don't have a job." She finished with a small chuckle in order to ease the tension brought on by their serious conversation.

"Okay, bye then. I'll talk to you later," Natalie said.

"Talk to you later, Natalie." Then Desiree added, "And thanks."

<hr>

That evening Desiree hurriedly left work, Natalie's words playing over and over in her head as she distractedly walked with her head bent deep in thought. Suddenly she collided with something rock solid and almost had the wind knocked out of her. She would have stumbled to the ground had it not been for the hands that steadied her. Looking up she gazed up at the enigmatic green eyes of Tyler Banks. *They're not contacts.* His hands felt protective as they steadied her, and she felt a jolt of excitement. Embarrassed, she broke free and, once she stepped back, she saw the smudge of her lipstick on his white shirt. "I'm so sorry," she stammered, "I've ruined your shirt."

Tyler Banks looked down at the stain, which was a perfect imprint of her full lips, and gave a crooked smile. "I wouldn't say that. If anything I think you've made it look far more attractive."

Desiree didn't know how to respond and stammered, "I would like to pay the cleaning bill for your shirt."

"I wouldn't hear of it. You bumping into me is a pleasure. This has been a good day for me."

And with a tilt of his head he strode off, leaving her to wonder what he meant as she stared at his retreating back.

Once at her apartment, she began to prepare dinner. She made a salad and covered it tightly with saran wrap to keep it fresh. Then she mixed the spaghetti sauce and left it on the stove for the seasoning to soak in. "I'll cook the noodles and heat up the garlic bread after Travis gets here," she said aloud, talking to herself.

Glancing at her watch, she saw that it was only seven o'clock. She had an hour before Travis's usual arrival time. *Natalie's right. Travis and I need to get our act together and set a date for our wedding.* Wanting everything to be perfect for their talk, she decided on a bath. Afterwards, Desiree stood in front of her bedroom mirror and assessed her naked body. She stood five feet, nine inches, but looked taller because her legs were so long. Her complexion was light honey like her mother's, and her eyes were so dark the outline of her pupils was barely visible. Her ebony black hair was shoulder length and she twisted it into a topknot that showed off the lines of her long neck.

During elementary school the kids on the playground had nicknamed her "the ostrich" because she was so gangly. Now that she was older and had filled out considerably, she thanked God that her limbs were so long. She didn't have to constantly watch her diet like so many other women.

She had rubbed on her favorite body oil, and now followed it with body lotion, then its matching perfume. Desiree took lace panties and matching bra out of her dresser drawer and slid them on.

Walking over to her closet, she searched for something that Travis had not seen a million times. She found a pair of black silk drawstring pants with a matching off-the-shoulder lace top.

"Well, I can't wear a bra with this!" She quickly rid herself of the bra before she put on the blouse and headed to the bathroom to apply some makeup. *I'll wear just a little makeup. The natural look is in. And besides, I don't want to look like I'm trying too hard.*

Desiree went back into the living room, put her on her favorite CD by Kem, placed candles on the table, and settled down to wait for Travis.

Startled awake, Desiree heard three successive taps at her apartment door. She had dropped off to sleep waiting for Travis. She continued to sit in her recliner until she heard a much louder knock.

Angrily, she looked at the clock on the wall and noted the lateness of the hour. Walking slowly over to the door she threw it open and let it bang against the wall with a loud thud. Even in her anger, Desiree noticed how good he looked. Physically, Travis personified her idea of male perfection. He was tall, slender, and black. His facial features were bold, but not intimidating. Travis's eyes were his most outstanding feature. They were an unusual light brown, and because they were combined with high cheekbones and a thick mustache framing full lips, women always looked twice whenever they saw him.

Travis's eyes widened as he took in Desiree's slightly disheveled appearance. Her eyes glittered in a way he had never seen before, and the hair that had been pinned earlier that evening in a topknot was askew with locks on one side escaping and falling past her ear.

The expression on his face became slightly apprehensive as he looked past her into the dining area and saw the burned down candle and the wine bottle floating in what had once been a bucket of ice.

Travis pushed past her into the apartment, closed the door, cleared his throat nervously and began, "I'm sorry that I'm late, Desiree. I got held up on a photo shoot." Then, hesitantly, he added, "You look like you went to a lot of trouble."

"Why didn't you call?" Desiree was so incensed her words were barely audible.

Travis calmly walked over to the sofa and sat down. "I'm sorry, Desiree. I just got so involved that I lost track of the time. You know how important this photo shoot was for me. This could be the break I need to sign on as a photographer with a top-notch modeling agency. It was my first big solo layout, and everything was clicking." Travis snapped his fingers for emphasis. "The models were responsive, the lighting was excellent. All the while I'm taking the photos I was thinking, this is it. I'm finally on my way. When we were finished, we all went out for drinks as a sort of celebration, and the next thing I knew it was after midnight. I figured that you would be kind of upset so I came straight here."

Desiree planted her body in front of Travis. Her eyes were narrowed into slits, her body was rigid with anger, and her mouth was pursed. Mentally she counted to ten in an effort to quell the angry words she wanted to hurl at him. She swallowed the lump that had risen in her throat.

At the look on Desiree's face, Travis felt the need to defend himself. "You didn't tell me that you had planned anything special. I thought tonight was going to be like every other Tuesday night we spend together."

Desiree swallowed the lump in her throat and fought back tears. "I wanted us to set a date for our wedding. We've been engaged for three years now. Don't you think it's time?"

Travis's only response to Desiree's question was a brooding silence.

"I haven't pressured you, Travis, because of your responsibilities, but I think that it's time we made some decisions. Don't you?" Her words were deceptively calm.

"Desiree, three years is not that long a time when you're talking about spending the rest of your life with someone. This is really a bad time for me to think about getting married. You know how hard it is out there for a black man to be successful. The odds are stacked against us. I need to spend all of my energy trying to become established as a photographer." He drew a deep breath, "I want to get married when the time is right." Suddenly his voice got louder. "Why are you pushing me for a commitment all of a sudden? Has Dominique been talking to you again?" He sounded exasperated, and now it was his turn to glare.

"No, Dominique has not been talking to me again." Desiree mimicked his words and voice and she pointed her index finger at him. "This is about you and your casual attitude about our relationship. This is about you and your lack of planning for our future. Did you ever stop to think that I might need you to be there for me sometime?"

Travis expelled a long sound of annoyance. Upon hearing this, Desiree picked up the wine bottle and slammed it down. She pointed her finger in his face and screamed, "I'm sick and tired of being treated like a second class citizen by you. And I'm really fed up with black men crying about how hard it is out there for them." She tapped her index finger on a spot in the middle of her chest. "It's hard out there for sisters, too, but you don't hear us whining about it all of the time. We just take care of business. What does it take for you to show me a little consideration?"

Travis's whole body stiffened. "Look, Desiree, I know that you're upset. And maybe you have a right to be, but do not talk to me like this. You're not my mother."

"I know I'm not your mother. If I were your mother, your ass would have been here on time! She's the only person you show any respect for anyhow," she screamed. "The next time you want some sex maybe you should go and get it from her."

"That's a disgusting thing to say." He paused. "Obviously you're overwrought." His voice was cold. "And I didn't know that you felt that way about my mother. What did she ever do to you to make you disrespect her so? Go ahead, while you're having your tirade you may as well diss my handicapped sister, too." He expelled another deep breath, stared her straight in the eye, and said, "Well, it's better to know now than later."

"What the hell is that supposed to mean?" she screamed. "Does this mean that you don't want to marry me? Big surprise!"

"Look at us," he shouted. "Look at this fight we're having. We're not ready to get married. Obviously we have some real issues that need to be resolved!"

Desiree stared at Travis as if seeing him for the very first time. "This is your way out," she whispered quietly. "This is just the excuse that you needed to haul ass."

"Look, Desiree, I can't marry you or anyone else," Travis declared loudly.

"Why not?" she shouted.

"I made a promise to my father, and I can't break it."

"What promise? How could you have promised him that you wouldn't marry me? He was dead before we even got together."

"I didn't promise him that I wouldn't marry you. I promised him that I would take care of my mother and sister."

"So what does that have to do with anything?"

"I can't do both."

"I don't need you to take care of me, Travis. I can pull my own weight. I always have, haven't I? But I need a partner." Her voice had quieted, but it held a warning tone.

Now Travis's voice was so low Desiree had to hold her breath in order to catch his words. "I can't be that for you, Desiree. My mom and sister are my responsibilities. I can't run out on them. They don't have anyone else. I'm the only man that they have."

"Man!" she scoffed. "You need to get a dictionary and look the word *man* up. You may be many things, Travis, but you're not a *man*."

"I know that you're mad, Desiree, so I'll overlook that. It's very simple; I can't be everything to everybody. Someone has to lose out."

"And of course that someone is me, isn't it, Travis?"

Travis's response was no response.

"If you felt this way, why did you ever get involved with me in the first place?"

Travis dropped his head, avoiding her eyes.

"You knew from first meeting me the kind of woman that I am. Why have you been wasting my time? Why do you think I've been sleeping with you for so long?" He didn't answer her. "So you've been stringing me along all of this time." Again Travis didn't answer her. "If you never intended to marry me, why did you ask me to marry you in the first place? Remember that, Travis? You asked me, not the other way around."

"I knew that you were getting tired of our relationship the way that it was. The night that I proposed, I was carried away by the wine and the atmosphere and I didn't want you to leave me and sleep with another man."

Upon hearing this, Desiree unconsciously took a step back as if the cruelty of his words could topple her.

"I temporarily forgot about my responsibilities. Then I didn't know how to take it back. I just didn't know what to do."

"You never know what to do, do you, Travis?" she mimicked, and again Travis didn't answer her. He just stared past her at some far-off place on the other side of the room. Incensed, Desiree whipped around and stormed down the hallway to her bedroom. When she returned, she held in her hand a small promise ring Travis had given her the night of their pseudo-engagement. "Now I know why you never replaced this with an engagement ring like you promised. It was never about finances. It was about honesty." Desiree threw the ring at Travis and, reflexively, he reached his hand out to catch it. He missed and it bounced off his forehead and rolled away somewhere. "I'm going to make it easy for you; I'll say the words that you aren't man enough to say."

He just stared at her.

"Travis, we're through!"

Angry and a little embarrassed at being hit in the head by a ring, Travis merely shrugged his shoulders nonchalantly.

His ready acceptance of their broken engagement enraged her even more. "Get your black ass out of my apartment and don't ever come back!"

Travis slowly stood up, adjusted his jacket, picked up the ring, and walked over to the front door and opened it. His eyes were narrowed in a way she had never seen before. "Whenever black people get angry, the first thing they do is they start calling names and talking about skin color. Obviously the only reason you've been with my black ass all these years is to prove a point. You want to prove that you're high yellow, but not color-struck, but you're no different from anyone else." He turned on his

heel walked out the door. The only sound in her apartment was that of her front door closing.

Leaning heavily against the wall, Desiree slid to the
floor in the hallway of her apartment. Somehow she
managed to drag herself to the bedroom and she sank
onto her bed. Travis had left her, and the fear of loneliness caused her body to be racked with tears into the
early morning hours.

At the end of the next day, just as Desiree was getting
ready to leave work, she heard her name being paged
over the intercom. Her heart began to leap. *Maybe it's
Travis. He's had time to think and he wants to work things
out.* She drew in a deep breath in order to quell her
pounding heart before answering the phone. "Desiree
Diamond!" she deliberately made her voice sound brisk
and businesslike.

"Hey girl, it's Darcy." Once realizing who the caller
was, Desiree immediately became guarded. She had gone
to high school with Darcy, but she never heard from her
unless she wanted something. Desiree had never hung
out with her in school because Darcy hung out with a
group of oddballs. Desiree remembered comments she
had made at social gatherings about Desiree being in the
smart class at school, and that she hadn't associated with
her in those days.

Once Desiree had started dating Travis, she often
found herself thrown into Darcy's company. Desiree
tried to stay on friendly terms with her because Darcy's
longtime boyfriend was Travis's cousin Donald.
Although Donald and Travis were related, they looked

absolutely nothing alike. Travis was tall and lean and Donald was short and fat. Desiree liked Donald. He was a really nice person and what he lacked in physical appearance he more than made up for in personality. Whenever he was around, people could count on having a good time. However, she didn't care for Darcy. She always had some gossip about someone, and usually it was downright nasty.

"Hey, Darcy, how are you doing?" Desiree's response was unenthusiastic.

"I'm just doing great," Darcy oozed over the telephone. "I'm right around the corner from you and wondered if you could meet me."

"This is kind of short notice. I'm really very busy." Desiree tried to make excuses.

"But you have to eat, don't you? Look, I'm at A Little Taste of Italy. It's right around the corner from you. I'll go ahead and order, and by the time you get here it should be about ready."

Still Desiree hesitated.

"Come on, girl." Darcy begged, "I have some really big news and I don't want to tell you over the telephone."

Finally Desiree agreed. "Okay, I'll be there in about ten minutes."

As Desiree walked the short distance to the restaurant, she wondered if Darcy had heard about her breakup with Travis and was going to pry in her business. *If she is, I'm going to really let her have it. She's been dating Donald for years and they're not engaged. That can't be it. Darcy said that she has some news, so it must be about her.*

Once Desiree entered the restaurant, she immediately spotted Darcy sitting in a booth on the other side of the room. Darcy was frantically waving her arm at Desiree, calling her over. Once Desiree reached the table, Darcy said breezily, "At first, I didn't think you saw me."

Stevie Wonder would have seen you. Desiree immediately felt remorseful at her thoughts. Darcy's happiness at seeing her seemed genuine. *If she's really trying to be nice, I shouldn't let my bad mood ruin her day, too.*

Darcy had been overweight throughout high school, and each time Desiree saw her she looked as if she had gained at least another ten pounds. Today was no different, but she seemed to have a glow.

"I ordered us calzones and diet cokes."

"That's fine," Desiree said, giving her a half smile. "Now what's your big news?"

At once Darcy held out her left hand. On it was a small diamond ring.

"Donald and I are engaged." Darcy was deliriously happy, and her face showed it.

"That's great!" Desiree replied. She was genuinely happy for Darcy. "How exciting. When's the wedding?"

"As soon as possible. Now that Donald has popped the question I want to get him to the altar as soon as possible." She quickly added, "It's not that I'm worried or anything. I know that he's not going to back out." And then she paused before adding, "He doesn't want what happened to Travis to happen to him."

Desiree was caught off guard by the sudden change of subject. "What do you mean?"

"I mean about the two of you breaking up. Travis called Donald and told him that you were trying to pressure him into marrying you, and he just isn't ready, so the two of you broke up. I'm really sorry about that."

Desiree couldn't tell from the look on her face if she was being catty or not. "The next thing I know Donald proposed. I guess he's smart enough to appreciate a good thing." Darcy leaned across the table and laid her hand consolingly on Desiree's arm. "But don't worry, Desiree. One day you'll find a man to marry you."

Desiree stiffened at the insult. "I'm not worried about finding a man to marry me, Darcy. After all, you found someone to marry you, didn't you?" Darcy's mouth fell open at Desiree's uncharacteristically harsh tone and words. "At least I can say that there's one good thing that came out of my broken engagement. Now that I don't see Travis anymore, I don't have to put up with you." She saw the waiter approaching their table with their order and, standing up from the table, she stated coldly, "I don't think I'll stay. You can eat what you ordered for me. You look as if you're eating for two anyway." With these parting words, Desiree turned on her heel and left the restaurant.

Desiree quickly walked down the sidewalk, maneuvering her slim body through the throngs of people. Once she ran out of steam, Desiree sat down at a table at a nearby café. She had no appetite, so she ordered only a diet soda. She sat watching the couple seated next to her, who were holding hands. Then she looked at another couple seated nearby. The woman was laughing uproariously at something her date said. Desiree surveyed the room and it seemed as if everyone but herself was paired off. One lone forlorn tear slid down her cheek and she didn't bother to wipe it away. *How come everyone has someone and I don't? Lord, what am I lacking that makes men not want me?*

Shaking her head in an effort to clear her thoughts, Desiree realized that she had arrived at her parents' house and was parked in the driveway. She stiffened her shoulders and forced herself to push away all of the events of the last few days.

Then she realized one of her favorite songs of all time was playing on the radio, and as she listened to the lyrics she felt for some unknown reason that things were going to get easier and brighter.

Foot in Mouth

CHAPTER TWO

As she walked slowly up the steep driveway bordered by tall elm trees, red-gold autumn leaves fluttered to the ground around Desiree's feet. She smiled when she spied her sister Dominique playing in the front yard with her five-year-old twins, Nichelle and Nicholas. The twins spotted her and ran eagerly towards her shouting, "Auntie Desiree, what took you so long to get here?"

The twins looked adorable in matching red and white overall outfits paired with white sneakers. Bending down, she embraced them with a hug. She straightened and took each one by the hand. As they bounced by her side, she walked towards her oldest sister.

Dominique was the shortest person in the Diamond family. Standing about five feet, five inches and weighing about 125 pounds, she wore her shoulder-length hair parted in the middle. Her face was always perfectly made up and she was usually dressed like a fashion model. Today, however, she was clad in sky blue Capris, a blue and white striped knit shirt, and white sneakers.

Holding out her arms, Desiree warmly returned the hug from Dominique. The twins ran off after

Dominique instructed them to go and play Frisbee together. The two sisters strolled arm and arm up the driveway to the house that had been their home and haven since childhood.

"Everyone's already here. What took you so long? Dad's been waiting until you arrived to put the hot dogs on the grill."

"Sorry I'm so late. I had some paperwork that I needed to get out of the way this morning before I could come and enjoy our annual Labor Day picnic." Desiree avoided her sister's eyes, feeling guilty about the lie she'd just told. The truth of the matter was that she had waited until the last minute to get out of bed because she had tossed and turned for half of the night wondering how to tell her family that she and Travis were through. The last thing in the world she wanted was for them to be angry with Travis or feel pity for her.

"Don't worry about it," Dominique said. "It's only three o'clock. Where's Travis? I thought that you were probably waiting for him and that had held you up," she added dryly.

"No," she stammered, avoiding Dominique's eyes. "He couldn't make it."

Abruptly changing the subject, she pointed to an old, beat-up Chevy that she had never seen before parked in the driveway.

"Whose car is that?" she asked, pointing at it.

Dominique grimaced. "Sasha's boyfriend is driving that wreck. His name is Abdul. He's a Muslim, and you should see how he's dressed," she continued, rolling her eyes. "And for that matter, you should see how *she's* dressed." Dominique paused, then added, "I don't know where she gets her ways. Mom and Dad are so normal."

Sasha was the youngest sibling of the Diamond family. Whenever Desiree thought of her sister Sasha the word *saucy* came to mind. Secretly Desiree envied her. Sasha did exactly what she pleased, regardless of what anyone else thought.

Desiree and Dominique walked onto the screened back patio and took in the familiar scene. Marcus Diamond, their father, was a tall, stately man with smooth, jet black skin, gray hair, and twinkling eyes. He stood over the barbecue pit, turning spare ribs, chicken, and hamburgers.

Staying away from the cloud of smoke that enveloped him, Desiree smiled at him and waved her hand. Smiling and waving a fork in response, he reached into the Tupperware dish and added hot dogs to the fire.

Desiree turned to her mother, Nadine Diamond. She was about five feet, nine inches in height. All of the Diamond girls had inherited their skin and hair color from their mother. Though Nadine's hair was now gray at the temples where it had once been black, she had aged gracefully and looked far younger than her sixty-two years.

Nadine Diamond smiled, showing pearl white teeth, and quickly beckoned Desiree to follow her into the house. "Can I see you in the kitchen for a minute?"

Breaking away from Dominique, Desiree trailed after her mother into the kitchen. She knew from past experience that when her mother asked to see her in the kitchen that something was up.

"What's wrong?" Desiree asked with a furrowed brow.

"Nothing really," her mother quickly responded, giving her a hug.

Desiree felt a gulp of emotion rise in her throat from the comfort of her mother's arms around her. Tears formed in her eyes but she willed them back, not wanting to upset her mother.

"I'm real glad to see you, Desiree. First of all, how's everything going?"

"Oh, just fine, Mom. I've been real busy at work, but I enjoy it."

"Good. I need you to do me a favor. Sasha has brought her boyfriend, Abdul, and I want you to make him feel at home. Dominique has hardly said two words to him since they arrived, and when I said something to her about it she said that she doesn't talk Muslim," her mother added with a note of exasperation.

At this Desiree convulsed with laughter. She had always been caught in the middle between Dominique and Sasha's squabbles. Desiree looked upon it as the punishment of the middle child.

Her mother continued, "Honestly, Desiree, someone has got to do something. Marcus Junior is in the den watching football. He asked Abdul if he wanted to join him, but he declined. He mumbled something about white people using black men's brawn to get rich. Benjamin is in the library writing a report or something.

He said that it has to be finished by tomorrow, and I can't be everywhere at once."

For as long as Desiree could remember, her mother had been the mediator in the Diamond clan. She always wanted everyone to be happy, and she was the head peacemaker when they were not.

"No problem, Mom, and don't worry about Dominique. She would never be outright rude to Abdul. She has too much class for that. She'll just ignore him, that's all."

Desiree chuckled and smiled as she re-entered the back patio and walked around to the side of the house where there was a table with four chairs. Desiree found Abdul and Sasha seated at the table playing a fierce game of cards.

Blowing a kiss at Desiree, Sasha motioned for her to sit down in the vacant seat next to Abdul. "Hey, big sister, I thought I saw you going into the house a minute ago."

Desiree reached down and hugged her sister's neck. "You did. Mom wanted to speak to me privately for a moment."

"I'll bet she did." Sasha grinned with a knowing look in the direction of Abdul. Sasha had a strong physical resemblance to Desiree, but it ended there.

Sasha had been adventurous all of her life. She was a leader, not a follower. During her adolescence their parents had been called to the principal's office on her behalf more than once because of some stunt she had engineered. In junior high school she had led a school boycott in protest of the lunch menu, and once had been caught soaping the principal's car during homecoming week. Sasha now worked as an R.N. at St. Mary's Hospital in New York City. Sasha acted the part of a white collar professional during the day, but her evenings and weekends were another story. Looking at her and Abdul, Desiree could understand Dominique's comments regarding their appearance. Abdul was dressed in a dashiki. *Where did he get that?* Desiree wondered. He had completed his outfit with a pair of well-worn jeans and leather thong sandals. He had a medium brown complexion and a large Afro that seemed to overshadow his facial features. Glancing surreptitiously at his hands, Desiree was impressed to see that his fingernails were impeccably clean; they looked as though he had just stepped out of a nail salon.

Sasha was dressed in dark green shorts that showed off the long length of her legs. They were topped by a red, black, and green tee shirt. Desiree recognized the tee shirt Sasha was wearing as a relic of their father's. The words, *Free Nelson Mandela, Free South Africa* were emblazoned across the front. She had large gold hoops in her ears and her hair was twisted up and sectioned off into little balls all over her head. *I wonder how long it took her to get her hair like that?* Desiree thought.

Sasha made introductions by airily waving her hand in the air. "This is Abdul. I met him in the Village, and he's an artist. This is my other sister, Desiree. I told you about her."

Smiling politely at Abdul, Desiree stepped forward and reached over to shake his hand. He greeted her by saying,

"*As salaam alaikum.* Peace be unto you." His voice was gruff, but his manner and expression were smooth.

"*Wa alaik salaam,* and unto you be peace." She responded. Desiree noted with satisfaction the surprise that stole over Abdul's face at her response.

"Your sister told me a lot about you, but she did not tell me that you are a sister of the Muslim faith. Maybe you can convince her to visit the mosque and join me in prayer."

Desiree quickly shook her head in denial. "I am not a Muslim. I had the pleasure of taking a world religion course while in college and I learned a few phrases, but I am not in any way knowledgeable." She paused. "It seems as if I'm at a disadvantage here. Sasha has told you about me, yet the last time we spoke, which was just last week," at this Desiree gave Sasha the long look that was so characteristic of the Diamond girls, "she neglected to tell me about you."

"Oh, I can explain that," Sasha interjected. "I've only known Abdul for a couple of weeks. Besides, I wanted to surprise all of you. Abdul cannot be described adequately by mere words. You really need to see him in order to get the full impact."

At this point Dominique arrived, placed her hands on her hips, and yelled to the twins to come and wash their hands. Hearing what Sasha said, she rolled her eyes in their direction, then walked back to the patio.

"I think the food's ready," Desiree said. "Let's go and join the others." The minute her words were out she heard her father shout, "Come and get it."

Sasha immediately dropped her cards onto the table and rose to her feet. Linking her arms with Desiree and Abdul, she declared enthusiastically, "Let's go join the others."

The barbeque started out as a joyous occasion. A long picnic table with various foods was the central focus. Marcus Diamond told everyone as they sat at the table, "Eat up. There's enough food here for an army."

As they passed around bowls of corn on the cob, potato salad, and baked beans, they filled each other in as to their activities since they had last congregated as a group.

All of the women except Sasha reached for the ribs first. She took one chicken thigh and wing from the platter that held the meat. "It's not like you to bypass barbeque ribs, Sasha." Her father eyed her slender figure. "I hope that you're not watching your weight?"

"Not really, Dad, I'm just trying to give up eating pork. It's really not good for you; maybe you should think about giving it up for health reasons also."

"Nonsense," he replied. "Nothing in this world that God created is bad for you if you have it in moderation. As a little boy, I ate grits and grease, bacon, and sausage all the time and I'm as healthy as a horse."

Sasha simply shrugged her shoulders in her good-natured way as a response to her father's statement.

Marcus Diamond looked around the table and couldn't help smiling indulgently as he took in the obviously different personalities of his children. Each time they had a family gathering, he was amazed at the uniqueness of each. Dominique, so straight-laced, reminded him of a little general. Desiree was the epitome of predictability. She knew what she wanted out of life, made a plan, and followed it to a tee; and Sasha was a chameleon. One never knew from one visit to the next what to expect from her, and today was no different from the rest. He always silently prayed on her behalf that she would mature.

Marcus Junior briefly ventured out onto the patio at half-time to prepare a plate of food for himself before excusing himself and disappearing back inside the house to finish watching his football game.

"What made you become a Muslim, Abdul?" Nadine Diamond was seated next to her husband, directly across from Sasha and her friend. She gestured to Abdul to help himself to the platter of meat in front of him. He took a piece of chicken but declined the pork ribs with an unconscious frown.

"I found too many unanswered questions in the white man's bible. My question is, if God loves us, why would he sit back and watch men of color be persecuted generation after generation? The Nation of Islam teaches us how to be self-sufficient and not slaves to a society that treats us less than the men that we are. We black men should break the ties with a white society that binds us and holds us captive. I got tired of being the white man's pawn, playing the white man's game, abiding by the white man's rules, and subjecting myself to being treated as a second class citizen at work."

"What is your occupation?" Dominique's tone was droll, and Desiree braced herself for what was to come next.

"I used to be an engineer, but now I work independently. I am the master of my own destiny," Abdul answered obligingly.

"And what do you do now?" Dominique asked.

"I'm an artist."

Upon hearing this Dominique rolled her eyes again and asked, "Do you have health insurance?"

Nadine Diamond's voice immediately broke into the conversation. "That's enough, Dominique." She gave her a silencing look.

Dominique stood, grabbed her plate of food, and said to Desiree, "Will you keep an eye on the twins for me?"

"Of course I will," Desiree mumbled.

"Good!" Dominique then said to no one in particular, but with a look that spoke volumes, "I'm going to take my husband a plate of food and eat with him in the library. He could probably use a break. Besides," she added sarcastically before stomping off into the house, "I think that he's done enough white man's work today to pay for my Mercedes and his Jag."

"Don't mind her," Sasha instructed Abdul as she watched her sister's retreating back. "She treats everyone that way. Dominique feels that anyone who has beliefs different from her own is an alien. Isn't that right, Desiree?"

Desiree didn't answer and pretended to busy herself making sure that the twins didn't turn anything over as they enthusiastically attacked their hot dogs and hamburgers.

Marcus Diamond cleared his throat. "Do you mean to tell me that you don't believe in the Bible?"

"My bible is named the Koran, and it is the guideline of all true Muslims," Abdul answered affably.

"Sasha has been raised Baptist, and we follow the King James version of the Bible. It seems as if faith would be a real problem if the two of you ever decided to get married. What faith would my grandchildren be raised in?" Marcus Diamond's eyes and voice were hard.

Aghast at the sudden turn of conversation, Sasha interrupted, "Everyone needs to chill out. Abdul and I have known each other only for a short time. There's no need for this intense conversation. We're just friends, after all."

Abdul responded as if he didn't hear Sasha. "I would not marry a woman whose religious beliefs were different from my own." His voice was quiet, yet uncompromising.

With eyes fixed on Abdul's face, Marcus asked, "What exactly are your religious beliefs, Abdul?"

"I pray to Allah five times a day, and I practice the teachings of the Koran. Allah is the higher being, and we will all be held accountable to him."

"The higher being? By that you mean God, don't you?" Marcus Diamond's voice became even more heated.

"The god that I believe in is called Allah."

At hearing this, Marcus Diamond's eyes began to bulge in his head. "Young man, if you don't believe in God, how can you believe in the Son of God, Jesus Christ?"

"The Nation of Islam does believe in Jesus. He was a prophet," Abdul responded with conviction.

"He was that and so much more. Jesus Christ is the Son of God, the only God, and one day you will rue the

39

day that you ever doubted it." Marcus Diamond's tone was stern.

At this point Nadine Diamond broke in. "I think that we should table this conversation." She now gave her husband a warning look. In an obvious attempt to change the conversation she said, "Desiree, why didn't you bring Travis with you? I so looked forward to seeing him."

"We broke up." Desiree surprised even herself when she heard the words she had blurted out.

In an effort to help her mother defuse the situation between Abdul and her father she had spoken without thinking. "We decided to go our separate ways," she ended lamely, staring down at her plate in an effort to avoid the astonished looks of Sasha and her parents.

The rest of the meal was completed with desultory conversation. The only people who seemed happy as they ate were the twins. Desiree pushed her remaining food around her plate with a fork. Sasha kept her head bent, looking as if she could slide under the table, and neither Abdul nor Marcus spoke or looked in the direction of the other person. Even Nadine Diamond didn't attempt to lighten the atmosphere.

Immediately after helping to clear off the picnic table and with an apologetic look at Desiree, Sasha hugged her and whispered in Desiree's ear, "I'll call you." Then she muttered her excuses and left with Abdul.

That evening Desiree threw horseshoes in the backyard with Marcus Junior. He was the oldest of the

Diamond siblings and the mirror image of their father. Her brother never spoke of his time in the military or of the son that he never saw. They had seen baby pictures of him, and Desiree knew that he had her brother's eyes, but the only information they had was that his name was Ahmad and the mother's name was Alexandria.

After serving time in the Persian Gulf War, Marcus Junior had gotten a job as a postman in Brewster and lived a stone's throw away from their parents. Desiree was glad that he lived so close to them because she felt secure knowing that they could count on him if they ever needed him. Her brother was an enigma. One never knew what he was thinking, and his quietness sometimes unnerved those who did not know him. But Desiree was proud of him. He was a recovered alcoholic, and had recently celebrated eight years of sobriety.

"How's the job going, Marcus?"

"Quite well, actually. I'm up for a promotion as a supervisor in the spring and I have an excellent chance of getting it. The only other person competing for the job hasn't been at the post office nearly as long as I have. He's also missed quite a few days of work and has had some complaints from customers on his route."

"I'll send up a special prayer for you, Marcus Junior. You certainly deserve a promotion. You hardly ever take a day off from work, and you're flexible. I remember last year, as a favor for your boss, you worked third shift for three months because the post office was shorthanded and no one else would do it. That should count for something."

"I sure hope so," he said. "I really want this promotion. It's a desk job, and that sure beats delivering mail. It gets mighty cold here during the winter and insufferably hot during the summer months. The air is so stagnant, it can be difficult to breathe walking block after block. I'm getting older, and I need to think about that sort of thing. Also, this job is so right for me. I was a supervisor at the post office on base while I was in the military, so I have the experience. The only reason I might not get it is because of my alcohol abuse history. Having those two DUIs certainly doesn't look good on my record."

"They can't hold that against you," she replied encouragingly. "A lot of American soldiers had a problem with alcohol after the Gulf War. You've been sober for years now, and you faithfully attend AA meetings to keep you on track. You should be fine." Desiree hadn't seen Marcus Junior this excited about anything in a long time, and she was pleased that he felt comfortable discussing his feelings with her.

Marcus Junior abruptly changed the subject. "Dad said that I missed the fireworks during dinner. Had I known it was going to be that interesting, I think that I would have forgone the game and hung outside. Leave it to Sasha to always get something going."

"You're right about that. But Mom and Dad have probably gotten upset over nothing. I don't think that Abdul will last any longer than the others," Desiree said. "By next month, he'll probably be a thing of the past and Sasha will have moved on to a new and different experiment."

"How are you doing?" Marcus Junior eyed her searchingly. She knew he must have heard about the bombshell she had dropped during the barbeque, and she loved her brother all the more for being so sensitive.

"I'm okay," she replied. "Of course, the night that Travis and I split I thought the world was coming to an end. But somehow I managed to drag myself to work the next day and the day after that. I'm coping."

"Well, beware of Dominique. Before you arrived today, I overheard her telling Benjamin that she wished Sasha would grow up, and that the two of you would find men worthy of you. She asked Benjamin if he knew of any single available men that he could introduce you guys to."

"Oh, no!" Desiree grimaced. "The last thing I need is for her to start matchmaking me with someone she approves of. Don't get me wrong, I love Benjamin to death as a brother-in-law; he's gentle, kind, and extremely tolerant, but I don't want to be paired off with one of his friends. I'm sure because of what she said he's going to rack his brain in order to try to do as she asks. You know that Dominique leads him around by the nose."

"Oh I do, do I?" Dominique had approached Desiree and Marcus Junior from behind. Neither had heard her footsteps over the clanging of the horseshoes. "That's not true. Benjamin and I argue, too, you know. He can dig his heels in and be as obstinate as the next man. A lot of disagreements are interrupted when he goes to deliver a baby. When he returns, he's so exhausted that I feel sorry for him and realize that the important things in life are family and our children. They mean more to me than anything thing else in the world. And it's about time you and Travis started thinking that way, too."

Desiree heaved a deep sigh. "I may as well tell you and get this over with. You were inside and didn't hear. Travis and I have broken off our engagement. We've decided to go our separate ways."

Dominique's mouth fell open with astonishment and she exclaimed, "You mean to tell me after all of this time he's not going to marry you?" Dominique's voice was incredulous.

Desiree flinched at her sister's words. "The break up was a mutual decision. Neither of us was happy, and we just decided not to waste each other's time anymore."

"Then good, I never really liked him anyhow." Dominique's voice was filled with satisfaction. "You need someone with more ambition. I mean, how much brain power does it take to snap pictures with a camera?" She pointedly ignored her brother's glare for her to be quiet. "The field of photography is over-saturated with a lot of broke people trying to get that one picture that will make them famous."

"Lawyers are a dime a dozen too, Dominique," Desiree quietly responded.

"But not young, black, female lawyers," she countered. "You're beautiful and smart. That alone will give you the edge over other people." Dominique continued, wagging a finger at Desiree. "Make sure that the next man you get is an asset to you and can help your career."

"The way you help Benjamin's career?" Desiree asked.

"Exactly," Dominique agreed without rancor. "All the luncheons and charity work I participate in are not just for me. They also help Benjamin with connections. A good luncheon can help him get privileges at the best hospital. But still, no matter what, there are doors closed to us. Just last week it was one thing after another. The country club we were supposed to join denied our petition for membership. Their excuse was that a relative had to put your name to the board. I know for a fact there are several members that they didn't exercise that rule for. And then to top it off, I went shopping at this jewelry store and this shop girl tried to snub me. It wasn't obvious. She just took her time wiping off the glass case with some Windex. I walked out of there, purchased a watch from the competitor across the street and went back and showed it to her. It was just like a scene out of *Pretty Woman*. Things like that make me so angry. It reminds me of when I was a little girl. Things haven't changed all that much. I seethed for days."

Dominique suddenly halted her tirade and looked squarely at Desiree, refusing to be sidetracked anymore, and said, "But we were discussing you, not me. Desiree, you need someone with more ambition than Travis. And that family of his is a nightmare. His mother is the worst leech I've ever laid my eyes on. I mean, if he had actually made it as a pro basketball player, then I could maybe see you hanging in there. But 'Loser' is his middle name." She held up one hand in the shape of an L and touched her forehead with her fingers.

"It's not Travis's fault that he lost his college basketball scholarship and had to quit school. And it's not his fault that he has to help out so much financially. You know that his sister has cerebral palsy and someone has to look out for her. One of the things I always admired most about Travis is the fact that he takes care of his mother and sister. It made me feel that if we ever had a family he would always be there for us."

"Sometimes black people don't use their heads for anything but a hat rack. They should have gotten a decent lawyer after that truck driver ran into his father and killed him. The city would still be taking care of them, and his life would be a different story. To look after your family is one thing, but to take let them use you is another."

Dominique continued, "After she became a widow his mother should have taken night classes at the local community college or something. Because of her circumstances she could have gone to college for free. That way she could have gotten a better job, and not be so dependent on other people. What was she thinking? She knew she couldn't take care of his handicapped sister on a nurse's aide's pay, didn't she?"

Dominique threw her hands up in the air. "Then when I found out that Travis bought a house, put the mortgage in his name, and moved them into it, I immediately thought to myself, 'What's left for Desiree?'"

"Well," Desiree replied quietly, "that isn't my problem anymore. They're not my problem anymore. Now I'd like to drop the subject, if you don't mind."

"Fine by me. The Saturday after Thanksgiving Benjamin and I are having a retirement party for his colleague Victor."

"No way," Desiree said, shaking her head. "Just because I'm on the market again it doesn't mean I'm going to allow you to throw anything walking on two legs my way."

"I was going to invite you anyhow. Come on, Desiree," she wheedled, "you're helping me out of a jam. I don't know of any other single females to invite. You only have to be sociable to Victor's replacement, Adam. Make him feel welcome. He's single, recently moved here from Arizona, and doesn't know anyone. Please say you'll do it."

"All right," Desiree acquiesced. It was easier to give in to Dominique than to battle with her. Besides, what did she have to lose? "But if he's a dud I'm out of there."

"Thanks." Dominique hugged her neck and kissed Marcus Junior on the cheek. "The kids are tired, so Benjamin and I are going to leave."

"Later," Marcus Junior said and kissed her back. As they watched Dominique trot happily away, her brother patted her consolingly on the shoulder.

Close Encounters of the First Kind

CHAPTER THREE

Thursday morning, Claire Worthy was seated across from Desiree at the desk in the main conference room of Buchanan & Buchanan. Tyler Banks had instructed Desiree to record details of the specific things Bernard Slaughter had done to Mrs. Worthy at work that had made her feel threatened or sexually harassed.

Tastefully dressed in a navy blue double-breasted dress with gold buttons, with her ash blonde hair pulled back from her face and secured with a chiffon bow, Claire Worthy was a beautiful woman. She had large, hazel eyes, and she wore so little makeup that she looked naturally beautiful. Her only pieces of jewelry were small diamond studs, a watch, and a wedding band. *I would have never looked at this woman and pegged her as the type to have a torrid affair with her boss for three years,* Desiree thought.

Desiree was also tastefully dressed. Anticipating the interview, she'd dressed in a black business suit. Because she wore no blouse under her jacket, she had slid a matching print scarf in the neckline. Her long black hair was pulled back from her face in a ponytail, and gold hoop earrings complimented her perfectly made up face.

The rings on her fingers were eye-catching but not gaudy. She looked professional yet comfortable.

"Would you feel more at ease if I asked Mr. Banks to be here while I ask you some questions?" Desiree asked.

"No, not really." The hesitation in Claire Worthy's voice was completely opposite to the air of confidence she exuded. "Some of the things Mr. Slaughter said and did are extremely embarrassing, and I would rather talk to a woman alone first."

"Do you mean the things while you were having the affair, or after you broke it off?" Desiree mentally kicked herself the minute the words were out of her mouth. *It's not up to me to judge this woman. My job is just to get the facts.*

Claire Worthy looked at Desiree with understanding, and her voice was low. "You can't understand how I could have had an affair with my boss for three years." She paused. "I was a very unhappy woman with very low self-esteem. Bernard Slaughter paid me attention. He flattered me and made me feel intelligent. He asked my opinion about things and acted as if he really took my opinions into consideration." Again she paused, and then her words came rushing out. "I married my husband the month after I graduated from college in Florida."

Claire Worthy avoided Desiree's eyes and stared at some unseen object on the wall. "We were happy until we moved from Florida to Danbury, where he took a job as a salesman. Everything seemed to change with the move. Our three children came one after another. We're Catholic, so Neil didn't allow me to take birth control pills. I had no friends, no family, and Neil was so busy I rarely saw him. Sometimes he slept on the couch at his office. He even kept a spare set of clothes there. His job has made for a difficult marriage. I was a stay-at-home mom until the kids were all in school full-time.

"I started looking for a job. I found that in Connecticut my degree in marine biology wasn't worth the paper it was printed on, so I applied for a secretarial position at Reynolds and Smythe. I had absolutely no experience as a secretary, but Bernard Slaughter hired me on the spot. The pay was good enough that I felt that Neil could work less and we could spend more time together. But things didn't work out that way. The train commute from Danbury to New York turned out to be longer than I thought. And then Neil got a promotion so he didn't have to travel so much, but with the promotion came more responsibility and he was home even less." Her voice broke and she said, "I was so lonely.

"Bernard Slaughter made me feel important. He sought out my company and paid me attention. Before I knew it I was sleeping with him. All along the guilt was killing me. That was not the life I had envisioned for myself. I love my husband and my children. After awhile I tried to end the affair, but I was afraid. Bernard threatened to tell Neil, so I continued to sleep with him." She paused at the look of disbelief on Desiree's face. "It's true." Her voice became emphatic. "Not only that, he said that he would not give me a recommendation to work anywhere else. And by this time Neil and I had accumulated bills that depended on my paycheck, so I had to keep working." There was a heavy silence that lingered in the air. Then she continued. "Ms. Diamond, for months he put me through hell; he made cutting remarks to me, shot down every report I sent to him, and verbally criticized me in front of others. But behind closed doors, he would have sex with me. The final straw was the most humiliating thing I've ever experienced. Bernard walked into my office, unzipped his pants, and pointed to the floor and demanded that I drop to my knees. Right then and there, I ended the affair. Then he fired me. Eventually, I told Neil. I couldn't sleep at night, and he knew that something was wrong. I had started going to confession again and I was advised by my priest to go to Neil and beg his forgiveness. I've recommitted myself to my marriage and my children."

"Did he forgive you?" Desiree gave Claire Worthy a long, probing look.

Mrs. Worthy hesitated. "Divorce is not an option for us, and Neil wants to try because of the kids, but he doesn't trust me. I need to prove to him that he can trust me, and that takes time."

As she spoke these words, Claire Worthy clasped her hands together so tightly that her knuckles turned white. Her voice trembled when she said, "I never thought that I would be someone that you read about in the newspaper, but I feel this lawsuit is something I must do. Bernard Slaughter has blacklisted me. I've gone on job interview after job interview, and the minute they called him or anyone who works at the company for a reference, I'm turned away without explanation. I would have thought that before he fired me he had humiliated me enough, but this is adding injury to insult." She stared Desiree straight in the eye. "Even though Neil makes good money, we're struggling to stay afloat because of credit card debt. Nowadays, it's virtually impossible to declare bankruptcy. I baby-sit some of the neighborhood children during the day, but that money barely makes a dent. Connecticut is an expensive place to live. I know that I'm to blame for this mess, and I take ownership of that. There's no excuse for why I am in the predicament I'm in, but now you know the reasons."

"I have no right to judge you." Desiree felt ashamed of her rash judgment of Claire Worthy. She reached over to touch Mrs. Worthy's hand.

"Ten years ago, if our positions were reversed, I would have judged you," Mrs. Worthy replied.

The rest of the interview was long, tedious, and embarrassing for Mrs. Worthy. Desiree instinctively knew that she spoke the truth. Mrs. Worthy loved her husband and her kids and wanted to go on with her life, but Mr. Slaughter had made it impossible for her to do so.

"What do you think?" Desiree stood in the doorway of Tyler's office.

Looking up from the notes Desiree had left on his desk earlier, he smiled and beckoned her into the office to sit in the leather chair opposite his desk.

"I think that you did an excellent job. Your questions were direct, and your notes are clear and concise. These are facts that I can work with."

"Do you believe her?" Desiree persisted. She had no idea why it was important to her for him to believe Mrs. Worthy. She knew from past experience that it didn't always matter what the lawyer thought. What mattered most was whether or not there was a strong enough case to win.

Surprise etched his features. "Hell, yeah! I believe her. Unfortunately, sometimes even when even the truth is on a woman's side she isn't treated fairly. Sexual harassment is never black or white. Its guidelines in the courtroom are a real gray area, and the bottom line is what the jury believes. The woman has to prove once she ended the affair that was it, and in no way did she deserve to be terminated from her job.

"The crux of the problem is the fact that Claire Worthy had the affair with Bernard Slaughter for so long. I have to prove that she ended the affair but continued to do her job well. I also have to prove that she was fired out of spite."

"It's totally unfair that he fired her. A woman is allowed to change her mind, isn't she? I mean, just because people may have been lovers at one time in their life, it doesn't mean that they shouldn't be allowed to end things without being brutalized." Desiree frowned as she had a fleeting thought of Travis. She was glad they didn't work at the same place so she didn't have to deal with the drama of seeing an ex-boyfriend every day.

"I agree, but things don't always work out the way they should in the real world. What would really cinch this case is if another victim of Mr. Slaughter was to come forward to corroborate Claire Worthy's allegations."

"What do you mean, another victim? Do you think there's a possibility of that happening?" Desiree leaned forward eagerly.

Tyler's eyes twinkled. "I don't know. Sometimes people will come out of the woodwork and corroborate stories in cases such as this. The behavior Bernard Slaughter exhibited towards Mrs. Worthy is not usually reserved for one person. For some men, sex is a power thing and any attractive woman will do. It's all about control. Whether or not anyone else has the guts to come forward is another matter. Look what happened to Anita Hill. Some people believe she made up her allegations about Judge Thomas because she was angry that he got married to a white woman."

"Mr. Banks, what do you believe?" Desiree probed questioningly.

"Please call me Tyler," he quickly corrected her. "We're going to be working together daily, and it would be tedious for me to hear you refer to me so formally. I don't think that's the reason she came forward. As a matter of fact, she didn't willingly. Someone who knew their history leaked the information to the press and she had no choice. I do believe that because of their previous relationship Ms. Hill knew that Clarence Thomas has little respect for women, and it would be a mistake for him to be in the position to vote on laws that would affect the lives of so many women. And she was right; Clarence Thomas has not voted favorably on one issue that will enhance the lives of minorities or the lives of women in general. Look at his track record since he took office. I'm positive the people in charge of the selection process knew the real facts and deliberately ignored them in order to have him chosen as a Supreme Court judge. They knew that he would vote conservatively on issues, and that's all they really cared about."

"My parents feel the same way you do." Desiree's eyes met his and she liked what she saw. "Tyler Banks, how did you end up being so open minded and sensitive to women's feelings?"

"It's simple. I think all women should be treated the way I would like to have my mother treated," he responded.

At five-fifteen Desiree was standing outside Buchanan & Buchanan. She frantically waved to a cab as it sped hurried past her and snorted a sigh of exasperation when she felt the beginning drizzle of rain. *My hair is going to be a mess*, she thought forlornly.

Tyler Banks strode out of the glass doors of the building and walked over to Desiree. "Can I give you a lift somewhere?" he offered.

"No thanks," she said, anxiously looking around. "I'm trying to hail a cab so I can pick my car up from the shop. The law of averages deems that I will be able to get the next available cab that drives down the street."

"There's no need for you to wait any longer; it would be no trouble for me to take you to pick up your car. You should have mentioned earlier that you needed a lift," he gently chided as he cupped her elbow with his hand and guided her over to where his car was parked. Leaning over he opened her car door, ushering her inside.

"Are you sure that I'm not inconveniencing you?"

"No, Desiree, you're not. I have nothing else to do this evening. What garage is fixing your car?"

"My car is at the Ford dealership on Calypso Boulevard," she replied, settling back comfortably on the sumptuous leather seats of his yellow Corvette.

She slid a sidelong look at Tyler. He was wearing an expensive suit that had to be tailor made, since it fit him like a glove. The muscles of his thighs strained against the fabric as he shifted and pressed down on the clutch of the car. *He must work out.* She had seen too many professional men with bellies from far too many lunch meetings. Tyler expertly maneuvered the car onto the street, weaving in and out of traffic. "This car seems a little bit out of character for you. Not saying that I know you all that well, of course," she added hastily.

Tyler's warm, throaty laugh filled the interior of the car. "So you think it's a little too fast for me? When I bought this car it was supposed to fill a void in my life and make me happy, but of course it didn't. I had a Mercedes, and I prefer to drive that, but my wife has that in Ridgefield, along with the house, and the kids."

She looked at him in surprise. "I didn't know that you're still married." Immediately, Desiree could have kicked herself for letting Tyler know that she had listened to the office grapevine about his personal life.

Tyler cast Desiree a knowing look and smiled good-naturedly. "I'm not any longer. I still refer to her as my wife. It's an old habit. My father is a Baptist preacher, and he reminds me every chance he gets that God doesn't recognize divorce except in cases of adultery. And that situation didn't pertain to us."

Glancing at his hand she said, "Is that why you still wear a wedding band?"

"When I joined Buchanan & Buchanan Law Firm I wasn't open to an emotional involvement with any of the staff members. I still wear my wedding band out of force of habit, even if it is on the wrong hand, not because I harbor any feelings of love for Nancy. I once thought that when I got married, it would last forever. But life doesn't always turn out to be what you want it to be."

"What happened?" Desiree inquired gently. "No, don't answer that. I really am just too nosy about other people's business. I guess it's the aspiring lawyer in me, or it's because I don't have a life of my own." She had muttered the last of her sentence only for herself, but Tyler heard her and shot her an inquisitive look.

"I don't mind answering that. We split because we are incompatible. The things that I thought were important didn't seem to matter to her and vice versa." He slid a look at Desiree. "Nancy, my ex-wife, warned me years ago that if I left the law firm in Ridgefield and joined one in New York that it would probably be the end for us. And it was. We lasted only six years after that. I wanted to practice law in the city because I wanted to do pro bono work for civil rights cases, and you don't have as much need for that in the affluent area of Ridgefield."

"I find it most surprising that she had a problem with that. Most women like to champion worthy causes."

"There was a time Nancy wasn't so hard. When I first began practicing law I was a public defender. She was pregnant with twins. They run in my family. Nancy miscarried one night and a neighbor had to take her to the emergency room. I couldn't be found because I was out looking for a witness in a drug-infested area of New York. I arrived home about one o'clock in the morning and found out what had happened. Nancy blamed New York City and me for what happened. She accused me of caring more about being viewed as a champion of lost causes than I did about being a good husband to her. After our loss, things were never the same for us. Even the words 'New York City' can anger her."

"But you had other children."

"Yes, we tried to make our marriage work. Chad is fifteen and Tiffany is eleven. I tried because I had been raised to believe that divorce was only a last recourse, and Nancy tried because she hated to admit she'd made a mistake by marrying me in the first place. Nancy and I decided go our separate ways a year and a half ago, but the marriage was over long before that. In reality, once the divorce was final it was as if a weight had been lifted off my shoulders. While married, Nancy and I argued constantly in front of the kids; I think they were as relieved as we were. She kept the house in Connecticut, and I took the penthouse in New York. The divorce was actually very civilized. We occasionally get together for special events when it affects the kids."

Not knowing what else to say, Desiree softly said, "I'm sorry."

"I'm not. Even though my life is lacking emotional involvement with a special woman, I'm happier now than I have been for years."

"Well, that explains the wedding band," she said, glancing at his hand on the steering wheel.

He glanced briefly at his right hand. "I'm not actively looking for love, but I'm willing to give it another try. I'll know when the time is right to take it off."

Even though their conversation hadn't been exactly upbeat, Desiree had enjoyed Tyler's company and she was startled to realize they had already entered the parking lot at the car dealership. Once the car stopped Desiree said, "Tyler, thank you for the lift. I really appreciate it."

"Go and check on the status of your car. I'll wait here to make sure that it's ready before I leave," he instructed.

Desiree nodded her head in assent and gave him a smile before she grabbed her purse and quickly walked into the service department.

About ten minutes later a slight quirk formed at Tyler's mouth as he watched Desiree hurry back towards his car. The drizzle had turned into an onslaught and, even though she ran with her head bent down to shield herself, he could see a petulant droop around the corners of her mouth.

Once she reached his car, he leaned over from the driver's side and pushed the door open for her. She once again sank into the comfort of the car.

"Not ready, huh?" He hid a smile at her annoyed expression.

She snorted in disgust, shoving a list at him. "They say it won't be ready for a couple of days. Supposedly," she crooked her fingers in the quote unquote mannerism, "my car needs all this work and they have to order some of the parts because they don't have them in stock. My God, my car's not that antiquated, is it?" she ended in exasperation.

"I don't know, Desiree, is it?" He smiled teasingly. "Wait here a minute." Before she could say anything, he opened his car door and ventured out into the rain, nimbly jumping over the puddles.

Desiree sat with her arms folded in Tyler's car. She enviously stared at all of the new cars for sale and amused herself fantasizing which car she would buy if she had the money.

Tyler returned ten minutes later and dangled a set of keys in front of her face. "This is a loaner from the dealership. They should have called you and explained that your car isn't ready. That would have saved you the trouble of a wasted trip, and you could have made arrangements for transportation in the interim. That's the way business is done. The car is yours to drive until yours is ready. I'll drive you to the back lot where it's parked."

Knight in Shining Armor

CHAPTER FOUR

As Desiree drove a new Ford Explorer to her apartment her thoughts were of Tyler. *He's a catch. Why, oh why, couldn't he be black?*

Later that evening, as Desiree ate her Chinese takeout, her thoughts were again of Tyler. She felt respect, and admiration, and if it hadn't been for him, she would have been forced to pay for a taxicab back and forth to work while her car was in the shop.

In the ensuing weeks, as they worked on the Worthy case, Desiree and Tyler fell into a routine that was comfortable for both of them. They usually worked together mornings, and the first one to arrive at work started the coffeepot.

They had managed to secure the conference room adjacent to the library because it was more accessible to Desiree, who was constantly looking up precedents that would be helpful to Tyler once he went to court.

He was in and out of court most afternoons, and Desiree did research and left her typewritten information on his desk before she left at the end of the day. Tyler had hired a private detective to follow Mr. Slaughter in hopes of catching him in another affair with another employee, but so far nothing had turned up.

Mrs. Worthy gave them a list of associates that she had been on cordial terms with while employed at Reynolds & Smythe, but either Desiree's numerous phone calls were not returned or the contacts denied knowledge of a relationship between Claire Worthy and Bernard Slaughter.

They'd had several meetings with Mrs. Worthy, and Desiree had squirmed uncomfortably as she listened to the sordid details of the sexual relationship between Mrs. Worthy and Mr. Slaughter and the humiliation she had suffered at his hands before her subsequent dismissal.

Tyler's face was impassive as he listened, and he scrutinized Mrs. Worthy's body language as she spoke. She commented on this to him one day before it was time to break for lunch. "It seems almost as if you watch Mrs. Worthy's mannerisms more than you pay attention to her words."

"Mentally I'm role playing as if I am a juror, and trying to gauge if Mrs. Worthy comes off innocently or as someone trying to make money off her own indiscretions."

"Really? How does she do?" Desiree asked.

"Pretty well, actually. She's an excellent witness. I wanted to save her more exposure to the media by settling out of court, but all of her associates at work have clammed up out of fear for their jobs."

"You could subpoena them."

"I could, but they would only resent it, and that would make them very hostile witnesses. Then again there could be a backlash against them at work for their participation, and I would like to hurt as few innocent people as possible. Besides, the only thing they could testify to be the truth is that they heard there was an affair, and that won't help us. We're not suing because they had an affair. That's not illegal. We're suing because of what she suffered because she ended the affair, and as far as I know there are no witnesses to the verbal and physical abuse."

"With the media coverage and all, I'm surprised his company is backing him. He's such a liability they should dump him." Desiree's facial expression showed her distaste for a company backing an employee who didn't deserve its support.

"If they fire him they would be admitting that he did something wrong and would be handing me the case without me having to do any work. Also, if they fire him and he actually beats this charge, he can then counter-sue them for wrongful termination."

"And being the rat that he is, he would sue." Desiree's eyes were snapping, and then she added hotly, "He's as guilty as sin. He should be ashamed of himself for what he's done."

Tyler burst into laughter at the indignant expression on Desiree's face. Reaching over, he touched her nose with his index finger. "Don't you worry, Desiree, we'll get him. I'm not about to let that misogynist get away with this." He strode confidently out of the room.

Desiree sat in surprise at Tyler's action. A warm feeling had stirred inside her from his touch. *I've gone too long without a man if I get that excited by casual contact.*

Friday afternoon she heard her name being paged over the intercom system and picked up the phone at the desk where she was sitting. "Desiree Diamond speaking."

"I guess now that you're working on this big case you're too busy to call your friends."

She was thrilled to hear Natalie's voice. "Natalie, it's great to hear from you. I can't believe you're calling me in the middle of the day! Your phone bill is going to be out of this world."

"I'm bored. The doctor put me on bed rest until after the baby comes."

Desiree felt immediate guilt because she hadn't been keeping in touch as she should. "Are you okay?" she asked in concern.

"Yes, it's really nothing. I was spotting, which is in fact quite common, but I'm so tired all the time. Martin said that I really need to take a hiatus from work because I'm so cranky."

Desiree laughed, "That sounds just like Martin. He really wouldn't care, though, if you never went back to work."

"I know, but I would care. I like having my own money. I think the ideal situation would be for me to work part time. I could have some play money and spend more time with my kids. I'm going to look around after the baby's born and see if there's a small firm looking for a part-time lawyer."

"That sounds like a great idea. Then you would be having the best of both worlds."

"Well, what's going on? Talk to me. Let me know what's happening in a world not full of soap operas."

Desiree hesitated before saying, "Travis and I are finished." She heard Natalie's quick gasp of astonishment over the phone.

"Oh, no, are you okay?" Now concern was etched in Natalie's voice.

"Surprisingly, I am. I think the reason that I never left Travis was because he was sort of a safety net for me. I was used to him and he was used to me. But now I've also gotten used to not having him around. I wonder if I'm a shallow person or something. I shouldn't have adjusted so easily. Of course, I haven't had time to dwell on our break-up because I've been extremely busy at work and all, but there was a time that I thought I couldn't live without Travis. For years all I thought about was marrying him and having his children. I now know that will never happen, and I'm okay with it. There are no romantic highs in my life, but there are no lows either. But I'm tired of being alone. Even though my split with Travis was fairly recent, I feel as if I've been by myself for a long time. At this time in my life I'm ready to date a custodial engineer just for the companionship."

"I know that those jobs are important, and someone has to do it, but what you need to do is find someone that you have shared interests with. The only things you and Travis have in common are that you are single and black. That isn't the blueprint for a happy marriage."

"I know you're right," Desiree agreed.

"What brought everything to a head?" Natalie questioned softly.

"The last conversation I had with you." She interrupted Natalie's next words, which were sure to be an apology asking if she had interfered too much. "You were right; I did need to find out where I stood with Travis." Then she repeated word for word the events and the drama that led to her break-up with Travis.

She waited patiently as Natalie guffawed when she repeated what she had said to Travis about his mother and the names she had called him. Once Natalie's laughter simmered down, she continued, "I do feel bad about the things I said, and I feel as if I should call him and apologize. He thinks that I hate his family and that's just not true. And you know how sensitive he is about his complexion, so what I said really hit him where it hurts."

"Don't call him. It's too soon. If you do, you might be opening yourself up to more heartache and become involved with him again. Travis has known you for six years and been engaged to you for three of them. He knows that you're not that small-minded. You were just angry, and rightfully so. Don't you dare stress yourself out about what you said. There are never any fair fights. People aren't like that. You said what you needed to say and did what you needed to do long ago. What he said to you about his complexion was just his own insecurity talking. Let him think what he likes, and you look out for yourself. For years you've been waiting for him, and now that you're free of him, staying away from him is the best thing."

"You're right," Desireè agreed sadly. "I'm just wondering if I'll ever find true love."

"You'll find true love," Natalie promised. "It will show up when you least expect it, and when it does you'll fall so hard you'll forget all this nonsense about thinking you're a shallow person. I do have to hang up because now Martin is paying all the bills, and he never understands what we find so much to talk about."

After Desiree hung up, she sat with her chin in her hand and wondered if Natalie was right. When she wasn't looking for love would it someday find her?

Friday morning Tyler asked Desiree, "What's on the agenda for today?"

"At one o'clock we have to meet the Worthys at Red Lobster for lunch. It's around the corner from Mr. Worthy's job, and it's the only time he can make it because he's leaving this afternoon on a business trip."

"Good. I have yet to meet him, and I need to see how they interact with each other."

"I know. Every time Claire Worthy and her husband are scheduled to come in she shows up alone with the excuse that he was too busy at work to get away."

"I hope he shows up this time so I can assess their relationship. It's very important that the jury see that he has forgiven his wife's indiscretions and that they want to move on with their lives but they haven't been able to because Bernard Slaughter has hindered them. Even though Neil Worthy won't be on the witness stand, the jury will study him as closely as they do anyone else."

"I'm kind of surprised that he wants to sue at all. Mrs. Worthy told me that he's the one who suggested that they get a lawyer and pursue this. I find it odd that a man would want to expose his wife, and especially his children, to this kind of gossip." Desiree mulled the situation over in her mind.

"We should be able to tell at this luncheon today whether he's asking his wife to do this because of the money or because he feels that it is the right thing to do under the circumstances."

Desiree and Tyler arrived at the restaurant at one o'clock sharp. She knew from the previous time she had ridden in the car with him to remain in her seat and wait until he came around and opened her door for her.

Quickly walking into the lobby of the restaurant, she saw Claire Worthy looking around anxiously as if she were searching for someone. When she saw them she waved them over. "Neil isn't here yet. He left a message with the hostess that he was running late, and for us to get a table. He said he would be here as soon as possible."

Desiree immediately looked at Tyler and saw his mouth tighten in the way she had come to recognize as an indication that he was annoyed.

Once seated in the non-smoking section of the restaurant, Tyler ordered a bottle of white wine and they nibbled on bread as they bided their time waiting for Neil Worthy.

After about fifteen minutes, the waiter reappeared for the second time and asked if they were ready to order. Curtly nodding his head in agreement, Tyler signaled for Mrs. Worthy to tell the waiter what she wanted for lunch. They each ordered and the waiter left.

Neil Worthy casually walked into Red Lobster just at the time the waiter was bringing out their food. He was an ordinary-looking brown-haired man of medium height. A protruding belly pulled at the buttons of his shirt. After offering Tyler his hand to shake, he gave his wife a slight peck on the cheek, and then slid into the booth next to Desiree without acknowledging her presence.

Neil Worthy apologized. "Sorry I'm late. I'm completely swamped at work."

Claire Worthy nervously said, "I ordered shrimp pasta for you."

"Whatever," he replied with a flip of his wrist.

Then he reached in his pocket and withdrew a gold-plated cigarette case. Until then Tyler had been quiet, but noticing Mr. Worthy's action he stated, "You can't light that here. We're seated in the non-smoking section."

Mr. Worthy put it away and abruptly asked Tyler, "Was there a specific reason you wanted to meet with me?"

Desiree fumed. *We've been sitting here cooling our jets for forty-five minutes and he acts as if he's doing us a favor by showing up.*

Tyler's eyes glinted angrily in a way she had never seen before. He was silent for a long minute and then he began to speak directly to Mr. Worthy, outlining the strategy he intended to pursue once inside the court-room. While they talked, Claire Worthy and Desiree silently ate their meal.

"Our court date is set for the third week in February," Tyler added dryly. "I understand that you're a busy person, but I need you in court every day to show the jury a united front."

Leaning forward, Neil Worthy eagerly asked, "How much money do you think we'll get?"

"As you know, we're suing for ten million dollars. I doubt that we'll get that, but it's better to start high. So far they haven't offered a dime for an out of court settle-ment, but I'm hopeful." He paused, and then added, "Can I count on you to be in court every day?"

"Anything to support my wife," Neil replied smoothly.

Tyler filled Mr. Worthy in on things that the jury would be looking for, the behavior, mannerisms, and facial expressions he expected him to exhibit during the trial.

As Desiree finished eating her lunch, she felt a foot lightly bump against her ankle underneath the table. Knowing at once that it was the deliberate action of Neil Worthy, she moved farther over to her side of the booth.

Several times during their meeting, she felt Neil Worthy's eyes on her. Towards the end of lunch Mr. Worthy continued to eat with his right hand; then dropped his left hand casually under the table and began sliding it up the length of Desiree's thigh. Angry at the unwanted attention, Desiree placed her fork on the edge of her plate, stood up, grabbed her purse, and felt the knowing eyes of Tyler and Claire Worthy. Muttering "Excuse me," Desiree escaped into the ladies' room.

Once inside the bathroom she exclaimed to the empty room, "This is just what I need. Lunch with an octopus!" This wasn't the first time she'd found herself in an uncomfortable position, and unfortunately she was pretty sure it wouldn't be her last. Desiree hid inside the bathroom for a few minutes before she realized that it was ridiculous. She couldn't stay in there forever. Walking over to the sink, she washed her hands, drew in a deep breath, and then went to rejoin the others.

When she reached the table, Tyler signaled to the waiter to bring the check. Not bothering to reclaim her seat, Desiree stood next to him as he signed the check, stared directly at Claire Worthy, and said in a gruff voice, "I think I've found out all I need to know at this time. Ms. Diamond will call you with any pertinent information about the case."

⁓⊘

As Desiree was tidying her desk before she left for the day, she looked up to find Tyler watching her intently. His mouth was set and his features were grim.

"Because of what happened at lunch today, I will understand if you don't want to be the paralegal on the Worthy case any longer."

Desiree immediately knew that Tyler was addressing Neil Worthy's lecherous behavior. "Do you think it was my fault, that I did something to make Mr. Worthy feel that he could take liberties with me?" Desiree felt a small knot in the pit of her stomach at that thought.

In spite of the gravity of the situation, Tyler smiled at Desiree's old-fashioned description of Neil Worthy's behavior. "Of course not, Desiree. You're a beautiful woman. And unfortunately, in this world, some men don't know how to behave around one," he responded quietly.

Desiree gave a start of surprise at Tyler's words. She dropped her eyes and, nonplussed, began nervously moving things around on her desk.

Tyler continued, "Men like Neil Worthy have no respect for boundaries. I would hate to lose you, but I don't want to subject you to an uncomfortable situation. You've already laid the groundwork and completed a size-able amount of work. Your notes are excellent, and another paralegal should be able to pick up from where you left off."

Desiree looked at Tyler closely. "That's not the first time I've been subjected to unwanted advances, but this is the first time that I was so crudely manhandled in a work-related situation. If it were any other situation I would have known what to do, what to say, but I was completely caught off balance." She hesitated and eyed Tyler search-ingly, then shrugged her shoulders. "What do you think I should have done? Made a scene or something?"

"I don't think you making a scene would have done any good. Claire Worthy would have been even more embarrassed if she had been confronted with his behavior. It's obvious that Mrs. Worthy knows the kind of person her husband is, and she's made her choice to stay with him. Now I have a clearer picture of why she was so vulnerable to Bernard Slaughter. Their marriage is in trouble. All of the previous meetings Mr. Worthy canceled at the last moment made me suspicious of him, but his actions and conversation today confirmed it. He's in it only for the money."

"She ought to divorce him before she gets a settlement." She paused, giving Tyler a sideways look. "I guess you think that's pretty mercenary of me."

"Actually no, I was thinking the same thing after lunch. But she won't. For whatever reason, I think she feels that this is her lot in life, and she's accepted it as such. So what's your verdict? Are you going or are you staying? It's entirely your decision."

Desiree didn't know why, but she felt that if she didn't stay on the Worthy case it would be a great loss to her.

"I'm staying." Desiree saw something that looked like an expression of relief flash across Tyler's face. "I probably won't be having a lot of contact with Mr. Worthy anyway, and if I do, I'll make sure that I'm not alone with him or seated near him under any circumstances."

"Good," he said, "I was hoping you would say that."

Later that night, Desiree lay in bed thumbing through her latest issues of *Cosmo* and *Ebony* as she thought about her day. As the conversation with Tyler replayed in her mind, she felt something warm curl inside her loins. *He said I'm a beautiful woman,* she thought. Then she mentally chided herself. He was probably just being nice. *Am I so unused to compliments that I make a mountain out of a molehill when I actually do get one?*

The following Thursday morning Desiree was running late to work and practically bumped into Neil Worthy as he exited the elevator.

Her body automatically stiffened at the sight of him, but he only gave her a curt nod of his head as he hurriedly left the building.

When she joined Tyler in the conference room he was pouring himself a cup of coffee. She always grimaced when she saw him gulp it down without cream or sugar.

"Good morning." He smiled broadly, showing even, white teeth.

"Good morning," she responded. "You know, I just saw Neil Worthy leaving the building. What's he doing here? We didn't have an appointment this morning, did we?" she finished in a puzzled voice.

"Did he say anything to you?" Tyler's eyes searched Desiree's face.

"No, he didn't. And that was a pleasant surprise after his behavior at lunch. He barely looked my way."

"Good, that's how I expect someone being represented by Buchanan & Buchanan to behave."

"What did you do?" Desiree demanded, putting her hands on her hips and scrutinizing Tyler. "I called him last night and asked him to come in because I needed to talk to him alone. I informed him that if he exhibited any more behavior such as what he displayed at lunch last week towards you, or any other employee at Buchanan & Buchanan, he and his wife could get another lawyer. I also warned him that he needs to watch himself or one day he might find himself needing a lawyer to defend his actions, and I might be his opponent."

Desiree shyly smiled at Tyler and teased him, "Be careful, Tyler, you're quickly turning into my knight in shining armor."

A couple of weeks before Thanksgiving, Desiree stood in front of her closet scanning the clothes that she had hung neatly on hangers. "I have absolutely nothing to wear that Dominique and her friends haven't seen before. I need to go shopping!" she exclaimed in disgust.

That afternoon, as she pushed her way through the throng of people in downtown Danbury, Desiree didn't relish the thought of spending a lot of money on a dress to wear to a party that she didn't exactly want to attend. She knew that the people Dominique usually had as guests to her shindigs were usually dressed to the nines. Purchasing a new dress was a necessity, because she didn't want to embarrass herself by looking like a poor stepchild in front of her sister or friends.

After several hours browsing stores, Desiree began to lose hope of finding something she wanted that she could afford. Then she stopped in front of the window of Saxon's Specialty Store.

The mannequin in the window had on a royal blue dress that fell to the ankles. The dress had a straight skirt with a split that slid above the knee on one side. The waist was cinched with a gold belt and the sleeves were sheer. Excitedly she went inside. *Oh God, please let me be able to afford it,* she prayed as she entered the store.

Immediately a small gray-haired woman approached her. "May I help you?" Her smile was genuine and Desiree mentally crossed her fingers.

"I'm interested in the blue dress the mannequin in the window is wearing."

"Oh dear, that's the only one we have. But if you can wear a size six I would be more than happy to get it for you."

Desiree eagerly replied, "That's my size. How much does it cost?"

"The dress was originally three hundred and fifty dollars." On hearing Desiree's gasp, the saleswoman quickly added, "But we're having a half-price sale because this is a part of last year's fashion line."

A few minutes later, Desiree eyed herself in the dressing room mirror. With the dress on, she felt beautiful and seductive. *I wish I had someone special to wear this for. Maybe I'll actually meet someone at Dominique's party.*

The next week was an extremely hectic one because everyone was trying to accomplish five days of work in the three days before they broke for the Thanksgiving holidays. Tyler was in and out the office and Desiree was constantly buried in the library stacks either looking up precedents or typing notes to leave on Tyler's desk.

Desiree had begun to bring her lunch to work and usually ate alone rather than venturing into the lounge, where most of the other secretaries and paralegals ate, constantly complaining with every bite.

She had sensed a distance from some of the single paralegals since she had been designated to work with Tyler, but she had been much too busy to let it bother her.

Desiree had just finished eating when Tyler entered. She looked in surprise at his briefcase and jacket.

"I'm leaving early today. Chad and Tiffany are spending the holidays with me, and I have to go and pick them up from their mother's house in Ridgefield."

"That sounds nice. Do you have anything special planned for them?"

"I won't be cooking, so we'll eat out Thanksgiving Day. I purchased tickets for Barnum and Bailey's Circus on Friday evening. I know Chad will be bored with that, but I'll let him decide what we're going to do on Saturday and that should appease him. What are your plans?"

"I'm going to my parents' house Thanksgiving morning, and I'll spend Friday there also. But on Saturday night my sister is having a party for a friend of her husband's and I'll be attending that."

"Well, have a good time and try not to break too many hearts." Tyler turned on his heel and left the room.

Later that evening, Desiree was sitting in front of her television set watching the news and waiting for her nails to dry when her phone rang.

"Hello."

There was a brief pause. "Hello, Desiree, this is Tyler. I hope that you don't think it's presumptuous of me to call you at home."

"No, that's quite all right. Is something wrong?" There was another long pause. Desiree had never known Tyler to struggle for words, and she instinctively knew that he was upset. "My plans fell through with the kids. Tiffany has the chicken pox, so she couldn't come this weekend."

"Oh, no, I'm sorry to hear that. The itching is horrific." She hesitated before asking, "What about Chad? You're still going to be seeing him, aren't you?"

"No, he's never had the chicken pox so Nancy sent him to stay at a friend's house while Tiffany's contagious, and then he was out with that friend so she couldn't reach him to tell him to come home so I could pick him up. I guess they were somewhere hanging out. I'm kind of at loose ends, and I know that it's the last minute, but would you like to have dinner with me tonight?" Tyler sounded depressed. It was obvious that he loved his kids and was upset that he wouldn't be spending time with them for the holidays. But she was caught off guard at his invitation. *Oh my God! What is he asking me? A lunch with a colleague is one thing, but I can't go out on a date with him. Someone might see us and get the wrong idea. I like Tyler and enjoy his company, but he's my boss. No,* she thought, *he's not my boss. He's become sort of a friend, but he's really not my friend because he's sort of over me. Well, he's not over me and I'm not under him. Whatever he is, I know that I can't go out with him.* Desiree felt flustered. Her thoughts scattered, she realized that Tyler was waiting for a reply. She felt sorry for him, but fear instantly clutched at her heart at the suggestion that they spend time together after hours. Desiree stammered her refusal, "I'm sorry, Tyler, but I can't. My nails are wet, and I still have to pack to leave for my parents' house in the morning."

"Oh, I understand completely. I'm sorry to have bothered you at home. Good night," he paused, "and drive safely." Even though he abruptly hung up the phone, he seemed to have accepted her flimsy excuses as to why she couldn't have dinner without rancor.

Seeing is not Believing

CHAPTER FIVE

Thanksgiving Day at the Diamond house was uneventful in comparison to the Labor Day barbecue. When Desiree arrived at twelve o'clock, Dominique and her family were already there. She was helping their mother put the finishing touches on everything.

Their mother traditionally stayed up late the night before Thanksgiving baking pies and cakes. She'd put the turkey in the oven to bake that morning. She had already prepared most of the other dishes and the only thing left to prepare were the yams and mashed potatoes. Desiree volunteered to make the yams and left the latter for Sasha to do when she arrived.

Sasha arrived an hour later, and Desiree was somewhat relieved to see that she was alone. On her arrival, Sasha gave each of them a kiss on the cheek. It was obvious that she felt guilty about causing confusion the last time they had gathered as a group and was trying to make amends. Once Dominique realized Sasha had not brought Abdul, she cast her eyes towards the heavens and mouthed so that only Desiree and her mother could hear, "Thank you, God, for answering my prayers." Sasha immediately sat down at the kitchen table and began peeling potatoes. Dominique took this as a favorable sign and pounced on her. "Are you coming to the party on Saturday night?" she asked.

"No way, Jose!" Sasha quipped.

Even Dominique had to laugh at the old familiar cliché they had frequently used as children. She gave in easily and turned to Desiree.

"You're still coming, aren't you, Desiree?" Dominique asked.

"Yes, Dominique." She dragged out her response as if she were a person being forced to walk the plank. Her voice turned into a whine. "I don't see why I have to come and Sasha doesn't."

Sasha cut into the conversation. "Dominique doesn't pressure me into coming because she's afraid of what might happen if I do. She only asks me because I'm her sister." Dominique looked a little shamefaced by the accuracy of Sasha's statement, and seeing this Sasha continued, "Don't feel bad about that. I know that you love me. We're just different, that's all." Looking at Desiree she said, "Dominique loves showing you off, and she knows that you won't embarrass her. She also knows that you don't stand up for yourself. That's why she always barrages you until you give in. You are so malleable."

"That's not a very flattering opinion you have of me," Desiree retorted, stung by Sasha's assessment of her character.

"Don't worry about it. I have hope for you yet. One day something is going to matter so much to you, you're going to do exactly what you think and to hell with anyone who doesn't like it!"

"Watch your language," Nadine Diamond piped in, eyeing Sasha. "This is still a Christian household, even if once in a while you decide to veer off course." All of them were seated at the kitchen table, and Desiree and Dominique smirked from behind their hands at each other because of their mother's statement. Upon hearing obvious reference to Abdul's religious beliefs, Sasha fell silent.

Dinner was a feast: mashed potatoes, cranberry sauce, green beans, collard greens, sweet potato pie, pound cake, and, of course, turkey and dressing. Family camaraderie was at an all time high, and even the usually quiet Marcus cracked jokes and told amusing anecdotes about delivering mail and some of the unusual customers he had on his mail route. Suddenly thoughts of Tyler being alone on Thanksgiving entered Desiree's mind. *I wonder what he's having for dinner. I can't believe I'm worried about him. After he hung up with me he probably called someone else. A man like Tyler Banks never has to be alone.*

After dinner the men retreated into the den to watch football while the women cleaned up the dishes and wrapped up the food that would be eaten for days until it was gone.

"How is it that the men sit on their butts all day while we do all of the work? They were in the den watching football when I arrived and immediately after dinner was over they marched back there to do what? Relax? Relax from what?" Sasha complained.

"Okay, Ms. Women's Libber. You didn't exactly break out in a sweat yourself. All you did was peel some potatoes. Mom did the majority of the work," Dominique said.

"I purposely arrive late because it irritates me to see Mom work like a dog every Thanksgiving. She's trained all the men in her life to expect this kind of treatment, even the ones that marry into the family."

Dominique knew that was a reference to Benjamin and replied, "Benjamin hardly ever has a chance to relax. He rarely gets a day off, so I don't want him to help in the kitchen."

"I love Benjamin to death, but him working all of those hours doesn't help me out with my bills, so I guess I'll let you do his part." Sasha threw the dishcloth she had been using on the counter and took the twins outside to play.

Desiree placed her hands on her hips and said, "That leaves even more work for us." She watched from the window as the twins kicked leaves. Dominique also placed her hands on her hips in the familiar Diamond mannerism, watched the scene and snorted, "Humph!"

Nadine Diamond patted both girls on the shoulder. "Well, at least she's keeping the twins occupied."

Saturday morning Desiree sat with her mother enjoying a cup of coffee. Sasha had left the previous evening after playing with the twins. She had plans in the city. No one had ventured to ask her if they were with Abdul.

Dominique and her family had also left early that morning to return home in order to prepare for the party that evening.

"Are you okay, Desiree?" Nadine's gentle voice broke the silence.

"Sure, Mom, I'm fine. Why do you ask?"

"You've been awfully quiet. At times I look at your face and you seem deep in thought." Nadine Diamond's eyes searched her daughter's face.

Desiree's response was brief. "Everything's fine, Mom."

"I don't mean to pry, but how are you handling your break-up with Travis?"

Desiree gave a start of surprise at the mention of his name. "I'm good. Believe me, I don't miss Travis half as much as I thought I would." Thoughts of Tyler crept into her mind, but she pushed them away.

Her mother looked at her and said, "I worry about you being on your own in Danbury. At least when you were seeing Travis I felt comfort in knowing that someone was around to look out for you."

"Mom, I mean this from the bottom of my heart. You and Daddy don't have to worry about me. Travis is the furthest thing from my mind."

Mrs. Diamond looked deeply into her daughter's eyes and immediately felt at ease.

Dominique's party was handled with her usual style and elegance. Throughout the house cherry wood furniture was complemented by wheat walls and carpet. Accent pieces of cherry wood and brass hung on walls and tasteful pictures African American art was hung in every room.

Soft music was played by a deejay who was set up inconspicuously in one corner of the room, and several couples swayed to the music in the space that had been cleared in the middle of the room.

At the far end of the living room the wet bar was being hosted by a bartender hired for the evening. Perpendicular to the wet bar was a long buffet table crowded with hors d'oeuvres. In the center of the table was a large white sheet cake. *Happy Retirement Victor- We'll Miss You!*

Suddenly, a tall black man walked towards Desiree, extending his hand. She automatically looked at his left one and saw that it was completely unadorned by jewelry.

"You must be Desiree Diamond. You're every bit as beautiful as Benjamin described you." His smile was beautiful, and he had a big dimple in his right cheek.

Shaking his hand she replied, "I'm Desiree, and thank you very much for the compliment. However, I feel at a disadvantage. I don't have the pleasure of knowing your name."

"My name is Adam Westlake. I've just joined the neurological staff at Yale New Haven Hospital."

"Oh," she said, eyeing the gorgeous man standing in front of her. "You must be Victor's replacement."

"You give me far too much praise," he replied humbly. "I don't think that I could ever replace Victor.

After observing him in the short time I've been at the hospital, I can only hope that I can fill half the void he leaves with his retirement."

His manners and conversation impressed Desiree. Thank goodness, he wasn't a braggart. She had come in contact with far too many professional men who constantly tooted their own horns. It was a real turn off.

There was admiration in Adam's face as he took in Desiree's appearance. The blue dress she had purchased at Saxon's fit her as if it were a second skin. Her hair was feathered back from her face and hung smoothly down to reach the small of her back. Her face was lightly made up, and she had taken extra pains to accent her eyes with different hues of blue eye shadow to complement her dress.

The admiration she saw in Adam Westlake's eyes was reflected in her own as she took him in. He was truly a commanding presence. He was several inches taller than Desiree's six feet, two inches height in her spike heels. His skin was a smooth cocoa brown offset by a pair of round eyes, short curly black hair, and a thick mustache.

"I must say, I expected you to be older." She studied him through long eyelashes.

"Why, because I'm a doctor?" He had a wry look on his face.

"Yes," she replied bluntly.

"I started school at four and went straight through to medical school, never taking time off, even for good behavior. That makes me all of thirty-five, and that's not exactly a babe in arms," he added with a smile. He was obviously flirting with her as he held her eyes with his.

She smiled a response. She was going to have to congratulate Dominique. Her matchmaking attempts might have finally hit pay dirt. This man was personable, and he seemed on the fast track for success.

"I was beginning to get worried. Practically everyone here is coupled off. It can be really awkward being the odd person out at a party." Adam made an over-exaggerated shudder of distaste.

Desiree laughed at his mannerism. "I totally agree. And because of that, if Dominique weren't my sister, I wouldn't be here," she added, tapping her chest with her index finger.

Adam imitated her, tapping his index finger to his chest. "If Benjamin weren't my business associate, and if it wasn't a retirement party for Victor, I wouldn't be here. But I must say, your sister really knows how to throw a party." Adam surveyed the room, obviously impressed by the festivities.

Desiree glanced around and noticed how quickly the room had become crowded. The party was in full swing, and people walked from the living room out the French doors to the garden, braving the brisk autumn air.

People were laughing and greeting each other and Desiree recognized many of the guests as business acquaintances of Benjamin's or fellow charity drive co-workers of Dominique. There were two other single people that she knew at the party. Nathan was a doctor at Mt. Sinai, a rival hospital of Benjamin's. He and Benjamin had a mutual respect for each other and occasionally played golf together and had had a friendly rivalry going for years. Desiree had been introduced to him several times, and every time he said that he was going to call her and take her out to dinner, but he never did. One time Desiree had causally asked Benjamin about him and he had replied he hadn't seen Nathan in a while, but had heard that he was working full time at Saint Anne's Hospital and was also volunteering his services at a free clinic.

The other person she recognized was Susanna, one of Dominique's sorority sisters. She was a nurse and could be counted on to attend any party where a single doctor could be found. She had latched on to Nathan and had him cornered on the other side of the room. Nathan's eyes met Desiree's across the room and Susanna looked around to see what had drawn his attention away from her. On seeing Desiree, Susanna turned back towards Nathan, slid her hand possessively in his and drew him onto the dance floor. She wrapped her body around his to Luther's soulful voice.

Desiree nodded her head at the dancing couple. "They're single," she told Adam.

"They also seem occupied." Adam's tone was droll. He again had a wry expression on his face. "They didn't know we were coming, or else they would have waited before hooking up."

At this comment, Desiree hid a grin behind her hand. She liked his sense of humor.

"There's a lot to be said about taking your time at parties," he continued. "Wait until all the guests arrive, and then make your choice as to who you want to spend your time with."

Desiree agreed. "You're right." She smiled at Nathan as his eyes met hers. His head lay on top of Susanna's as they slow danced.

Turning her attention back to Adam, she smiled at him. "So do you enjoy living in Connecticut?" she queried.

"I do. It is a beautiful state. The green grass and the change of seasons are phenomenal. Children could grow up playing every sport imaginable here. It's such a nice change from dry, dusty Arizona."

"Wait until winter comes," she said with an exaggerated shudder. "They can be wicked."

"So I've heard, but I've come well prepared. I've already purchased a long wool overcoat and a pair of leather gloves. I don't want to be caught unprepared." They lapsed into a companionable silence.

"Would you like to dance?" His eyes were intense as he admired her.

Desiree agreed and they joined several couples as they swayed to the music. "Luther seems to be getting a lot of mileage tonight," Desiree murmured from the cocoon of Adam's arms.

"I know. He's sorely missed. No other singer can rival his voice. His passing was a great loss." Adam held her close to him, but not so close that she felt uncomfortable. Adam hummed softly in her ear. "I don't want to sound like a cliché, but I can't help agreeing with Luther, here and now is all that's important."

They moved sinuously to the music and Desiree felt heat in her stomach, and with that, hope. It had been too long since she had been intimate with a man.

She looked over Adam's shoulder and encountered the criticizing look of Mildred Brown. An inexplicable feeling of apprehension made Desiree shiver and Adam looked questioningly at her. "What's the matter?"

"Oh, nothing," she said, "a ghost just walked over my grave, that's all."

"You're cute," he said, recognizing the adage. He gathered her close again. "You know, Desiree," Adam murmured softly in her ear, "I really could use a tour guide. It's hard trying to learn a new city and not really worth the effort to do it alone. How would you feel about taking some time off from the host of admirers you must have and helping a lonely bachelor learn his way around?"

"I think that can be arranged, Mr. Westlake." Desiree's response was low and throaty and he drew her even closer in order to catch her words.

"Call me Adam," he whispered as they moved slowly.

Desiree opened her eyes at a feeling that she was being watched and again met Mildred's gaze. She closed her eyes in an effort to black out Mildred's stare.

Mildred was chairwoman of one of the charity organizations to which Dominique belonged. Desiree knew there had been an undercurrent of antagonism between the two ever since high school when Dominique had beaten her out of the position of color guard captain. Mildred's husband Richard worked at the same hospital as Benjamin and they had been friends ever since they had interned together at Harvard, so for Benjamin's sake, Dominique put up with her.

After they had danced consecutively to several songs, Adam lightly propelled Desiree over to the buffet table by placing his hand in the small of her back and they joined the line of people. Leaning towards her he said, "I haven't had a bite to eat since lunch."

"I could use a bite myself," Desiree agreed. She placed a few boiled shrimp on a platter and added a scoop of pâté and crackers and cheese.

Adam followed her around the table, filling his plate with a sample of everything that was offered: salmon croquets, crackers with pâté, chicken wings, meatballs, and shrimp cocktail. At Desiree's sidelong look at the amount of food he seemed willing to devour, he grinned at her and said, "I'm a bachelor. It's expected."

She laughed because she knew that it was true. If a woman had put that amount of food on her plate it would have been considered tacky. They sat down next to several other couples seated in chairs lined up against the wall on one side of the room.

"How are you enjoying yourself, young man?"

Desiree recognized the booming voice of man who spoke. It was Peter Finch, one of Benjamin's coworkers. He had been at Yale New Haven Hospital for more than a decade.

"I'm enjoying myself immensely, sir," Adam said, smiling at Desiree.

Peter Finch's wife Bernice was seated next to him, and she smiled pleasantly at Desiree when she and Adam joined them. "I haven't seen you in a while, Desiree. What have you been doing with yourself?"

"I'm employed as a paralegal in Danbury, trying to save enough money to go to law school."

"That must be interesting work."

"I enjoy my job," Desiree agreed. "I believe the experience will be invaluable to me later."

Peter Finch piped in, "I'm sure it would be if you needed it. With your looks you don't need to work. Find yourself a good man to take care of you. My Bernice did, and it's the best decision she ever made."

Bernice shot him a look of annoyance. "That's debatable. I dropped a very promising acting career to move to New Haven with you."

"Oh honey, you still get to do those community theater activities with teenagers every summer."

"That's a far cry from Broadway," his wife retorted.

Desiree tactfully decided to change the subject. "Did you to move into a house or apartment when you moved to Connecticut?" she inquired of Adam with an encompassing look at the Finches in order to make sure they felt included in the conversation.

Taking her cue that she wanted to channel the conversation into safer waters, Adam responded, "I'm renting an apartment for the time being."

"Waiting for that fiancée of yours to come and set up housekeeping, I bet. I don't blame you one bit." At these words from Peter Finch, an uncomfortable silence fell over the group as Desiree looked questioningly at Adam.

Bernice turned to her husband in frustration and declared, "Peter Finch, sometimes I could just brain you!" she said. She handed her unfinished plate to him and stomped off with an apologetic look at Desiree.

"Angel, what did I do?" he exclaimed. He hoisted himself out of his chair and scurried after his wife, carrying her plate of food.

"It's not what you think." Adam looked at Desiree for understanding. "Please give me a chance to explain."

Desiree agreed only because she was interested in hearing how he was going to explain his obvious attempt to portray himself as unattached when, evidently, he wasn't.

Adam began, "There is nothing definite about Vanessa and me getting married."

"Then why does Mr. Finch think you're that you're engaged?" she asked quietly.

"He was on the panel that interviewed me for the position at the hospital. I knew that it would be to my advantage if they thought that it was only a matter of time before I was married. Being married is a big plus when you're interviewing for a job these days. Bosses like you to be tied down with responsibility. They feel you're not as apt to move within a short time span."

"Engaged, or not engaged, whichever it is, where is she?" Desiree shrugged her shoulders and looked around.

"Vanessa is in Arizona in graduate school. She's in the process of completing her dental internship."

"So she'll be here when she's finished?"

"She may be coming in June, but that remains to be seen. She's been offered a position in Arizona." Adam's eyes fell from Desiree's unwavering stare. "I'm five years older than Vanessa; we grew up together. Her older brother and I have been friends since grade school. The reason I didn't mention her right away is because everything's still very much in the air." He waited a moment for Desiree to digest what he was saying, "You see, I don't want my wife to work. As a doctor for a prominent hospital like Yale New Haven Hospital, I need my wife to be a partner to me at home, not a competitor in the business world. Vanessa won't need a job, and it's totally unacceptable for her to work if she and I are to get married. Because I'm African-American, I need every advantage I can get to help me achieve my goals. A beautiful, intelligent wife at my side can open doors for me that nothing else could."

"Oh, I see. You need a wife to take care of the home." Desiree quietly responded to his explanation.

"Yes," he said almost eagerly. "So you do understand."

"Someone to make sure you know the right people and attend the right functions." Desiree deliberately made her voice sound amenable to his way of thinking.

"Yes."

"So it's a waste of time for her to continue her education?"

"Exactly."

Since the beginning of Adam's explanation anger had begun to build in Desiree, and now she was at the boiling point. He didn't care how Vanessa would feel about having to give up a career that she had pursued for years for her own personal fulfillment. Adam expected Vanessa to submerge all of her wants and desires to further his career, completely forgetting about her own. She felt sorry for the unknown Vanessa because of the decision she had to make. She hoped she wouldn't throw away the chance of a lucrative career for a marriage that might not last.

Relief echoed in Adam's voice. "I'm glad you understand why I didn't tell you. I find you very attractive, Desiree, and I hope we can get to know each other. Maybe we can be friends and see what happens. I would still like for you to show me around. June is a long way off, and as I said, nothing's definite."

"No thanks, Adam. I'm not interested in hanging around, hoping that one day I might be able to step into another woman's shoes, in case it doesn't work out for her. I'm not that predatory. Also, in the long run you would be faced with the same problem with me that you find in Vanessa. One day I'm going to be a lawyer. That's not a dream I would give up for anyone. Besides, you misled me. You would never have told me about Vanessa if Peter Finch hadn't spilled the beans. If you had, we could have at least become friends. But as far as I'm concerned, half a lie is no better than a whole lie. If there's one thing an aspiring prosecutor despises, it's a liar."

Desiree abruptly turned and stood up. Speedily she threaded her way through the crowded room to the curved staircase that led upstairs. She felt winded when she reached the landing at the top of the stairs and stopped to catch her breath.

After a slight hesitation, she crossed over to the rooms where the twins slept in Nichelle's canopy white bed. Dominique had put them in the same bed so she could check on them during the night.

Nichelle had snuggled close to Nicholas under the covers. Reaching over, she kissed each lightly on the cheek.

"What's wrong? Are the twins all right?" Dominique had seen her rush upstairs and followed her. She looked worriedly at her children.

"They're fine," Desiree whispered. "I'm just checking on them."

"Good," Dominique responded with relief. "I saw you hurrying up here and followed you, thinking that something was wrong. What do you think of Adam? He's a looker, isn't he?"

"He's also engaged. And he had no intention of telling me. Peter Finch did it for him."

"What?" Dominique exclaimed. "Are you sure?" Desiree repeated the conversation she'd had with him.

"I'm going to kill Benjamin!"

"Don't bother." Desiree held up her hand. "I'm sure Benjamin doesn't even know. It's kind of on the down low," she added derisively.

"What a bastard!" Dominique exclaimed.

At Dominique's uncharacteristic use of profanity Desiree stepped back, holding her hands out in mock horror. "Such strong language from such a pillar of society. I'm aghast."

Dominique gave Desiree a crooked smile. "Oh, Desiree, I'm so sorry. I just so wanted something to happen between the two of you." She gathered her sister close and hugged her.

Desiree bent her head and laid it on top of Dominique's. "So did I," she mumbled. "So did I."

"People are beginning to leave, so I'd better go downstairs. Are you coming?"

"I don't think so. I've had enough for the night. I think I'll just go to my room and lie down."

Dominique gave her a brief kiss as she left the room. "I'll see you in the morning."

The next morning, the Diamond sisters sipped their coffee in the breakfast nook as they watched Benjamin and the twins cavort in the snow that had fallen during the night.

Benjamin had Nichelle and Nicholas's rapt attention as he showed them the correct way to make a perfect snowball. They squealed in delight and ran around in circles when he smilingly threatened them.

Immediately they both bent down, formed a ball barely recognizable to the one their father had made, and aimed. Nicholas hit Benjamin in the middle of his stomach while Nichelle's snowball hit him on the thigh. Playfully Benjamin clutched his stomach with one hand and fell into the snow on his back, sticking his legs straight up into the air.

Upon seeing this, the twins ran to their father and bent down to peer at him. He simultaneously dragged each of them on top of him and tried to tickle them through their snowsuits.

Desiree felt a pang of envy as she turned away from the window to face her sister. "They seem to be having a good time."

"Yes, Ben's great with the kids. I'm sure now they have a new way to torment each other. They'll be hitting each other with snowballs until spring." Now the three were rolling a huge ball of snow, which looked like the beginning of a snowman.

Dominique's face was a mixture of apology and self-anger. "Desiree, I'm sorry about last night. It seems as if I put you in an awkward position."

"It's not your fault. On the surface, Adam seemed as if he could be everything that I want in a man. He's handsome, ambitious, and intelligent. But his ideas about the proper role for a wife are antiquated. I want a man who would feel my career is as important as his. I don't want to feel as if I am an extension of him, but a part of his life that is valid and respected. I want to have it all. I want husband, a beautiful home, children, and a rewarding career." Desiree expelled a long sigh. "Sometimes I feel as if I'm asking for too much. Do you think it's possible to have it all?"

"I think I have it all," Dominique quietly responded.

"But you gave up your career. You had to make a choice."

"I gave up my career in fashion design because I wanted to, Desiree. That is the difference. I had to make a choice, and I chose him. I have never felt one moment of regret. The minute I saw Benjamin I wanted to marry him. Everything else seemed to pale in comparison to having a life with him. It seemed as if fate brought us together and we were perfect for each other; but I do realize that everyone wouldn't feel the fulfillment that I feel. Different things make different people happy."

Dominique reached across the table and covered Desiree's hand with her own. "I believe in soul mates, and because of that I know that one day you will have everything you want, the way you want it."

"I think a person's soul mate may not be so easy to recognize." Dominique looked perplexed at Desiree's statement, but before she could ask her what she meant Desiree abruptly changed the subject.

"Come on," Desiree said, standing, "I'm going to help you put your house in order and then I should be going. I don't want to travel at night just in case we get some more snow."

After they finished, the two sisters walked arm and arm down the driveway to Desiree's car. The twins were in their room taking a nap. Benjamin had already started her car to let it warm up. He stood at the open trunk where he had placed her suitcase and overnight bag.

Closing it, he reached down from his burly height to give his sister-in-law a big hug. "Drive carefully, and give us a call to let us know that you got home safely."

"Will do," she replied.

Dominique turned to her sister and held her close. "I love you, and I want you to be happy."

Desiree hugged her tightly, then broke the hold and got into her car, put on her seat belt and backed out of the driveway.

Desiree looked at the picture of her sister with Ben's arm around her shoulders and felt happiness for her sister because she had managed to find a wonderful man to share her life with.

As Benjamin watched Desiree depart he had a sudden premonition. He looked at his wife and said, "Don't worry about her so much. She's going to be just fine."

Carpe Diem

CHAPTER SIX

Desiree felt bored after she arrived back at her apartment. She made the quick telephone call to Dominique as promised and then sat in the living room, idly channel surfing. Throwing the remote aside, she declared aloud, "I'm bored. There's nothing good on television. I may as well walk down to the gym."

The gym was located on the other side of the clubhouse at her apartment complex. Desiree hadn't done any real working out since before she and Travis broke up. She hadn't really had the desire. It wasn't as if she was expecting anyone to see her naked any time soon.

Once she entered the gym she walked over to the Stairmaster. Whenever she worked out she made it a practice to use the machine she hated the most first. After half an hour she walked over and climbed on the cross trainer for twenty minutes, and then toweled away the sweat from her forehead and tackled the treadmill.

Desiree continued her workout with weights, working her biceps and legs, and then finishing with abdominal exercises. She used the machines as if some unseen force drove her. Three hours after entering the gym, she gave herself a pat on the back. *I haven't worked out in months, yet I was able to do my usual routine and more.*

Back at her apartment Desiree broiled a steak and coupled it with a baked potato. She had eaten so much food the last couple of days that she felt as if she should cut back before she couldn't fit into her favorite black dress.

Looking at the clock on the wall, Desiree was surprised to see that it was past eight o'clock. The telephone rates were down and she wanted to touch base with Natalie and see how her Thanksgiving holidays had gone.

Natalie answered on the third ring.

"Hey Nat, how are you doing?"

"Desiree! I'm fine, how are you?"

"I'm good," Desiree replied. "I just got back in town this afternoon, and I wanted to call and see how your holiday went."

"Everything went real well. My parents flew out for a couple of days. Martin left just a little while ago to take them to the airport. As usual, Mom cooked everything, so of course the food was delicious."

"I would have called earlier if I had known they were there. The next time you talk to them tell everyone I said hello."

"Will do. What's new with you?" Natalie queried.

"Thanksgiving was nice. Of course I went to my parents' house for Thanksgiving. That night we just sat around a watched some DVDs. On Friday, my sisters and I went shopping to catch some sales, and last night I went to Dominique's because she was having a party."

"How was the party? Were there any good-looking men there? Let me live vicariously through that wild single life you're living," she teased.

"Actually, there was one unattached man at the party. His name is Adam and he is fine, good-looking, and black."

"What? Tell me more. Did you go for it?" Natalie eagerly listened for some gossip.

"Well, I did, and then I didn't. He's sort of engaged."

"What's up with that? How can a person be sort of engaged? Either you are or you aren't."

"He's sort of engaged to his childhood sweetheart, and he didn't tell me about it. I wouldn't have known anything if a colleague of his hadn't let the cat out of the bag. She's in Arizona in dental school and they're going to get married if she decides to turn down a job offer and move to Connecticut to be with him."

"Bummer, but anything may happen. It does seem to be sort of up in the air," Natalie mused. "Are you thinking about going for it? Engaged does not mean married. Technically, he's still fair game."

"Not as far as I'm concerned. And with all that he has going for him, he doesn't seem that much of a catch. His ideas about the role a woman should play in a man's life are way too old-fashioned for me."

"Oh, so he's a bit of a Neanderthal, huh?" Natalie laughed.

"In the worst way," Desiree replied.

"You can still have yourself a little fun. When you get tired of going out with him, you can quit him without feeling guilty because he already has someone."

"I think that would be a big mistake. Many times women start relationships just planning on having a little fun, and then they fall in love, and can't get out of a triangle or hurtful situation. That's why I'm not that into casual dating. I don't want to risk it. As far as I'm concerned, engaged men are taboo, or in other words off limits."

"I agree with you, Desiree. I wasn't really serious. I can't think of a worse way to begin a relationship than trying to outlast the residue from an old one. If they were serious enough to get engaged you know that he must have strong feelings for her. Most likely he would go back and forth between the two of you until he finally made up his mind."

"It doesn't really matter about him. There's something else going on." Desiree struggled to form the words that she was about to say. "I may have already met someone."

"What? When? Who?" The surprise was evident in Natalie's voice, which had risen slightly with excitement.

"Slow your roll, Natalie. He's totally unsuitable for me, and my family would just die," Desiree added sarcastically.

"Why? Is he unemployed or something?"

"No, he's, not unemployed. It's just that," she hesitated, "they wouldn't approve."

Natalie demanded, "Who paid your rent last month?"

"I did," Desiree responded.

"Who paid your light bill, phone bill, and cable?"

"I did."

"And your water bill?"

"I get your point, Natalie! I'm an adult."

"Right. You are an adult. Desiree, you have always tried to please everyone but yourself, and look where it's gotten you. You went to college, returned home as expected, and hooked up with Travis because it seemed as if he fit the bill for what you and everyone else felt was acceptable. Look how that turned out." Natalie paused, and then said, "What looks good isn't always good for you. If you like this man and enjoy being with him, then go for it, and the hell with what anyone else thinks."

"But . . ." Desiree started to explain that Tyler was white, but broke off when she heard something that sounded like glass breaking and Michael crying in the background.

"Honey, I've got go. Michael has gotten into something in the kitchen. Remember what I said." And then Natalie hung up.

❧

Desiree woke up the next morning in excruciating pain. Her body was sore from head to toe, her neck hurt, and she had a headache. She lay there for a few minutes before she forced herself out of bed.

Gingerly swinging her legs to the side, she stiffly walked to the bathroom to grab a bottle of Tylenol out of her medicine cabinet. She placed three tablets in her mouth, and grabbing the glass off the counter she gulped down some water from the faucet. She made a face in the mirror as she swallowed because the water was tainted with the taste of Listerine as it went down her throat.

Even bending over to turn on the shower made her groan, and she regretted having been such a dynamo the previous evening.

That morning at work Desiree didn't accomplish very much. Earlier she had been subjected to sharp pains in her neck, her shoulders, and arms. Now she could barely lift her arm to retrieve a book she needed on the top shelf.

Later that afternoon she had to get down on all fours in front of the stacks. Drawing in a deep breath, she struggled to her feet after finding the law book that she needed to complete her research for the day. Rubbing her neck with both hands, she turned around to see Tyler. He had noiselessly entered the room and apparently observed her stiff motions.

"What's the matter with you?"

"I went to the gym last night and I ache all over," Desiree complained in a plaintive voice.

"Did you stretch before you worked out?" He looked worriedly at her.

"No, because sometimes when I stretch it seems to tire me out, and then I end up cutting my routine short."

"You should always stretch before you begin working out. It stops your body from tightening up later. If you like, I can show you some quick and easy exercises that should help you so you're not so sore the next day." And then he said abruptly, "Where do you hurt?"

"All over," she said, rubbing her neck with one hand. "I hadn't worked out for some time. It's so strange. Last night I felt perfectly fine, but when I opened my eyes this morning, I couldn't move. At first, I first thought I was paralyzed," she finished with a half laugh.

Real concern was etched in his face as he watched her slowly walk to her desk.

She groaned aloud as she bent her knees to sit. "My neck is killing me, and I think that it's behind this piercing headache."

"Let me see something." He walked over to her and stood behind her.

"What are you doing?" Desiree couldn't turn her head to see what he was doing and it made her nervous.

"I'm not doing anything. I'm just checking to see if anything is out of alignment." Tyler placed the palms of his hands on each side of Desiree's face. "I'm not going to hurt you. Just be still."

Desiree closed her eyes to the feel of Tyler's hands. They were gentle, and the smell of his cologne wafted to her nostrils. She was concentrating on trying to figure out what the scent was when he suddenly snapped her neck to the left and to the right.

"Ouch," she yelled. She swiveled around in her chair to face him. She was eye level with his belt buckle, and he bent down to look her in her face.

"If I had told you what I was going to do you wouldn't have let me help you. That's a technique I learned during my football days. Now, does your neck feel any better?" he queried softly.

She slowly moved her head from side to side. "Amazingly, it does. But that doesn't mean I appreciate the fact that you tricked me."

"I know." Tyler didn't sound a bit apologetic. "Sometimes the end justifies the means."

"Well, I won't be doing that again anytime soon." Desiree grimaced.

"Doing what?" Tyler asked.

"Working out. I can't spend a day in bed letting my body heal. Something's got to give."

"Your not working out anymore is the worst thing to do. You do remember the hair that bit you philosophy, don't you?"

"I've heard of it, but does it really work?" She looked up at him questioningly.

"In this case it does. So do you want me to show you how to stretch properly or not?"

Throwing caution to the wind, she replied, "Sure, why not. What time do you want to get together?"

"I have to leave the office for a meeting, but if you're free around seven o'clock that would be fine with me."

"Great," she said. "That will give me time to soak in a bathtub of warm water."

"Add some Epsom salts to your bath and that should take some of the soreness out," he instructed.

"Which gym are you a member of? Do I need a pass to get in?" he asked.

"No, I use the one in my apartment complex. I'll give you my address." Desiree tore a piece of paper from the notepad on her desk and quickly scribbled down her address and where the gym was located and handed it to him. After Tyler left her office she thought to herself, *What have I let myself in for?*

The gym was empty and Desiree nervously sat on the floor and waited for Tyler. When he entered, he immediately spied her sitting with her back against the wall. He glanced appreciatively at her appearance in her workout clothes. She had dressed in a matching tank top and shorts. She had not worn her spandex biker shorts because she felt that they were too revealing and she wanted to feel comfortable mimicking any movement Tyler might choose to show her. He walked over to stand in front of her.

"Hello," he said. Tyler's voice made the simplest words sound sexy.

"Hello," she responded softly, feeling shy at finding herself alone with him after work.

"Feeling any better?" Tyler watched Desiree's movements to see if her face showed any of the signs of the pain she had had earlier that day.

"A lot." She gingerly moved her head from side to side. "And thanks for the tip about the Epsom salts. I think it helped."

"Good." He held out his hand, and Desiree placed hers in his and he hoisted her to her feet.

Tyler was an excellent teacher. First, he modeled the movement he wanted her to copy. Then he watched her to make sure that she did it correctly. Starting with the feet, he showed her how to stretch every part of her body without straining herself. They worked their biceps, quadriceps, hamstrings, and thigh and leg muscles. Desiree was unaware that whenever she lifted one of her legs she gave Tyler a full view of her thigh area from her knee to her crotch.

Stretching took out most of the soreness that was left and she felt more relaxed and limber. They stretched for about twenty minutes before he stopped, saying that was enough for the day.

Later, they lay on the floor of the gym. Desiree sat drinking out of the liter of water she had brought with her and eyed him speculatively. She brought up the subject of his unexpected phone call. "I'm sorry that I couldn't have dinner with you when you called last week, but I had so much to do before I left for my parents' house." She broke off, feeling guilty at the flimsy excuse. Averting her eyes, she asked, "Did you end up going anywhere?"

Tyler took her apology at face value. "Out of the blue, an old friend called me. She was in town unexpectedly, so I was saved from dining alone."

Immediately Desiree felt a surprising twinge of jealousy. She wouldn't ask if it was an old girlfriend. That question was too personal. She had no right, especially since she'd turned him down.

"Anyhow," he continued, and a teasing light twinkled in his eyes, "you more than made up for that tonight."

"How did I do that?" she asked. "You helped me; I didn't help you."

"Yes, you did," Tyler grinned. "Every time you lifted your leg, you gave me a thrill I haven't felt in a long time."

Immediately Desiree realized what he meant and she felt herself flush.

Seeing this, Tyler laughed loudly and then made an effort to stop. "I'm sorry, Desiree. I didn't mean to make you uncomfortable. I would have never said anything if I had known it would embarrass you like that." Reaching over, he took her chin in his hand. "You really are quite shy, aren't you?" He dropped his hand and then, in an effort to lighten the atmosphere, asked, "Is there a water fountain in here?" He swung his head around, searching the room.

"There's one in the lobby, but it's broken." She showed him her water bottle, not yet meeting his eyes. "That's how I knew to bring my own. I'm sorry, I should have warned you."

"I'm parched," Tyler complained. He sounded like a little boy who was jealous because his friend had candy and he didn't.

She glanced sheepishly at her empty water bottle. "I should have offered you some of mine. My apartment is a five-minute walk from here. Would you like to walk over to my place and get some water?" she hesitatingly asked.

"I thought you'd never ask." He stood, extending his hand to help her off the mat. They walked in silence to her building. Butterflies danced in her stomach. She hadn't planned on inviting Tyler back to her place. Things were moving a little too quickly for her, but she didn't see a way out that wouldn't make her look like a silly schoolgirl.

On entering her apartment, she motioned for him to sit down while she went into the kitchen to get him a bottle of water. He glanced around with admiration. Desiree's apartment looked just like her. The décor was tasteful and classy.

Handing him a bottle of water, she sat on the couch far enough from him so that they didn't touch.

"Desiree, what's your story?" he suddenly asked, turning his piercing green eyes on her.

She was caught off guard at his unexpected question. "What makes you think there is one?" she responded noncommittally.

"Everyone has one. You're a young, beautiful, single woman coping alone in the tough corporate world."

"There isn't much to tell. I met a nice guy after I returned home from college. We got engaged and then disengaged."

"I bet there's more to it than that," he responded.

"Well, there's the fact that I want to be a lawyer, so I'm putting money aside out of every paycheck so I can go back to school."

"I kind of figured that." His tone was matter of fact.

"Kind of figured what?"

"That you want to be a lawyer. Your mind is far too sharp to be satisfied with being a paralegal for the rest of your life. It would be such a waste." He paused, taking a gulp of water. "What kind of law do you want to practice?"

"I haven't decided. I want to help people, but I also want to be comfortable financially."

Tyler said suddenly, "He's a fool."

"Who?" Not understanding, Desiree looked at Tyler inquisitively.

"The man who let you get away." The room was silent and Desiree was uncomfortable. She was out of her depth and she knew it.

She looked pointedly at the clock and Tyler took the hint. Straightening his long limbs, he hung his workout towel around his neck, smoothed down the pants leg of the sweat suit he had donned for warmth over his gym shorts, and studied her.

"Desiree, would you like to go out to dinner with me tomorrow night?"

Desiree didn't know why, but she was unprepared for his question. She should have expected it from the look in his eyes when he looked at her. Her response was automatic and without thinking.

"I'm afraid that I can't, Tyler. It's just not a good idea." Desiree avoided Tyler's eyes and focused on some imagined spot on the wall past his shoulders.

"For me, or for you?" His expression was wry as he waited for her answer.

"Well," she said slowly, "you said out to dinner. That means that you're asking me out on a date, aren't you?"

"Yes, that is exactly what I meant." His eyes glinted as he teased her. "Do you find the concept of the two of us going out on a date so reprehensible?"

"No," she replied, "it's not that. It's just that I don't think that it's the smartest thing in the world to do. It might cause problems."

"For who?" he replied seriously.

"For me, for you, for both of us." She averted her eyes.

"You're making a lot of drama out of a simple dinner invitation, Desiree."

"I know that, but it could lead to something else, and that would open a whole can of worms. I just don't want to create problems."

"Why would it be a problem? There's no rule that two people employed at the firm can't go out together. Actually, I know of two other couples at the firm that are in a relationship. There's even a husband and wife team."

"Yes, but they're all of the same race. You and I dating would be a whole different scene. We would be the subjects of gossip, and that would make me uncomfortable." She hesitated, "It's not you, it's me." She placed her hand over her nervously beating heart. "I'm just not brave enough to withstand that sort of thing."

Tyler said gently, "I think that I'm brave enough for two people."

"Maybe you are. But there's more to it than that. For me, it's black men. They're the only ones I've ever been attracted to. They just do it for me. It's hard for me to put it into words, but I feel them. They have depth and a deep heart and soul," she replied softly, not wanting to hurt his feelings.

"So you've never dated a white man before?" He looked at her quizzically.

"I think you already know the answer to that," she replied, avoiding his eyes.

"Well, I think that you should know that black men don't have the market on hearts and souls. White men have them too, Desiree. We feel things deeply also, and we too search for love," he replied with conviction.

She made no answer but only continued to look away.

Tyler continued, "And as for the other, interracial relationships are a lot more common than they used to be."

At this Desiree faced Tyler and met his eyes with hers. "That's true. But many of the people who are in that sort of relationship live their lives only for themselves, or are stars, or are people who have gotten to where they're going and like to or feel they can flaunt tradition. They feel they don't need the approval of other people. Many times they come from very liberal families. Then, of course, there's the relationship itself." Her face took on a sad expression. "Relationships are hard under the best of circumstances, and an interracial relationship would be even harder. Why look for drama? Why test the waters?" Desiree paused. "There are a lot of white women at work that are dying to go out with you. Why don't you ask one of them?" The minute the words were out of her mouth Desiree wished that she could retract them. They sounded horrible. She didn't want to hurt Tyler's feelings, and she didn't want him to think she was callous or trying to put him off on another woman. But she was no trailblazer. She never had been and never could be.

Tyler had remained quiet throughout Desiree's speech, digesting her words.

"How old are you, Desiree?" Tyler's eyebrows lifted in query as he waited for Desiree's response.

"I'm thirty, but I think you already knew that."

"I did, but I wanted you to say it out loud. I'm thirty-six years old. When a man reaches my age, he realizes what's important in a relationship. What makes it work? It's not what looks good. It's what is good."

Hearing Tyler repeat verbatim the words she had previously heard from Natalie seemed surreal.

"It's having the same ideals, enjoying the same things, and having someone you like spending time with. That's not so easy to find. It's almost synonymous to finding a needle in a haystack. And if you do think there's a chance of having that, you need to go for it." Desiree had turned her head to one side to avoid looking at him. "Desiree," he said, and she turned and looked at him. He took his hand and lifted her chin. His touch was gentle and he held her eyes with his own. "I can't make you go out with me, and I'm not going to even try, but life is too short to base it on what everyone else thinks. I won't harass you, and I won't ask you again. If you change your mind, you're going to have to come to me." Tyler lightly touched her on the cheek before he walked out of her apartment.

Later that night, Desiree lay quietly in the darkness of her apartment, alone and lonely. Desiree's memory reverted to her sophomore year in college. She and Natalie had been with their suitemates Sophie and Tamara at a round table in the cafeteria when Dylan approached them.

In the winter, the cafeteria was the foremost social meeting place of the school. If you were looking for someone you could be sure to find him or her in the cafeteria sooner or later.

North Carolina Agricultural and Technical State University was a historically black college, and Dylan was the only white boy who played on the football team. He had been sitting at a nearby table with a bunch of his football cronies. After dumping his tray and placing it on the conveyor belt, he boldly walked up to the table where the girls were sitting.

"Desiree, may I ask you something?" Dylan's voice sounded loud and nervous and she looked up at him in surprise.

She had an English literature class with him, and several times they had sat next to each other during lecture and had shared notes. However, this was the first time they had seen each other out of the classroom and she was surprised that he had approached her.

"Sure, what is it?" she asked.

"Would you like to go out to dinner and the movies with me Saturday night?"

Tamara was in the process of drinking her soda and she began to sputter and cough, attracting the attention of people at nearby tables. Desiree was totally caught off guard. She had expected him to ask her about the term paper that was assigned to them earlier that day in class.

Becoming very flustered she stammered, "I'm sorry, Dylan. I can't because I'm going with someone."

Dylan's face turned slightly red as he looked at Natalie patting Tamara discreetly on the back. "Okay, I'm sorry to bother you. I didn't mean to step on anyone's toes. See you in class." He abruptly nodded his head at everyone sitting at the table before walking off.

Only then did Tamara stop her choking act. Desiree slid a sideways glance at the football players sitting a few tables down and two of them were slouched in their seats, convulsed with laughter. She noticed the boy that had been laughing the hardest had previously asked her out, and she had turned him down because at the time she had a boyfriend.

"And who do you go with?" Sophie demanded to know. "I thought you and Paul split weeks ago?"

"We did. I lied because I just didn't know what else to say." Desiree had broken up with Paul because he preferred hanging out with his buddies to spending time with her.

"Well, if you ask me, you should have gone. Live and let live is my motto," Sophie continued as she munched on a French fry. "Dating in the 21st century is a whole new ball game. What used to be taboo isn't anymore. Check out Demi and Ashton. Years ago, her dating and then marrying a guy that much younger probably would have affected her career, but after the first few raised eyebrows, people stopped making a big deal out of it. The new millennium is here and times are hard. War and terrorist attacks are always a possibility. You never know what the next day is going to bring. It's hard to find a college man with enough money to actually take you somewhere, and if he does you're lucky if he doesn't ask you to chip in on a six-pack of beer. We never get to go to the hotel to get some. You have to have sex in a hurry while your roommate sits outside and then reminds you for the next week that you owe her some huge favor." Her words trailed off as she stared at her roommate Tamara, who was glaring at Desiree with accusation in her eyes.

"I can't believe he asked you out. You must have been too friendly to him or he wouldn't have gotten out of place like that. You know white folks. Give them an inch and they'll take a mile." Tamara hated white people. Her father was in a Texas prison serving a life sentence for a crime for which Tamara insisted that he was innocent.

"I have not gotten out of place with him!" Desiree retorted hotly. "We have a class together, that's all!"

At this point Natalie championed Desiree. "I doubt if Desiree became too familiar with him. He's probably lonely. I wouldn't be in his shoes for anything. He's at a predominately black school and he lives on campus. The majority of white people that go here attend class in the evenings under the master and doctoral programs. Dylan falls on the dating list right below the Africans, and they're only shunned because they consider it unmanly to wash, and therefore smell. No decent girl will date Dylan because everyone cares what everyone else thinks. Think about how you would feel if you were him. It's wrong to be ostracized because you're of a different race. I feel kind of sorry for him. He must be lonely."

"I don't feel sorry for him. He's only here because he gets to come here for free. He's the minority, which means he gets a scholarship for attending. That's the only reason why he's putting up with our black asses. And as for feeling ostracized, you'll know how that feels soon enough," Tamara countered.

"What do you mean?" Natalie asked.

"After we graduate, just try to get a job in corporate America." At this Tamara became consumed with laughter and the others grudgingly joined in.

Once the laughter subsided, Desiree felt the need to explain. "I didn't only turn down Dylan only because he's white. I don't find him physically attractive. With all of these fine-looking black men on campus, why would I date him? I don't even date light-skinned black men. It's a known fact that girls date and marry men that remind them of their father. All of you have seen my family pictures and know my dad is dark-skinned."

"Yeah, he's burple," Tamara piped in.

"What does that mean?" Sophie looked confused.

"It means that he's so black he's purple," Tamara replied, laughing at her joke.

"You're not so far off that yourself," Natalie countered, giving Tamara a warning look.

"Yes, he is quite dark, and handsome," Desiree replied proudly, not at all offended by Tamara's remarks about her father's complexion. "I could never be with a white man!"

Although Desiree continued to see Dylan in class, he never again approached her. Sometimes she felt his eyes on her and her conscience felt a twinge when she saw him, but she consoled herself with the thought, "Well, at least I didn't use him for his money, and there ain't no way in hell he was going to experience the black woman through me."

Suddenly the telephone rang, shattering the silence and bringing her back to the present. As Desiree reached for the phone she half hoped and half feared that it was Tyler resubmitting his dinner invitation. "Hello," she mouthed softly into the receiver. Click! The sound of the dial tone was the only response she heard. Assuming it was a wrong number, she slowly placed the phone back onto its cradle. Rolling over on to her side she curled her body into the fetal position. Her last thought before she willed herself to sleep was, *Damn, Tyler is fine! Why do things have to be so difficult for me?*

❧

"Good morning." Desiree had already started the coffee brewing and was seated at the conference table when Tyler walked in.

"Good morning." Tyler's expression was inscrutable.

"Would you like a cup of coffee?" She made a conscious effort to make her voice sound light and breezy.

"No, thank you, I had a cup before I left home." His words were concise, and his tone was different.

"Oh," she said, sitting back in her chair. "Do you need me to translate some of the notes that I left on your desk yesterday afternoon?"

"No, thank you. Everything you did yesterday was crystal clear."

She searched his face to see if there was any hidden meaning in his words, but his expression was calm.

For the next few days, they worked seated across from each other at the conference table and in complete silence. The easy camaraderie which had been apparent before was lost.

His behavior had been above approach since he had left her apartment, but gone was the special attention and teasing from him that she had taken for granted. She was being treated simply as a paralegal working on a case with the firm's leading lawyer. No more, no less.

It was only Wednesday. The last few days at work had seemed endless, and were the most uncomfortable she'd ever spent in Tyler's company. She was relieved when it was time to break for lunch.

Standing abruptly, Tyler said, "I'm going to lunch. I'll be back around one o'clock."

Buying a ham and cheese sandwich and diet Coke from one of the vending machines, Desiree walked past the lunchroom and only nodded her head briefly at several coworkers on her way to the double glass doors that were the entrance of the building.

Feeling the need for some fresh air, she walked out of the building in a small park across the street from the law firm. The park was crowded with people enjoying the unusually mild weather. She sat on a park bench and began absently eating the sandwich she had purchased as she looked around.

Desiree spied a couple lying on a blanket under a large maple tree. The couple was older, each had hair tinged with gray and their faces were lined with wrinkles. Desiree instinctively sensed by their body language that they had been married for a long time, yet they behaved as if they were newlyweds. They were engrossed with each other and totally oblivious to anyone else. There was a picnic basket between them, and the woman withdrew sandwiches, opened them, and placed them on paper plates. Then she withdrew a thermos and poured what appeared to be juice into two plastic glasses, handing one to her husband. A plate of potato chips lay on the blanket, and as they alternated between eating the sandwiches and munching on the chips, Desiree could see gold wedding bands on their hands. The couple didn't talk, but sat in a companionable silence. The woman reached for her drink and knocked it over. Hurriedly, the man withdrew a linen napkin from the picnic basket and began to mop up the liquid, at the same time handing his wife his drink to finish. Desiree mused, "That's what I want. Someone to love and grow old with. I want to still have romantic feelings after years of marriage. I want to be able to spill my juice and have my husband give me his without hesitation."

Hurriedly devouring the rest of her lunch, she made a decision. The last couple of days had been the loneliest she had ever spent at Buchanan & Buchanan Law Firm. It was worse than before Tyler had begun to work there because, having spent time with him, it was hard to slip back into a routine without him. She didn't want to step backwards from a relationship with Tyler. She wanted to forge ahead, and it looked as if it was up to her to get things back to what they had been before her refusal to go out with him.

Tyler was surprised to see Desiree seated at his desk when he entered his office after lunch. Sensing something important was pending, he stopped, placed his hands in his pockets, and began to rock back and forth on his heels.

"I have something to say to you." There was a slight quiver in her voice.

Knowing she was nervous, Tyler sat in the leather chair on the opposite side of the desk in order to look less imposing.

"The night you were at my apartment you were right. There is more to my story than I told you. Almost three months ago, I ended a relationship with a man I had known for six years. We were engaged for three of them. He couldn't, or wouldn't, make a commitment. He had a whole lot of baggage, and yet I wanted to make a life with him. There's not one good reason why he didn't marry me, except that he didn't want to. I was afraid that if things didn't work out with him, they couldn't possibly work out between us.

"The cards are stacked against us. The odds are against a relationship between the two of us ever amounting to anything, and all I want to do is fight any feeling that I may have for you. I like you, Tyler, and I enjoy your company. When I talk to you, I feel as if you know how I feel about things that are important to me. I feel as if you feel the same way I do about things that matter. I am attracted to you, Tyler, but I am also afraid. I don't know that I have the gumption that it takes to have an interracial relationship, and I'm scared to take a chance and waste more years of my life on something else that is impossible."

Tyler had sat quietly listening and digesting what she said. Then he said, "Desiree, I'm a man, not a boy. I'm not searching for love, but if it comes knocking at my door I'll be sure to open the door, not close it. I don't make promises I don't intend to keep, nor do I waste a person's time. That's one of the reasons I haven't dated anyone consistently since my divorce. I know very early in a relationship whether or not it could amount to anything. I don't like to give women false hope. I would really like you to give us the chance to know each other. I won't pressure you for any more than you can give. And before we begin discussing how hard a future for the two of us would be, let's get to know each other on a personal level and find out if there can even be a future between us."

Desiree sat quietly for a few minutes; then she shyly looked at him. "Can you pick me up for dinner tomorrow night around eight?"

Point of No Return

CHAPTER SEVEN

Desiree was as nervous as a cat as she dressed for her date with Tyler. She stood in front of her mirror in the bedroom and drew in a deep breath, placing her hand on her ribcage in an effort to quell her heavy breathing. *Its just dinner; nothing has to happen. If it doesn't feel right after tonight, I'll just walk away. It will be easier to know that there is nothing to this than to wonder for the rest of my life what might have been.*

Desiree had applied her deodorant and face moisturizer before leaving the bathroom. Now she leaned over and picked up her favorite body oil off of her dresser. She sat down on the bed and began to lightly massage her limbs with the oil, from the soles of her feet to her neck, stopping before she reached her face. Next she reached for her favorite perfume. Obsession was her old standby and, for some reason, whenever she sprayed it on her body, she felt sexy and alluring. The next thing she grabbed for was her pantyhose; she always wore coffee bean. Many a day she had been asked if she was wearing any hose at all because the color of the hose so perfectly matched her skin tone. Crossing over to her closet, she reached for her off-black spaghetti-strapped after five dress. She knew that the weather was too cold for the dress to be worn by itself, but it had a matching jacket and, combined with her overcoat, the ensemble should be perfect. Desiree brushed her long hair, leaving it loose, stepped into her heels, and began to apply her makeup. *I want to look a little more sophisticated.* She applied makeup base a little heavier than she usually wore it, matted it with loose powder, and outlined her lips before coloring them with a dramatic red lipstick. Desiree carefully drew liner on her eyelids before she finished with new mascara guaranteed to make long eyelashes longer. Once she added large gold shaped earrings, she stepped back and eyed her reflection in the mirror. *I don't look the way I feel. I look ready and confident.*

Antonio's was an Italian restaurant located in the exclusive suburb of New Fairfield. The inside was opulently furnished in mahogany wood, and wallpaper with Renaissance designs clung to the walls. A huge candle chandelier was in the ceiling in the center of the room, throwing off subdued lighting. Against one wall a fireplace was burning, and the scent of pine lingered in the air.

Every table had a candelabrum of candles that exuded an air of intimacy. The table at which Desiree and Tyler were seated was in a secluded corner of the room near the fireplace. She felt as if they were alone on a deserted island.

"Tell me about your family," Desiree asked as she sipped a glass of white wine the waiter had poured for her. Once seated, she was too warm from the flames of the fireplace. Tyler had checked her coat in the lobby and she had also taken off the jacket to her dress. It lay across the back of her chair.

Tyler saw that one of the thin straps of her dress had slipped off her shoulder, making her even lovelier in the subdued glow in the room. "I'm the son of a Baptist preacher. My dad has a small congregation in Wheeling, West Virginia, where life never changes and neither does he," Tyler answered.

"You sound as if you don't really get along with him all that well." The thought of Tyler not liking a parent seemed foreign to her. "I hope that I'm not being too nosy, but may I ask why?"

"My dad is a difficult person to get along with. We rarely see eye to eye on anything. It's either his way or the highway. He's my father and I love him, but I don't admire him," Tyler quietly affirmed. "He always had time to listen to any petty problem one of his congregation members had, but he rationed out his time to my mother. I always tried to show her how much she meant to me, and I know to some degree it helped. But I could see the loneliness in her eyes for a husband who was a partner to her at home, not just in front of his congregation."

"I'm surprised. I would think that your father being a preacher would make him an ideal mate for marriage."

Tyler gave a small snort of derision. "Reading the words in the Bible and actually using them in life as a way to govern yourself do not necessarily go hand in hand. The Bible speaks of how a man is supposed to treat his wife, and how he is supposed to cleave to her. Sunday after Sunday, I would sit in the pew of the church next to my mother and wonder, why don't you treat my mother the way the Bible teaches a man to treat his wife? Why don't you practice what you preach?"

"Maybe he didn't realize that he was doing anything wrong," she responded quietly. "Some people don't, you know."

Tyler digested this for a moment and then continued, "When I became a teenager, I used to say stuff to him about how he treated Mom, but it fell on deaf ears." He shrugged. "Sometimes I would suggest little things that he should do for her on special days, but he never followed through, never listened, and after a while I just gave up. I vowed that I would never be so insensitive to my wife and children and then I ended up being divorced."

"It takes two for a marriage to fail, just as it takes two to make it work."

Tyler's face looked pensive. "Maybe. I sometimes wonder if I could have done more, but Nancy and I grew in opposite directions. I tried to give her the quality time that I felt she needed, but she divided that time between social clubs, friends, and me. She graduated from college with a degree in interior design, but she's never used it, except for her own personal use. She's amazing in that respect.

"Our house was beautiful. But it was more of a showcase to be admired than something to find comfort in. I used to encourage her to start her own business. I think it would have been good for her, but she was content to spend her time being a social butterfly. She comes from very old money, and there's a lot of it. Nancy's income is a combination of alimony payments from me and money from a trust fund left to her by her grandmother."

"Does she treat the kids well?" Desiree carefully probed, not sure how much personal information Tyler wanted to divulge.

"Yes, she gives the kids all the attention they need. She still fraternizes with the people she grew up with and spends a lot of time making sure our children continue to have the right connections."

"Are they very much like her?"

"Yes and no. They both attend private schools. Tiffany takes ballet, voice lessons, and piano lessons, but so far she seems very unaffected by the people she comes in contact with. She doesn't put on airs." Upon seeing Desiree's smile at his use of expression, Tyler explained, "I get that from my dad. He used to use that against my mom and me when we asked for things that he thought were too expensive."

Attempting to lighten the atmosphere, Desiree queried, "How about Chad?"

"Chad, on the other hand, is more like Nancy. He takes tennis and ski lessons through the country club. He's already looking at magazines, fantasizing about the sports car he wants the minute he turns sixteen."

"When he comes of age are you going to get him one?"

"I don't know. Thank goodness that's a few years down the road." He held out his hands, with his palms towards Desiree, as if he were holding off some hard decision he knew that he would have to make in the future. "I don't want to be as rigid as my Dad, and I want my children to experience and have all the things I didn't when I was growing up, but I don't want to overcompensate for being a part-time father by giving them too many material things. I think children are better off earning and getting things on their own. It gives them character and helps build discipline."

He continued, "When I was growing up in West Virginia, we were dirt poor. I went to the University of Virginia on a football scholarship, hence the bump on my nose." Tyler ran the tip of his finger down the bridge of his nose. "I broke it my senior year of college. After I graduated I worked my way through law school. That's one of the few times I felt my father was proud of me.

"The next time was when I married what he thought was the right kind of woman; but then I went and botched that up by getting a divorce, and once again I felt his displeasure."

There was a long pause. "I've seen a change in Chad. Last Christmas I took the kids to West Virginia to visit my parents. Chad wasn't out-and-out rude, but it was obvious by his behavior that he thought it was the worst Christmas ever, and I ended up feeling badly because there weren't more exciting things for him to do."

"How did Tiffany behave?" Desiree probed.

"She was great. We built a snowman; she helped my mom bake pies, and patiently listened to my mom's boring stories about me growing up."

"How did your mother feel about Chad's behavior?"

"My mom's wonderful. Even if she noticed anything about it she would never comment on it. It's not her personality. She's so docile that sometimes I want to shake her. Dad treats her more like he's her father than her partner in marriage. Mom's never worked outside the home. That would have been good for her; it would have made her more independent. But Dad wouldn't allow it because he didn't think it looked right for a minister's wife to work because she should always be accessible to the church flock. So what Dad couldn't provide for us, we did without.

"Throughout my whole life, Mom lived through me, and at times I feel guilty for living so far away. I often urge her to come up for a visit, but she won't leave Dad, even for a vacation." He drew a long, deep sigh. "I don't squawk about it a lot because she is content to remain in Wheeling with him, or at least she acts as if she is."

At this time they were finishing up their salads and the waiter came over to the table with their entrees. Tyler had ordered spaghetti and meatballs and Desiree the lasagna.

"Now it's your turn." Obviously it upset Tyler to talk about his mother, and he wanted to change the subject.

"My family is definitely a unique and varied mixture. First of all, my father's been a bricklayer since he and my mother moved north from Alabama right after high school. Dad's an outdoor person; he's real good with his hands. They're rough and callused, but whenever I fell down on my bike and scraped my knees they were the gentlest hands you could wish for.

"He's so comfortable with who he is. Even though Dad only has a high school education, he's always provided for us through hard work. It hasn't always been easy for them. I don't think it was easy anywhere for black people just starting out in the fifties, but they say Alabama was worse."

There was a long silence before she continued, "After my parents were married they didn't want to raise their children in Alabama, so after my mom got pregnant with my brother Marcus Junior they left. It was a struggle, but Dad worked two jobs and my mother went to school part-time to become a teacher."

"It takes a strong man to help his woman fulfill her dreams. I've had colleagues who got upset if their wife wanted to pursue a degree in higher education. I never understood the draw of the trophy wife syndrome. I would, and did, find that boring," Tyler said.

Desiree digested his words, happy that he didn't feel threatened by ambitious women, but she made no comment, instead preferring to continue her train of thought. She said with pride, "After all of us were in elementary school Mom went back to college again, this time for her master's degree. It was a dream of hers to teach at the college level, and she does so at the local community college. She always says that Dad helped her to fulfill her dream."

Tyler interjected, "Teachers have a special place in society. They're helping to shape the world's future, yet they're usually overworked and underpaid."

Desiree acknowledged his words with a nod of agreement. "One definitely has to have patience and a kind heart if they're going to be in it for the long haul and not use it as a temporary stepping stone to something bigger and better." Desiree reached for her glass and took another sip of her wine.

Tyler picked up his glass and slightly raised it in the air before he said to her, "Here, here." Then he took another sip. "Do you have any brothers?"

"Just one. Marcus Junior is the oldest and he has had a rather rough time of it. He served in the Persian Gulf War, but he never talks about the things he saw in combat, or how he feels about the United States' involvement in the war in Iraq. He had a bout with alcoholism after he returned to the States, but he conquered his addiction."

Desiree's voice dropped to a whisper. "Marcus Junior has a child from a woman he met overseas. She didn't want to continue a relationship with him, and he has respected that. Our family has seen baby pictures of his son, but never met him in person."

"That's a tough break and, unfortunately, too common." A dark silence descended on the table.

Then Desiree's face and tone brightened. "I have to tell you about my sister Dominique. She's my big little sister, short, petite, and baby doll beautiful. She can be domineering, but she behaves that way out of love for us. She's married to a doctor, Benjamin James. I nicknamed him Gentle Ben. He has a lot of ways like Daddy. I think that's what attracted her to him in the first place, even though she's not very much like Mother. They have the cutest twins one could ever hope for and a great big house on the outskirts of New Haven. Dominique doesn't work a regular job, but she does a lot of community work to champion black causes." Once again silence descended on the table.

"Why do you do that?" Tyler looked at her inquisitively.

"Do what?" Desiree had completed her salad and now began to attack her plate of lasagna.

"Hesitate anytime you mention anything to do with race?"

Desiree shifted uneasily in her chair. "My mother always taught us that it's ill bred to talk about race in mixed company or bring up to white people the bad things they have done in their past to their face." She finished in a prim voice.

Tyler laughed loudly, throwing back his head. "Oh, so it's okay to talk about us behind our backs?"

"You know what I mean," she muttered, sipping from her second glass of wine. Desiree was feeling warm and cozy from the combination of the wine and Tyler's company.

"Yes, Desiree, I know what you mean, and I do understand." Changing the subject, he asked, "Is that everyone?"

"Good grief, no! I could never fail to mention Sasha. She looks a lot like me, but the buck stops there. My youngest sister has a wild, outgoing personality and doesn't bind herself to many social conventions. She says anything she thinks. I wish I were more like her." A note of jealousy had crept inside Desiree's voice.

Tyler sat quietly watching Desiree in the candlelight. Unbeknownst to her, now both of the tiny straps on her dress had fallen down to one side, making her look alluring and kittenish.

"I happen to think you're perfect just the way you are." Their eyes locked as Tyler reached for her hand across the table; he lifted it to his mouth and briefly kissed it. Lowering their hands to the table, he continued to hold her hand within his warm clasp. In the dim lighting of the restaurant, Desiree didn't see or feel the malevolent gaze of several couples seated nearby.

As they stood in front of Antonio's and waited for Tyler's Corvette to be brought by the valet, she vigorously rubbed her hands together and stuck them inside the deep pockets of her wool overcoat. In Connecticut it was always cold in December, and the weathermen were predicting an unusually harsh winter.

"Why didn't you wear gloves?" With every word he spoke, a puff of cold air billowed like smoke in front of his mouth.

She pulled a glove out of her coat pocket and showed it to him. "I lost one, and you look crazy if you wear only one. The only place you can buy this particular brand of gloves is at Neiman Marcus, and we don't have that store in the Danbury Mall. After the feel of these I didn't feel like settling for any other kind; the next time I go to New York City I'll get another pair." Desiree bemoaned the fact that she lost one because they were a present from Dominique last Christmas and she knew it would be expensive to replace.

They looked as the valet speedily pulled up to the curb in front of them and parked. Tyler quickly ushered her inside the car and walked to the other side, discreetly handing the valet a bill before they left.

They were quiet on the drive back to Desiree's apartment, each deep in thought. Desiree studied his profile in the dim interior of the car and she realized Tyler was handsome, no matter the color his skin.

Tyler walked Desiree to the door of her apartment and she suddenly felt unhappy that the evening was coming to an end. She hadn't enjoyed herself so much in a very long time. "Would you like to come in for awhile?"

"If you're sure that it's not too late?"

She quickly glanced at her watch. "It's only nine-thirty. I think I can stay up a little while longer," she replied with a smile. "But not too late, because I'm working with a real tyrant at the office. He works me like a dog and never gives me a moment's peace."

He joined in the joke. "That means that he really likes you. On the playground, didn't you ever get pushed into the monkey bars when you were a little girl? That's how men behave when they don't know how to express themselves."

"Yes, I did. And I distinctly remember I didn't like it."

"Well, I'll remember not to play with you like that because I want you to like me because I definitely do like you, Miss Desiree Diamond."

Not knowing what to say, Desiree dropped her eyes from the spell of Tyler's gaze. She was playing with fire, and she didn't care.

Shrugging out of her coat and taking his from him, she hung them in the hall closet, gesturing for him to take a seat in the living room. She went into the kitchen and peered into the refrigerator, then called out to him, "I have some wine in here. Would you like some?"

"Only if you promise not to take advantage of me while I'm under the influence."

Desiree half-smiled at the thought. Walking into the living room, she smiled to see Tyler thumbing through her music selection.

"Nice taste in music," he complimented, showing her several CDs, one of which was Marvin Gaye's greatest hits, and then he handed her the last one he'd picked up. They sat close on the love seat, each of them drinking a glass of wine, and felt completely relaxed. The atmosphere, the alcohol, the music, and Tyler's presence all combined to extinguish her inhibitions and Desiree closed her eyes.

The lyrics 'I can't stop loving you' filled her with longing and desire. She let her head fall backward and she felt the light touch of Tyler's fingertips as he began to massage her temples. His touch was caressing, and she felt a fire ignite in her.

Tyler turned Desiree so that she was cradled in the crook of his arms as he began to massage the base of her neck. Flickers of desire began to mount as Desiree responded to Tyler's touch. Her body curved into his and his mouth began to nibble lightly on her ear. Gently turning face her to his, Tyler's lips touched hers. At first they were gentle; then they became firmer, more demanding and insistent. She melted at his touch. Her mouth opened against his and he slid his tongue into her mouth. Their tongues danced together until Desiree felt she would explode from the intimacy. *This doesn't feel weird. It feels good.*

He moved his hand from her back and began to caress her breast lightly. There was nothing intrusive about his touch. Desiree arched her back and closed her eyes in anticipation. Slowly he began undoing her buttons in the front of her dress and lightly feathered a kiss on her skin as each button revealed more of her soft, pliant body.

The sensual voice in the background and the words mingled with Tyler's touch to create a potent combination. Tyler undid the back of her dress and slid the straps down her arms. Then he freed her breasts by unclipping the front of her bra. His moved his mouth across one breast and slowly he licked her nipple fully before he took in as much of her full breast that his mouth could hold. He suckled it while he caressed the other with his hand.

After what seemed to be an eternity he switched from left breast to right and gave it the same amount of attention. Desiree's hands cradled the back of his head, guiding him. Then again she arched towards him as Tyler moved his hands lightly across her stomach as his fingers found her belly button, his tongue played with its ring before his planted a kiss on the spot his hands had explored. Then his tongue licked the inside of her navel, and Desiree squirmed against his mouth as she felt wetness between her legs.

Tyler began to slowly move his hand up the inside of her thigh and then he hesitated, "Do you want me to stop?" His voice was laced with the sound of desire, and Desiree knew that there was no turning back.

"No," she denied huskily. Tyler swiftly stood and bent down to scoop Desiree into his arms. He instinctively walked down the short hallway to her dark bedroom and laid her on the bed. Desiree lay on her bed and Tyler slowly finished undressing her. He gently took off her shoes, then her stockings, dress, and very slowly slid her thong panties down her past her thighs to join the heap of scattered clothing.

Desiree watched Tyler rid himself of his clothes. Finally he stood naked. She gave a start of surprise at the sight of him. She had never seen a white man naked before except in the movies. His penis, which was fully erect, was not white as she had expected, but instead almost a deep pink in contrast to the rest of his body.

Tyler joined Desiree on the bed and she began to panic until he looked her directly in the eyes and whispered, "I hope you will still respect me in the morning." His teasing voice soothed her, and pulling her close to him, he gave her a long, languishing kiss. Tyler began to explore her body with his tongue. He slowly moved down the length of her body and, parting her legs, he gently probed inside her with his fingers, moving, touching, exploring. She arched her body against his hand loving his touch.

Tyler lightly kissed the inside of her thighs, then her center. Desiree gasped as he probed her center with his tongue. She spread herself wide open at the unexpected but welcome intrusion. She writhed underneath him, squirming with pleasure. Desiree lost track of how long Tyler pleasured her with his tongue. As he did so, he caressed her breast with his left hand.

The other one he slid under her hips and arched her body towards his mouth for more complete access to her moistness. She felt a sensation building, moving towards Tyler's mouth and she tried to pull back, but instead her body convulsed and spilled her desire. That night they lay together, limbs intertwined deep in sleep.

Desiree awoke and turned her head, surprised to find herself alone. A note lay on the empty pillow next to her. She read the scribble she had become so used to seeing at work. *You looked so peaceful I didn't want to wake you. As you know, I have an early date in court. Sleep in this morning if you wish. Your boss won't mind. Smile, I will not be in the office until this afternoon.*

Desiree lay motionless, thinking about the events of the previous night. She searched her heart for regret and could find none. And then, with amazement, a thought came to her. *I am totally satisfied and didn't have to do a thing for it.* Then she turned over and drifted back to sleep.

Desiree was walking down the hall towards the firm's lunchroom when Tyler hurriedly strode into the building. Memories of what had last occurred between them surfaced, and she felt blood rush to her face at the sight of him.

Smiling at her, he held up the bag in his hand and spoke softly. "Court broke for lunch earlier than I had anticipated so I took the liberty of picking us up some lunch. Are you hungry?"

"Ravenous," she replied shyly.

"Good. Let's eat in the park. It's turned into an unusually mild winter day."

No words were spoken between them as they walked the short distance to the park across the street. The air was somewhat nippy, but the noonday sun warmed them. Handing her a diet soda he said, "You don't need to watch your weight, but I notice that's what you always buy from the vending machine at work."

"Every little bit helps," she quipped. "Thanks for picking up lunch, Tyler. That was very thoughtful of you."

"No, thank you for last night." He had a devilish expression on his face as he eyed her. When she blushed, he threw his head back and laughed. "I can see that you're blushing. I didn't know women did that anymore." He grinned. "But seriously, Desiree, last night was very special to me."

"It was special for me also," she replied softly.

"Any regrets?" he inquired.

Dropping her eyes from the intensity of his, she softly asked, "No, not really, but how can we ever go back to just being co-workers?"

"We can't. That's the last thing I want, and I don't think you do either," he said.

Desiree automatically shook her head no.

"Good," Tyler responded. "Then its time for us to build on what we have and see where that leads us."

They sat on the park bench eating sandwiches and chips in a companionable silence. Then Desiree cleared her throat. "Why didn't we . . ." She didn't complete her sentence, uncertain as to how to broach the subject.

"Why didn't we what?" Tyler finished. "Go all the way?"

She grinned because she hadn't heard that expression since she was a teenager. She nodded her head in confirmation. "What happened last night was unexpected, and I wasn't prepared. We didn't have our little talk."

"What do you mean?" Desiree inquired.

"I told you before that I would try to never hurt you, or make you regret having a relationship with me. I don't know if you are on any kind of protection."

Even though Desiree knew this conversation was very much needed, she still felt embarrassed and dropped her eyes from Tyler's. "I'm on the pill. Although I'm not with Travis anymore, I just never stopped taking it." She added, "They keep me regular."

He nodded in understanding. "I'm glad to hear that. In that case, I have a feeling the next time I get lucky I will be even luckier."

She laughed again. Tyler had a way of making any subject easy to talk about.

"I have to go. I'll be in court for the rest of the day." Before he left he leaned over and kissed her lightly on the lips, ignoring the sideways glances of the people in the park. "I'll call you at home tonight, and by the way," he added, looking over his shoulder as he walked off, "that belly button ring is a real turn on."

Tyler laughed at the look of consternation on Desiree's face when she realized that the couple seated on the next bench heard him and cast sly looks at her.

That night the doorbell to Desiree's apartment rang. She opened her door a tiny bit to see the Federal Express man standing there with a package in his hand. "May I help you?" she asked.

"I have a special delivery package for a Miss Desiree Diamond."

Opening the door wider, she held out her hand to sign the yellow slip he provided. "I haven't ordered anything," she muttered to herself. Confused, she saw the name Neiman Marcus on the outside of the box and opened it. Inside there was a pair of soft leather gloves exactly like her old one. A small note was attached to the lid, and even though it wasn't Tyler's handwriting, she knew the words were his. *Let these warm your hands and I will warm your heart. Tyler.*

A few minutes later, the phone rang. Turning down the sound on the TV she hurried to answer it. "Hello."

"Hello to you, too." His voice sounded sexy, and immediately thoughts of their sexual interlude resurfaced and she felt a wetness begin to form between her legs.

"Tyler, thanks for the gloves, but how did you manage that so quickly?" Her surprise was evident in her voice.

"I have an account at Nieman Marcus. When I lived in New York I did quite a bit of shopping there. I know the store manager, and he was very accommodating when I told them I needed them today as a birthday gift. He was also kind enough to fill out the card for me."

"You lied. Today's not my birthday," she gently admonished him.

"As I've told you before, sometimes the end justifies the means."

She tried not to sound too eager but couldn't help it. "Am I going to see you later?"

"Honey . . ."

The endearment was so natural it felt as if she had been hearing him talk to her like that for ages.

"I wish I could, but I'm so tired. Even though tomorrow's Saturday I have to go into the office in the morning. The next time we're together, I want us to wake up together."

"Okay, I understand." She was disappointed but tried to hide it.

"Let's set a date for tomorrow night. Do you want to do anything special?"

"I don't particularly want to go out anywhere. I'm kind of tired. It was hard going back to work after having those days off for Thanksgiving."

"Why don't I bring pizza and a DVD?" he replied.

"That sounds like fun," she agreed.

"What do you like on your pizza?"

"Anything except anchovies."

"I agree. If I don't get a chance to call you tomorrow, I'll be over to your place around eight."

"I'm looking forward to it." Her voice sounded breathless with excitement, and she didn't care.

"Good night." Tyler's voice was sensual. "Sleep tight, and don't let the bedbugs bite."

She smiled and softly repeated, "Good night, Tyler."

The following evening, Desiree smoothed clean sheets on her bed. A small candle was lit in her bedroom and it illuminated the room with a glow, casting off a sensuous scent.

Lying in a warm bubble bath, she thought about her developing relationship with Tyler. A lot of the preliminary work had been completed on the Worthy case, and Tyler was systematically readying himself for his day in court. Because she was not working with other lawyers, she had naturally drifted into performing any of the duties or research that he needed done on his other cases.

It pleased Desiree that she and Tyler worked well together with little friction. She knew that in some cases there was constant tension between the paralegal and the lawyer that they were assigned to.

Standing in front of the mirror drying herself with a big fluffy towel, her thoughts turned to a more personal level. She had never before had an office romance, but had heard from others that it could be deadly for your career and personal life if it didn't work out. Mentally she crossed her fingers. So far, so good! She wondered if this was the first interracial relationship Tyler had ever had. He seemed so comfortable with her that it made her comfortable with him.

Letting Tyler make love to her had been a revelation. She had never before been made love to in that way so thoroughly. Of course she had had other men to pleasure her, but she had always been expected to return the favor. His total unselfishness made her want to please him all the more.

Desiree continued to ready herself for her date. She applied light makeup. Earlier she had pinned her hair up for her bath and she now brushed it to hang loose.

Crossing over to her dresser she withdrew the lace thong underwear and matching bustier she had purchased from Victoria's Secret. Feeling naughty, she stepped into a pair of high-heeled sandals and eyed her reflection. Desiree felt too uncomfortable and, stepping out of the sandals, slid her feet into a pair of soft mule bedroom shoes.

When her doorbell rang precisely at seven forty-five, she was pleased. It seemed as if Tyler was a prompt person in his personal life as well as his professional. Hastily throwing on a casual dress that reached mid-thigh, she went to open the door.

Tyler stood there grinning and holding a large pizza box, a six-pack of beer, and a small bag that she knew must contain the movie. Smiling, she ushered him in and grabbed the beer out of his hand before he dropped it. Once Tyler's hands were freed, he turned and gathered Desiree in his arms. Tilting her face to his, he gave her a melting kiss on her upturned mouth.

"Hey you," he said.

"Hey you," she returned softly.

Desiree felt tightness in her chest at the somewhat unexpected intimate moment. Flustered, she reached over to pick up the sack to see what DVD he had brought. "What did you get?"

"I forgot to ask you what you liked so I brought *Ocean's 13*. It's been out on DVD for a while, but I never had the chance to see it."

"Sounds good to me; any movie that includes Brad Pitt or George Clooney is a winner to me."

"Should I be jealous?" Tyler asked.

"Not at all," Desiree vehemently replied. "Why on earth would any of those guys come to Danbury, Connecticut?" Tyler scooped her up into his arms and sat down on the couch with her in his laps, tickling her until she pleaded with him to stop.

"So I take it you haven't seen it?"

"No, I haven't. When I do go to the movies, I usually take the twins and then it's always a straight up Disney affair."

"I bet that you would be a great mother." When silence descended on the room, Tyler smiled and motioned to Desiree. "I'll cue up the movie and you go get some paper plates and napkins for the pizza."

Desiree leaned against Tyler as they watched the last credits of the movie roll across the television screen. Glancing at the clock, she was surprised to see that it was after ten o'clock. She thought of the old cliché that was so appropriate: *How time flies when you're having fun*! Stifling a yawn she glanced at Tyler from underneath her lashes. "Would you like to hear some music? Station 89.5 plays slow groove tunes from ten o'clock to twelve o'clock every night."

"That would be nice." Tyler's gaze was hooded as he watched Desiree saunter over to the radio. The sensual voice of Maxwell filled the room. She turned around, and at once she was enveloped in Tyler's outstretched arms.

Once again, he carried her into her bedroom and gently laid her down on the bed. Tyler's oral foreplay seemed endless and she bit her tongue to stop herself from screaming, afraid that her neighbors would hear. Once Tyler entered her, he paused momentarily, letting her body adjust to his long shaft. Her body was wet with desire and he slid in easily. Moving slowly inside her, Tyler continued to gently suck her nipples with his mouth as he gripped her hips and moved inside her with long firm strokes. Holding her tightly, he waited until she climaxed and then his body jerked as he whispered her name.

Desiree turned her head to see Tyler sleeping soundly next to her. He lay flat on his back, and she was able to examine his naked body at her leisure. Because of his position, his manhood lay limply to one side. The black hair surrounding it was thick and curly. His chest was broad and covered with silky hair, which met at his navel in the shape of an arrow and tapered downward. Tyler had very little hair on his legs and thighs, and she was amused to see that his feet were the whitest thing on him.

Last night had been extremely satisfying for Desiree, and if the sounds Tyler made during their lovemaking were anything to measure by she was not alone in her satisfaction.

All at once, Tyler moved in his sleep and she watched, transfixed, as his body slowly became aroused. He turned on his side and instinctively pulled her towards him. His penis was nestled against her hips as he ran his hand possessively down the smooth length of her body from her waist down the length of her thigh. In these early morning hours his need for her resurfaced, and when their bodies rejoined their lovemaking was short and furious.

Fighting Back

CHAPTER EIGHT

During the next few weeks, Desiree and Tyler developed a pattern at work and at home. On the days he was at the office, he asked her to choose whether she wanted to order take-out, which they ate in either the conference room or the park, or sometimes they went to one of the small cafes that were so prevalent downtown.

She noticed that the employees of the firm that she had been on friendly terms with for years now shied away from her, and the days that Tyler wasn't around she was her only company. At first she thought she was just imagining things, but the morning when she spoke to Blanche Harding, the firm's receptionist, and received no response to her greeting, she knew then that the office grapevine was out in full force.

She and Tyler were having lunch at a nearby bistro when she broached the subject. "Tyler, has anyone at work been behaving differently towards you lately?" Desiree was surprised to see his expression became guarded. "I mean, is anyone acting as if they are displeased with you?"

He tried to sidestep the question. "Honey, from day one some of the other lawyers at the firm have not exactly welcomed me with open arms."

"There's more to it than that. I think that we've become the hot topic at the water cooler."

Tyler averted his eyes as he thought back to the conversation he'd had with Arthur Buchanan the previous week. Arthur Buchanan had leaned back in his high-backed swivel chair and eyed Tyler penetratingly across his desk. "I'm extremely pleased with the work you've done since you've been at Buchanan & Buchanan. Your winning record to date is five for five, and I'm confident that after the Worthy case your record will be six and zero."

He coughed slightly and then cleared his throat. "However, there is something I feel that I should discuss with you, and I haven't known how to broach the subject."

Upon hearing these words Tyler became wary.

Arthur Buchanan continued, "I don't go in for idle office gossip. Even with an office as small as this, one week it's one thing and the next week it's another. In reality, small places of work are worse when it comes to people gossiping about each other's lives." Again he coughed slightly and reached over to a walnut pine box from which he extracted a cigar, and lit it with a solid gold lighter. "Have one?"

Tyler declined. Then Buchanan said bluntly, "You're a smart man, Tyler. People are talking. Don't you know not to get your meat and potatoes from the same pot?"

Tyler's body stiffened. "What exactly do you mean?" His voice was silky, but his eyes looked like steel.

Immediately Arthur Buchanan knew how a person on the witness stand felt when being questioned by Tyler Banks.

"Don't get me wrong, Tyler. Desiree is a beautiful woman. If I were twenty years younger I'd give her a try myself, but dating someone you work with can become a complicated matter."

"Is there a company policy that prohibits dating a co-worker?" Tyler's voice was deceptively quiet.

"No," Arthur Buchanan stammered, "but—"

Tyler cut him off. "I'm glad to hear that, because I know there are others at the firm who do date. We also have a secretary married to one of our junior lawyers, and they met while employed here."

"You must agree, Tyler, that this is a different situation."

"The only difference is that Desiree is African American and I'm white." And then he added, emphasizing every word, "I don't care if people are talking. However, I do concede that it might not be the wisest thing for us to work so closely together. After we go to trial on the Worthy case we shall no longer work together. I'll use either another paralegal or someone from the secretarial pool." Tyler drew in a deep breath and his eyes glinted like steel. "Remember, Arthur, you were the one who engineered the two of us working together in the first place."

"Only because she's the best paralegal with great secretarial skills that we have and you're one of the best, if not the best, lawyer we have."

"Exactly," Tyler nodded his head. "And those factors haven't changed, have they?" He raised one eyebrow in query at the man seated across from him.

"No," Arthur Buchanan agreed.

"There is one other thing I would like to say." Tyler's voice was hard.

"What is it, Tyler?"

"I would greatly appreciate it if you would not refer to Desiree as if she is a casual fling for me or some passing fancy, because she is anything but that."

His expression was stern, and Arthur Buchanan was quite happy to let the matter drop.

As Tyler left the room, Arthur Buchanan nodded his head in affirmation and deep respect.

Looking at Desiree now, Tyler sighed. "I didn't want to mention this to you because I know how sensitive you are, but last week Arthur Buchanan requested a meeting with me. It seems as if some of the other employees of the firm disapprove of our relationship."

Desiree swallowed hard. "That's no surprise." Her words dripped with sarcasm. "Did you confirm any relationship?"

"Yes, Desiree, I did. I'm not ashamed to be in a relationship with you. As a matter of fact, I'm proud, and I would never demean what we have by denying it."

"That's easy for you to say. You're established. You're already a lawyer. You are what I'm trying to become, but Buchanan & Buchanan Law Firm could find a replacement for me at the drop of a hat."

Tyler heard the small quiver in her voice and he rushed to reassure her. "Buchanan is a smart man. He didn't get where he is today by making decisions based on emotions. He wouldn't dare fire you, and don't you dare sell yourself short. For one thing, you could not be so easily replaced. You're reliable, you don't get involved with malicious gossip, and you are extremely hard-working and talented. Arthur Buchanan knows that. And then there's one more thing."

"What?"

"If they did, we would sue them so fast you wouldn't have to work for a very long time. You could go straight to law school and stop saving your pennies." Tyler leaned over and kissed her on the cheek.

Desiree smiled. It was wonderful having someone that she could count on to have her back.

It was the week before Christmas, and Desiree was clearing away the briefs she had been working on before she left for the weekend.

"Are you ready?" Tyler entered the conference room and watched Desiree organize the items on her desk.

"You bet. I can't wait to get out of here. Going to New York City this weekend is a great idea."

"Both of us need to go Christmas shopping, and I think it's high time I showed you my home there. I haven't asked you to spend the night at my place in town because it's not fit for company. It's too small, and furnished with only the bare necessities. When I moved here, I didn't care to buy a big fancy home. I wasn't sure that I was going to stay, so I was just looking for a place to lay my head."

"Well, I look forward to seeing your penthouse. The downer is Christmas shopping. Every year I put it off until the last minute and then I have to mix with the crowd of people pushing and shoving for bargains."

"Why do you wait so long?"

"I like to buy my family really nice gifts, and the stores don't put them on sale until it's the last minute."

"What do you do if they sell out of what you want?"

"Luckily, that has never happened. I always have at least two or three ideas for each member of my family. The only thing I ever have to worry about is the latest new toy craze that the twins want, and I took care of that over a week ago."

"You're a smart woman, Desiree."

At hearing this she swiftly looked around to make sure that they were alone and then kissed him fully on the lips.

The drive to the city the next day was relaxing. As what was now usual, Tyler had spent the night at Desiree's apartment and had roused her early so they could get on the road before the interstate became too crowded. She had been grumpy when he tried to awaken her, demanding that he leave her alone because weekends were the only time she had to sleep in.

Tyler had at first cajoled and pleaded for her to get up. Then he became firm, and when that didn't work, he became even firmer. Still, only the promise of a hot cup of coffee had coerced her to leave the warm comfort of her bed.

New York was an hour and a half away, and after Desiree's mood lightened they discussed everything from what they had seen on the news the evening before, to politics, to childhood memories.

When they arrived, Tyler carefully navigated his Corvette onto West Thirty-fourth Street to the large mall where Macy's East was located. He parked in the adjacent large parking garage. The mall was teeming with shoppers. Children ran around playfully while frustrated mothers and fathers tried not to lose them in the crowd. Tyler marched Desiree through the crowd, holding her hand with more thoughts of protection than romance on his mind.

Salvation Army men dressed as Santa Claus rang bells at the entrance of each store. Tyler stopped and dropped a fifty-dollar bill in the bucket of the first Santa he saw. Then he looked at Desiree and muttered, "Now I can walk by the rest of them and shop guilt free for the rest of the day."

Desiree had to smother a laugh. Tyler said the things most people were too ashamed to admit they felt.

They systematically shopped the stores in the mall. Desiree attacked her Christmas list with a vengeance. This was the time of year that she ignored her budget and splurged to purchase each of the gifts she had in mind for her family.

Tyler stood by patiently as she bought Benjamin a key chain that beeped when he clapped his hands. That way he could readily find his keys the nights he got a late call to deliver a baby. She purchased a beautiful designer handbag for her mother and a briefcase with his initials engraved on it for Marcus Junior. She explained the situation to Tyler. "At the beginning of the year Marcus Junior is up for promotion. Maybe this present will bring him luck." She added hopefully, "I want to buy my dad a tool chest with a lock on it. He's always complaining that one of us borrowed his tools and didn't return them. Now he can lock them up, and when they turn up missing maybe he'll be convinced that no phantom is stealing his tools. He just misplaces them, that's all."

"I don't know your sisters, but it's amazing to me that your dad would think that you would even borrow a hammer, much less a wrench or screwdriver. I would never consider you a possible suspect for my missing tools."

Desiree playfully screwed up her face and lightly punched him in the shoulder. She knew what he was referring to. He had had to come over to her apartment to fix a couple of things. Once, she had a leaky faucet in the bathroom adjoining her bedroom, and at night the drip had driven her crazy. Her apartment complex maintenance man had taken too long to respond to her calls. Another time her closet door had gotten off track. It had taken Tyler a total of ten minutes to fix both of the problems.

"What are you going to buy your sisters?"

"I'm going to buy Sasha a pair of black leather knee boots, and we need to go to a jewelry store for Dominique's gift. Benjamin bought her a beautiful pair of diamond studs for their tenth wedding anniversary and I would like to buy her a pair of jackets to match them." Desiree sounded wistful when she described the present Benjamin had bought her sister.

Tyler turned and pointed in the direction opposite to which they were facing. "Feinstein's Fine Jewelry is on the next concourse." Tyler led her to it and she oohed and ahhed at the bountiful selection. The hard task was to decide which ones to choose.

She told Tyler, "Each one of Dominique's studs is a carat, so I don't want to buy anything too small." She motioned the clerk over to her. "May I try on a pair of one-carat studs with these jackets? I want to see how they look together."

"Of course, ma'am." Sensing a sale, the clerk's reply was eager.

Desiree carefully placed the studs and jackets in her ears. "They're beautiful!" she exclaimed as she stared into the full-length mirror. Twirling around, she showed the combination of jewelry to Tyler. "Honey, what do you think?" Desiree didn't notice she had used the endearment to Tyler, but he did, and happiness surged inside his body.

Tyler positioned himself behind Desiree and their images blended together as if they were one. "The word beautiful does not describe what I see," he responded quietly.

An intimate smile passed between the two of them before she turned to the clerk. "How much do they cost?" Desiree grimaced when she heard the price, but she found it impossible not to purchase the jackets once she had seen them paired with the studs. Whipping out her emergency charge card, she handed it to the sales clerk. "Will you wrap them, please?" As the clerk happily sped off with her charge card, Desiree turned to Tyler.

"I thought you had some shopping to do?"

"I do. Chad is easy. He wants the latest video game and cartridges, and I bought them last week. Nancy called and said that he also wants a new pair of skis, so I told her to get them because I'm sure that he's already shown her the ones that he wants. She's supposed to call me and tell me how much money they cost so that I can mail it to her.

"Tiffany, on the other hand, is going to be a problem. I have no idea what to buy her. She's at that in-between age. I usually get her a doll, but I don't want to insult her by buying her something too babyish."

"Get her a doll. She's only eleven. Chances are she'll play with it when nobody's looking." After they finished Desiree's shopping, she dragged him to one of the mall's toy stores. It was bedlam. Children were crying, parents' faces were red, and the line was outrageous. Viewing the scene, Tyler looked at Desiree and then cast his eyes towards heaven. Walking up and down the aisle, Desiree and Tyler pulled doll after doll off the shelf until she spotted a doll the size of a toddler on the very last row.

It had curly blonde hair that was reminiscent of Shirley Temple. The doll was dressed in an old-fashioned pink and white gingham dress with matching shoes and purse. It was soft to the touch and, holding it out to Tyler, Desiree exclaimed, "Isn't she precious?"

"Yes, it's a very beautiful doll. What does it do?" He kept turning it around, reading the instructions on the box.

Desiree held the doll out to him and he took it. "It doesn't do anything. You use your imagination make the doll do anything you want."

"Then it's perfect for Tiffany, because if there's one thing my daughter has it's a vivid imagination." Before they went to the cash register, Tyler picked out several outfits in which to dress the doll and also and a pair of ice skates for Tiffany.

If it was possible, the line seemed longer than when they had entered the store. Whispering to her, Tyler said, "I have to go to the men's room. Can you hold my place in line?"

Desiree pretended to be indignant. "Don't leave me here. What should I do if a fight breaks out?"

"Tell anyone if they harm you they're going to have to deal with me." Reaching in his wallet he pulled out several bills and handed them to her and said, "I'll be back as quickly as possible."

Desiree was next in line by the time Tyler finally reappeared. Eyeing him speculatively, she gave his money back and teased, "Is everything okay? I mean, did everything come out all right?"

"Ha, ha, ha, very funny. The first bathroom I went to was out of order, so as you can guess the next one had an extremely long line," Tyler responded smoothly. He reached over and, unloading Desiree's arms, he placed the items on the counter for the cashier to ring up.

Tyler's penthouse was located in Central Park West. Desiree carried in as many presents as she could and, plopping them down on the sofa, smiled when Tyler went to the car for the remainder of their things.

While he was gone, she did some exploring and was impressed by the enormous size and exquisite furnishings of Tyler's home. The ceilings were vaulted, the carpet a warm toast color, and the walls slightly lighter in contrast.

All the kitchen appliances were bisque with nickel fixtures. Parallel to the kitchen was a dining room with a glass dining room table that would seat six, and a mahogany hutch filled with Lenox china.

In the living room there were two ecru suede sofas facing each other with a walnut coffee table in between the two of them. The room was illuminated by two identical floor lamps. A wet bar was located on one wall, and on the other was a large wall unit with a high-definition plasma television.

A small hallway led to two bedrooms, and sandwiched between them was a bathroom with a vanity made with double sinks and a step-down shower.

Next, Desiree opened the door to the master bedroom. A wrought iron king-size bed with a headboard and mirrors was the focus point. A dresser, mirror, and armoire completed the furniture. Tyler walked into the bedroom with their luggage as Desiree viewed the adjoining bathroom.

Whirling around when she heard him, she said playfully, pointing to the large sunken tub, "I'm in dire need of a bath, and I think you are, also." His only response was a wide grin as he dropped his pants.

When they entered Satch's, an exclusive restaurant in lower East Manhattan, Desiree didn't know why she was surprised to find out that Tyler had made reservations. He always thought ahead, no matter the situation.

The restaurant was crowded, and though the lighting was dim, Desiree thought she recognized some of the faces of the patrons from television. Turning around, she gave a small start at the intensity of Tyler's gaze on her. "What are you thinking?" she demanded.

"I'm thinking about the day we've had," he said, refilling their wineglasses. "I always enjoy myself when I'm with you. You have the ability to turn something as mundane as shopping into a fun adventure, and the generosity that you show others is intoxication in itself."

Desiree felt herself blush at the compliment. "I feel the same way when I'm with you. I cringe when I think about how close I came to walking away from you because I was afraid of what people might think. I would have lost out on the best relationship I've ever had." Her eyes locked with his across the table.

"Are you trying to tell me that you don't care what people think anymore?" He watched her face carefully.

"To be honest, I'm not sure. I've never been a maverick, but I'm more afraid of losing you than I am of what people say."

Tyler reached over and took her hand in his. "You're not going to lose me, Desiree."

At this time, the waiter wheeled to the table a tray laden with their order of seafood delicacies: lobster, shrimp scampi in butter sauce, jumbo fried shrimp, clams, and oysters. "I'll never be able to eat all of this!" Desiree exclaimed as she tackled her plate with relish.

They were quiet at dinner, each deep in thought. Desiree's mind was replaying their playtime in the bathtub earlier that evening. Afterwards Tyler had toweled them off and led Desiree to the bedroom, where they'd had a long, languid session of lovemaking.

After dinner they strolled down the boulevard. Shop windows twinkled with Christmas lights and decorations. People hurriedly walked with heads bent as they braced themselves against the cold wind. Desiree liked the feeling of anonymity. No one paid any attention to them, and she could be as affectionate to Tyler as she wanted without the raised eyebrows she sometimes felt she was getting in Danbury whenever they were seen out together.

Desiree clung tightly to Tyler's hand and said, "Do you know how dangerous this is? People get robbed more during the holidays than any other time of year."

"We'll be okay as long as we stay in the lighted areas," Tyler said.

"Then I want to go to Rockefeller Plaza to see the Christmas tree."

"You're pushing it now. It's not even twenty degrees tonight. I'll take you tomorrow during the daytime, when it's safer and warmer." His refusal was firm.

When he immediately smothered a yawn from behind his hand, Desiree tucked her arm in his. "I think I'd better get you home and put you to bed."

"Sounds good to me," he agreed.

The next morning, Desiree turned her head to see Tyler sleeping soundly next to her. As usual, he lay flat on his back. She had gotten into the practice of waking early and watching him sleep. As if aware of her scrutiny, Tyler moved restlessly under her gaze and, without opening his eyes possessively reached for her; he gathered her into his arms, buried his face in her hair, and curved her body into the folds of his.

After a late breakfast of coffee and croissants, they walked the short distance to Central Park. Tyler had asked Desiree if she wanted him to drive them but she had declined, thinking about all of the food she ate whenever she was with him.

Desiree stood within the circle of Tyler's arms and gazed with awe at the large, beautifully decorated pine tree. Kids in the crowd sang Christmas carols to no one in particular.

Her attention was drawn to a cluster of people who had gathered off to one side watching a photographer and his models at work. Desiree eyed the models as they posed for the camera. They were each about five feet, ten inches or five feet, eleven inches tall. One of them had copper-colored skin and full lips that pouted at the camera. The other model was obviously a mixture of Asian and black. Her eyes were slanted and her thick, black, shiny mane fell to her hips.

"Colette, lift your head a little," the photographer directed. The copper-skinned model turned her head.

Both models were dressed in full-length mink coats, and he snapped pictures as they posed in various positions in front of the fountain.

"Great job!" he replied enthusiastically, "Chanel, move a little over to the right." After Chanel did as he requested he said, "I think those are all the pictures we need with the fountain as a backdrop."

At this time the two models gracefully floated down off the three steps of the water fountain. The model called Chanel crossed over to the photographer, and as he straightened up from his equipment she wrapped her arms around his middle and gave him a long, possessive kiss.

There was something about way the photographer turned his head and the movement of his hands as they threaded themselves in the model's long hair that seemed familiar to Desiree.

The group of onlookers applauded the embrace, and Chanel threw them a bright smile. At this time the photographer turned to acknowledge his audience, and Desiree unconsciously stiffened when her eyes and met his across the crowd. It was Travis.

Travis murmured something to the models and started towards Desiree and Tyler. Hastily turning towards Tyler, Desiree gestured toward a vendor on the other side of the park where a line of people stood waiting to purchase a cup of hot chocolate. "Tyler, would you please buy me a cup of hot chocolate?"

"Sure." He hesitated and began to say something, but instead pressed his lips together and strode off.

"Desiree, what a surprise." Travis stared at her, and she fidgeted under his intense scrutiny.

"How are you doing, Travis?" She was taken aback at seeing him, and the quiver in her voice betrayed her nervousness.

"I'm doing okay. I tried to call you several times, but you didn't answer the telephone. Who is that?" He jerked his head in the direction of Tyler who was at the end of the line waiting to purchase Desiree's drink. Desiree didn't answer him. He hesitated and then continued, "I was going to stop by your parents' house during the Thanksgiving holidays, but I didn't think when we saw each other again that other people should be there." Desiree remained quiet, not giving Travis any encouragement or any indication as to what she was thinking.

At her lack of response, Travis's expression became surly, and his tone was slightly mocking. "Are you seeing that guy?"

"He's a friend of mine," she replied, stung by his attitude. "We work together." Her face was impassive and her words not forthcoming.

"It seems to me as if there's a little more to it than that." He said snidely, "Well, if he's your boss, I guess your job is pretty secure."

Travis's tone was derogatory and Desiree bristled at the insinuation. "My relationship with him, or any other man for that matter, is really none of your business."

"Desiree, we need to talk." He changed his tone and sounded like the Travis she had met years ago and jumped at the chance to go out with.

"Talk about what, Travis?"

"About us."

Desiree's only response was to raise one eyebrow in query. She glanced over to where Tyler was paying for his order. "Listen, Travis, if I had been home to answer the telephone when you called, I would have apologized for some of the things I said to you the night we broke up. Let me amend that. I don't want to apologize for what I said, but for the way I said it. That would have been all of the conversation between us."

"I'm sorry about what I said earlier. Don't get all hot under the collar at me for an innocent remark. I'm just surprised that you decided to go white. I must have really hurt you."

Desiree chose to ignore that. "Well, I must say that I'm not surprised to see that you're straddling the fence. You never could make a firm stand about anything, could you?" she retorted, looking past him to where the two models stood watching. Chanel's arms were folded and she was tapping her foot impatiently.

Travis frowned at her. "Chanel is mixed, but because her father is black she is considered African American."

"Well, all I know is that she's not a total sister. If you're going to do something, Travis, you may as well go all the way." She paused, "Be more like me. There ain't no half-stepping in my game."

She saw Tyler walking in their direction with a steaming cup of hot chocolate in his hand, and she looked at Travis dismissively. "My boyfriend is on his way back, so if you don't mind . . ."

Travis hesitated. "Desiree, again I apologize if I've offended you. I'm just a little surprised, that's all. May I please call you so we can talk?"

"What do you want to talk to me about? You ended our relationship, didn't you?"

Travis said hotly, "You ended our relationship, Miss Thang. Don't forget you dumped me; I didn't dump you."

"You readily agreed, though. You didn't even try to fight for me, for us. You just let it go," she retorted.

"You're the one," he said, pointing at her, "who forced me out of the relationship. You tried to force my hand, push me into a marriage that I wasn't ready for."

"Because you gave me no choice; I got tired of waiting. I got tired of you stringing me along. You flat out told me that you couldn't commit, and that was the straw that broke the camel's back."

Travis's voice became cajoling. "Come on, Desiree. If we sit down together, maybe we can straighten things out. This relationship that you're having with this white man is not right for you." She didn't respond, and Travis became exasperated at her stony silence. "Hell, you're lucky I would even consider taking you back after seeing this. A lot of black men wouldn't, you know."

On hearing this, Desiree's temper exploded, and she could barely contain her fury as she whispered to Travis, "This happens to be the best relationship I've ever had. That man treats me better than you ever did. You blew it, Travis. The smartest thing I ever did in our relationship was to actually try to pin you down to set a date for our wedding."

Travis whispered quietly, wishing he could take back his spiteful words. "Please, Desiree, may I call you?"

"I tell you what, Travis; don't call me if I don't call you."

She turned on her heel and went to meet Tyler halfway. As she walked away, she felt Travis's eyes boring into her back and she felt a chill run down her spine. Instinctively she stiffened her body and braced herself more against the eyes than the cold weather.

As Travis watched Desiree walk away with another man, he swallowed hard. He hadn't expected their split to last. He had been merely buying himself some time because he felt he wasn't in a position to take care of a wife. He'd never expected Desiree to get another man so soon after their breakup. Especially a white man! For the first time ever, he allowed his resentment for his mother and sister to flare up inside him.

Chanel walked over and planted herself in front of him. Her whining made him turn his attention to her.

Her plaintive voice pierced the air. "Are you ready? Why are we standing here in the cold?" Giving her a distant look, he let her lead him back to the waiting Colette and his camera equipment.

Neither Desiree nor Tyler spoke on the walk back to his penthouse. The silence hung heavy between them. Desiree slid a surreptitious look at Tyler and felt uneasy to see his dark countenance.

Once she entered the apartment she immediately walked into the bedroom to rid herself of her outerwear. Reentering the living room, Desiree was surprised to see Tyler had carelessly dropped his coat and scarf in a heap on the chair and was in the process of taking off his shoes. Without speaking he turned on the television and sat on the sofa, flipping through the channels with the remote control.

"Anything good on?" she asked.

"No." Turning off the set, he looked at her. "That's him, isn't it?"

"Who?" The abrupt change in topic and the tone of his voice threw her.

"The man you were involved with for all those years." Tyler bit off his words, and his expression was foreboding.

"Yes, that was Travis," Desiree slowly responded.

"Do you still love him?" Tyler's body was rigid as he sat on the couch.

Surprise etched her features. "What would ever make you think a thing like that?" she exclaimed.

"You got rid of me so that you could talk to him alone." Tyler's words were clipped, and his tone biting.

Desiree could hear Tyler's hurt, and she felt contrite that she had caused him pain.

"I'm sorry, Tyler. The only reason I did that is because I wanted to apologize to him for some of the things I said to him the night we broke up. I didn't want you to hear the things that I had said." She paused, embarrassed. "It's a side of me that you haven't seen."

"Breakups are rarely pleasant, Desiree. I know that Nancy's and mine wasn't. But it's disrespectful to dismiss me in order to talk to another man."

"I apologize, Tyler. I didn't think about it from your perspective." Remorse was evident on her face, and her tone was apologetic.

"Just don't do it again." Tyler's voice was stern and Desiree nervously drew in a sigh of relief, hoping that was the end of it.

The Dating Game

CHAPTER NINE

The next afternoon, the ride back home was peaceful. Laughter had been restored once she and Tyler talked at his penthouse, and it seemed as if they had never even had a slight disagreement. Inwardly Desiree was pleased to see that Tyler didn't sulk like a little boy and give her the silent treatment in order to teach her a lesson for her hurting him. She hated the payback game that so many couples played. She also felt a small thrill inside at the way he had put her in her place and called her on her behavior. Desiree looked over at Tyler, and when he glanced at her she smiled at him, reached over, grabbed his hand, and gave it a small squeeze that he returned.

Once back at her apartment, Desiree helped Tyler carry her belongings upstairs. After they separated everything, and Desiree went downstairs to check her mail. She was surprised to see Tyler on the telephone when she returned. "Who are you calling?" she asked.

"No one. The telephone rang, but once I picked it up, no one said anything."

"Oh," she said, "it must be a wrong number. I hate when that happens. The person could at least say something."

"You should get caller ID. I don't even answer the telephone if someone calls and I know it's a wrong number."

"I'll think about it. Because my number is unlisted, I never really felt the need before." Changing the subject, she asked, "When are you going home for Christmas?" Every year the firm closed down a few days before Christmas until after New Year's. Desiree knew Tyler usually went home every year to spend Christmas in West Virginia with his parents.

"Nancy called last week. Since I agreed to let Chad go skiing with his best friend and his family, she is going to keep Tiffany Christmas day, and I'm going to pick her up the next morning. We have an afternoon flight out of the Hartford airport."

"I don't like the idea of you spending all of Christmas Day alone," she said.

"Well, it was easier to get a flight out on Saturday so it sort of worked out."

"I won't leave for my parents' house until early Christmas morning. That way we can spend Christmas Eve together and wake up in each other's arms on Christmas morning. Since I'm going to be there for a few days I'm sure they will understand."

Tyler made no comment, but by the smile that spread across his face, he obviously appreciated her actions. "Are you ready for the Christmas party on Wednesday?" he asked.

Buchanan & Buchanan Law Firm had an annual Christmas party at the firm the last evening before it closed for the holidays. Attendance was not mandatory, but it was noticed if the employee wasn't there.

"Pretty much. It's always amusing to see some of the stiff-necked lawyers get tipsy. That's why the party is always held the last day of work before the holidays, so people can sleep it off the next day if they've had too much to drink." Desiree hesitated, "If we go together we'll be giving the gossip mongers even more to talk about."

"Good! That can be our Christmas gift to them," he responded.

"It should be interesting," Desiree agreed.

Blanche Harding smiled politely at the woman who stood in front of her desk. She admired the shoulder length brown hair streaked with blonde highlights and her obviously expensive tweed overcoat. "Good afternoon. May I help you?"

"Good afternoon," the woman replied in a haughty voice.

Blanche Harding's feathers were immediately ruffled by her tone.

"I'm looking for Tyler Banks's office."

"May I ask who wishes to see him?" Blanche's earlier cordial greeting cooled slightly, and she herself adopted a slightly disdainful attitude.

"I'm Mrs. Banks."

Blanche's mouth fell open. She slowly repeated the words. "You're Mrs. Banks?"

"Yes," she sighed impatiently, displeased that it seemed necessary that she explain. "I'm Tyler Banks's ex-wife."

"Oh." Blanche placed a hand over her heart, pretending relief. The gesture was an obvious attempt at cattiness. "You scared me for a minute when you said that you were Mrs. Banks."

"And the reason for that would be?" Nancy Banks looked at her inquiringly.

"Nothing." She lowered her voice to a whisper. "I really shouldn't speak out of turn."

Ordinarily Nancy wouldn't lower herself to acknowledge such an obvious ploy to repeat office gossip, but her curiosity got the best of her. "Whatever are you talking about?"

"Well," Blanche leaned forward conspiratorially, "it's just that when you said that you were Mrs. Banks I just got startled because everyone at the office knows that he's seeing a woman who works here."

"Oh, really? Who is the woman?" Nancy demanded.

"She's a paralegal. Her name is Desiree Diamond. She's young, beautiful, and . . ." Blanche hesitated, feigning decorum. "Well, maybe the rest you can see for yourself. They usually work together in the conference room down the hall to your right, room 111."

"Thank you." Nancy Banks was tight-lipped as she walked down the short hallway.

Left alone, Blanche leaned back in her chair with an air of satisfaction and muttered, "Serves her right. That should knock Mrs. Upper Crust down a peg or two."

Without knocking, Nancy Banks unceremoniously entered the conference room. Desiree and Tyler had taken a break and sat companionably drinking a cup of coffee.

Taking in the obvious look of surprise on Tyler's face, Nancy's expression became smug. Her eyes lingered momentarily on Desiree before dismissing her.

"Nancy, what on earth are you doing here?" His voice sounded unpleasantly surprised.

Desiree knew immediately that she must be Tyler's ex-wife.

"Darling, I came to see you." She crossed over and bent to kiss him on his cheek as he remained seated. Tyler immediately stiffened uncomfortably and he rose to his feet.

"That is an unusual greeting coming from you. Allow me to introduce Desiree Diamond," he said curtly.

It was now Nancy's turn to stiffen. Her mouth dropped open and she repeated his words. "This is Desiree Diamond?"

"Desiree works here as a paralegal and—"

"I know who she is." Nancy's voice cut across his words. "The office gossip reached me before I reached you." Pointedly ignoring Desiree, she asked, "May I speak to you alone?"

Desiree gracefully stood, gathering her things. "I'm going to go and freshen up before the party." Leaving before Tyler could stop her, she briefly nodded at the former Mrs. Banks and then left the room with a proud tilt to her head.

Once they were alone he said, "What do you want that is so important a phone call couldn't suffice?" His tone was cold.

Nancy's temper began to rise. "I happened to be in the area visiting friends, so I thought it would be easier if I just dropped by. I must say, I don't care for your attitude, Tyler."

"I didn't care for your attitude towards Desiree," he countered.

"My goodness, who is she supposed to be, the Queen of Sheba?"

"She's someone who's important to me," he retorted, and Nancy gave him a long look, noting the absence of his wedding ring. The last time she had seen him he had still been wearing his band.

"It's true, isn't it? You're actually seeing that woman." Nancy's tone was incredulous.

"I don't know from whom you got your information, and frankly I don't care. But yes, it is true. Desiree and I have been seeing each other for months, and I plan on marrying her."

Nancy sat down with a look of utter disbelief on her face. "Furthermore," he added, "I don't see what business it is of yours. We're divorced, or have you forgotten that?"

"We do have children together, and what you do affects them."

"Oh yeah?" He gave a snort of derision. "Since when?"

She ignored that remark. "I think that you're going through some early mid-life crisis, Tyler. A lot of men your age begin to do things that are unusual." She hesitated, then added, "If you're lonely, maybe I could introduce you to someone suitable."

He laughed harshly. "Nancy, I must say that you run true to form. You're not worried about the children, or me. You're worried your friends will find out that your ex-husband, and I must stress the word *ex-husband,* is involved with a black woman." Tyler noticed she didn't respond. He said abruptly, "Why did you come here today?"

Nancy's voice bridled with resentment. "Chad needs extra money for his ski trip, and I also need a check for the cost of the skis. They cost eight hundred and fifty dollars."

Tyler reached down into his attaché case and silently wrote out the check. He handed it to her with a condescending manner. "Here's a check, which includes extra money for Chad's trip. But you need to know something. I'm not interested in your friends' opinions or your shallow values. Tread carefully, Nancy, otherwise some of these extra fringe benefits you've become accustomed to asking me for at the drop of a hat could easily be obliterated."

After Nancy departed in a huff, Tyler found Desiree at her desk reading some notes. She looked up when he entered. "I take it that was your ex-wife."

"That's her, all right. I apologize for her rudeness."

"You can't apologize for her, Tyler. Only she can do that. What did she want?" She looked at him inquiringly.

"Money," he said simply.

"Did you give it to her?"

"Yes. I kind of expected it because of the holidays." There was a pause, "Nancy doesn't care about me. She hasn't for a long time. She only cares about how things look to other people. I told her about us, and she wasn't very complimentary."

"Do you think she'll try to influence the kids?" Desiree's voice was low. She was a firm believer in family unity, and hoped that her relationship with Tyler didn't put a strain on his relationship with his children.

Tyler's voice sounded hard. "She better not even think about it. I'm not going to let her jerk me around when it comes to them. The previous arrangements still stand. Chad is going to Aspen; that's what the extra money was for. And I'm picking Tiffany up on Saturday so she can spend the Christmas holidays with me in West Virginia. My parents deserve to see at least one of their grandchildren during the holidays."

Desiree stood. She looked quickly to make sure they weren't being watched, and kissed Tyler on his cheek. "You're a good man, Tyler Banks."

The firm's Christmas party was in full swing when they got there. Several employees cast knowing looks at each other when they entered the room together. Tyler bent down to murmur in her ear that he was going to the bar set up on the other side of the room to get them drinks.

Desiree pretended not to notice that other men in the room openly eyed her after he left her side.

As she glanced around the room, she realized she was being beckoned from across the room by a waving hand.

Desiree remained where she was, unwilling to approach the unfriendly looking group, but smiled when she saw her friend Jillian.

Jillian had been out on maternity leave for the last six months, and due to complications, had only recently returned. She broke away from the small group she had been mingling with and walking up to Desiree, gave her a warm hug. "It's so great to see you. A couple of times I looked for you at lunch, but could never seem to run into you."

"A lot of times I go out to lunch, or have it in the park."

"Oh, that explains it. Congratulations, I hear you're the brains on the Worthy case." There was a running joke among the paralegals that they were the brains and the lawyers were merely the mouthpieces.

"I bet that's not all you heard." Desiree's voice was mildly sarcastic.

"You got that right." Jillian had a teasing note in her voice. "I also hear that you're dating tall, white, and handsome over there. He looks like a younger version of Alec Baldwin." She pointedly looked at Tyler. Desiree's eyes followed Jillian's across the room in Tyler's direction. Desiree laughed at Jillian's statement and nodded her head in agreement. Jillian had always been a frank and honest person; that was one of the main reasons Desiree liked her so much.

Blanche Harding had waylaid Tyler at the bar. She placed her hand on his forearm and looked up at him with a beguiling smile. She found whatever he said to her enormously funny and giggled. Blanche's expression was seductive as she twirled a long strand of her chestnut hair through her fingers. Tyler smiled, and Desiree felt a sharp stab of jealousy when she saw that his amusement was genuine. Instinctively looking up, their eyes locked across the room. He excused himself at once and began to weave his way back in her direction.

"All the single females are extremely jealous," Jillian continued. "They said that he took off his wedding band once he started dating you."

After Tyler and Desiree had become intimate, he had removed his wedding band, and she hadn't seen it since. She never mentioned its absence, but was pleased when she realized it was gone.

Tyler rejoined Desiree. He gave Jillian a polite nod before he handed Desiree her drink.

Desiree introduced them. "Tyler, this is Jillian, a friend of mine. She's been out on maternity leave. Jillian, this is Tyler Banks."

Desiree didn't realize the expression of adoration she had when she looked at Tyler or the pride that was evident in her voice when she said his name. But Jillian did, and she was quite amused to see that her friend was so smitten.

Jillian and Tyler shook hands, carefully sizing each other up, and what each saw was that they had a mutual interest in Desiree's happiness.

Then Tyler said quietly, "I need to talk to Ralph Benson about a case before we break for the holidays. Are you going to be okay for a few minutes?"

"I'm fine; I'll hang out here with Jillian." Desiree's ease was genuine when she looked at him.

"Go ahead, Desiree and I can use this time to play catch up. Besides, we can't talk about you with you standing here," Jillian said, grinning.

Tyler's only response was a nod of acceptance that he would be the topic of conversation once he walked away.

That night as they got ready for bed, Desiree introduced the subject of the Christmas party. Walking into the adjoining bathroom to wash the makeup off her face, Desiree said to Tyler from where she was bent over the sink, "I had not been looking forward to attending the party, but it was better than I thought."

"I'm glad you enjoyed yourself. Jillian seems like an okay friend," he responded.

"She's pretty cool. We were hired around the same time. Because we were both the new kids on the block we sort of naturally gravitated to each other."

Just then the sound of the telephone ringing startled her. It was after midnight, and she usually didn't receive calls that late at night. As she walked back into the bedroom Tyler was reaching for the telephone on her nightstand.

"Hello," he said. A second later he repeated himself, "Hello." Replacing the receiver he looked at Desiree, who was watching him with a questioning look on her face. Tyler shrugged his shoulders. "They hung up. It must be a wrong number again. You should really get caller I.D."

"Okay, I'll do that," she replied.

Desiree changed the subject to what was weighing on her mind. It had been bothering her all evening long. "What did Blanche Harding say to you that was so amusing?" Her words were laced with an obvious note of jealousy.

"Is that the green-eyed monster rearing his ugly head?" Tyler looked pleased at the thought.

"So what if it is?" Desiree watched Tyler as he pulled back the covers and got into the side of the bed that he had he claimed as his own.

"Miss Harding felt compelled to tell me that she is the person who told Nancy she could find me in the conference room, and hoped that she hadn't caused me any trouble. She also said that if it did she would like to make it up to me while the firm is out for Christmas vacation."

"Oh she did, did she? What did you tell her?" Desiree was annoyed, and let Tyler know by placing her hands on both hips.

"At first I explained how irrelevant it was that she told Nancy where I was, and I was going out of town for the holidays but if she wanted to go out for drinks maybe I could do so after the first of the year."

Desiree walked over to where Tyler lay in bed and stood over him, glaring.

"I also told her that she could reach me at your home telephone number in the firm's directory, because that's usually where I am and she needed to clear this with you."

Tyler's eyes were twinkling with mischief and, seeing this, Desiree picked up a pillow and hit him with it. Tyler retaliated by pulling her on top of him and a boisterous pillow fight ensued.

As she lay snuggled in the comfort of Tyler's arms Desiree thought about Blanche Harding's behavior at the Christmas party and the jealousy she felt when she saw Blanche touch Tyler. Looking deep into her heart she knew. *I love him, and I want him.* There was no doubt in her mind about that. She had only one doubt. *What am I going to do about it?*

On Christmas Eve Desiree prepared a sumptuous dinner of veal parmesan and fettuccine alfredo for them. Candles lit the glass dinette table, and they were each excited about seeing their families for the holiday but saddened because they had not been separated for any extended length of time since they had begun dating.

After dinner Tyler leaned back, patting his full stomach, and declared, "If you keep feeding me like this, next year I'll volunteer to play the role of Santa Claus. I could save a store a lot of money on padding."

Desiree chuckled at Tyler and smiled. "If you play the part of Santa Claus, I'll be one of your elves."

"I'd much rather you play the part of Mrs. Claus. You're already acting out some of the roles, and I'm very, very satisfied," he said. The sensual look on his face caused her to blush. "It's sweet to see that you still blush around me. You're so shy and reserved during the day, but at night you're a regular little tigress."

Desiree's face was pensive as she thought about what he said. "I don't feel that I have to hold back anything from you. In other relationships, I was afraid to give my all because I wasn't sure it was being returned."

"My giving my all to you could only benefit me in the end. I firmly believe that whatever you do in life, you get out of it what you put in to it." Tyler reached into his pocket and held out a small square to Desiree. "Merry Christmas, darling."

Desiree smiled and said, "Wait a minute. I hid yours in the bedroom closet. Let me go and get it, and we can open our presents in the living room." Desiree hopped up out of the chair and rushed to the bedroom to get Tyler's gift.

When she returned she found he had grabbed the bottle with the remaining wine from dinner and two wine glasses. He was sitting on the loveseat, waiting expectantly. Reaching out for the large box she held in her hands, he said, "Hand my present here, girl."

Desiree stood quietly watching Tyler's face as he opened his gift. She had bought him a pair of navy blue Chinese silk pajamas, matching robe, and slippers. "I thought that you might like to leave them here all of the time."

Tyler's face shone with happiness as he looked up at her. "Desiree, they're beautiful. Thank you so much."

"Hold on," she said. She ran back into her bedroom and returned with a large basket with a large bow tied on the handle. Its contents held anything a man needed in order to be well groomed before he started his day.

Deodorant, alcohol, razors, after-shave, and cologne were teamed with several packages of underwear, undershirts, and a couple of pairs of argyle socks. At the bottom of the box, wrapped in tissue paper, was a key to the front door of her apartment.

"I put it together myself," she whispered shyly. "Now you don't have to get up early in order to go home to shower and change. Everything you need is here. I even cleared out a shelf in my bathroom for you."

Tyler looked as if he had just gotten the best Christmas gift he ever had. "I love it. Now it's your turn."

Desiree sat on the cushion next to Tyler. Carefully tearing the wrapping off the box, it revealed a velvet box without a name. Desiree opened it slowly, and gasped in astonishment when she saw that inside was the pair of diamond earrings she had tried on in Feinstein's where she had purchased Dominique's Christmas present. "Tyler, they're too much," she gasped.

"I think that you must be the only woman in the world to tell a man something like that," he laughed.

"But," she protested, "these studs must be at least two carats each."

Tyler laughed, "They better be; that's what the salesman said when he sold them to me."

Desiree digested this information and looked up at him curiously, "Did you think that I was hinting for a pair when we were in Feinstein's?"

"No, I did not," Tyler reassured her. "And that's what makes you so unique. You have no idea what a godsend it was for me that you decided to buy those earring jackets for Dominique. Until then, I had no idea what to get you, so when you were in line at the toy store I went back and snapped them up. Try them on. I want to see if they look as beautiful on you here as they did in the store."

Desiree walked over to the mirror she had hanging on the wall in the living room. Staring at her reflection she felt very special, and when Tyler came and stood behind her, their reflections seemed to blend together as if they were one person. Not moving from in front of the mirror, she stared at the image they made in the mirror. It looked beautiful to her.

"Tyler, the earrings are beautiful and I love them, but not half as much as I love you." Desiree's voice was choked with emotion.

"I know that, honey." Mirrored in his eyes was his love for her.

"It's getting late, so we better go to bed. I don't want you tired while driving home tomorrow."

Family Ties

CHAPTER TEN

When Desiree pulled into the driveway at her parents' house, she could tell by counting cars that she was the last to arrive. Gathering up an armful of gifts, she opened the back door to the aroma of coffee and of freshly baked pies. "Ho, ho, ho, Merry Christmas!" she shouted.

She heard the twins scream from the living room and the sound of running feet when they recognized her voice. The other members of her family were alone behind them, and she felt consumed with the holiday spirit as she received warm hugs from each.

The twins were jumping up and down demanding to know why she was so late. Avoiding an explanation, she replied, "I'm sorry, kids. I'll make it up to you by staying as long as you want me to."

She handed each of them their gift. Appeased, they ran back into the living room to unwrap their presents. "I have to go back to the car and get the rest of them," Desiree said.

At this Marcus Junior said, "I'll go and get them. You should relax after your drive." Shrugging on his overcoat, he opened the door and went outside.

Smiling at Desiree, Dominique said, "The twins already opened their other gifts. I couldn't contain them, but the rest of us waited for you."

Desiree followed the rest of her family into the living room. Everyone's gifts were sectioned off in a pile around the tree.

Sasha looked amused and told Desiree, "Nichelle and Nicholas did that so we wouldn't have to waste any time once you got here."

The Diamond family tradition was that everyone took turns unwrapping gifts while the others looked on. The order was always the same. Their parents went first, and then Dominique, Desiree, Sasha, and Marcus Junior. Ever since marrying into the family, Benjamin had insisted on being the last person to open his presents, not wanting to ruffle a long-standing order. Christmas was the time of year that everyone splurged on presents and the money each person, spent usually turned out to be almost equal each year.

Desiree's gifts were a hit, and she was extremely happy with her loot. Her parents gave her a gold necklace, and Sasha gave her a charm holder with several charms to start off her collection. Dominique and Benjamin gave her a DVD player, and her gift from Marcus Junior was a combination cordless phone and answering machine. When Desiree opened her present from Marcus Junior, she teased him unmercifully because she knew that he didn't own an answering machine. He replied that there had been such a good sale on them that he had gotten one for himself.

After the gifts were opened everyone leaned back, exhausted and relieved that another Christmas shopping extravaganza was over. Mrs. Diamond got up and said, "I'm going to the kitchen and put the finishing touches on some dishes." As her girls started to get up and help her she waved them back down. "Sit back, there's little left to do. It would be more trouble to tell you what to do than to do it myself." Without voicing any argument, they immediately sat back down in their chairs.

As she did so, Desiree tucked her hair behind one ear and Sasha exclaimed, "Oh, my God! Desiree, are those earrings real?" Everyone's eyes suddenly focused on her.

Dominique spoke before Desiree could say anything. "Of course they're real; glass doesn't sparkle like that."

Desiree felt as if she were standing under a spotlight as everyone waited for her to answer. Just then the telephone rang and Desiree's mother called from the kitchen, "Desiree, the phone is for you." Eagerly scrambling to her feet, she was relieved to get away from her family's intense stares.

"Hello." She felt excited because she knew the only person who could be calling her was Tyler.

"Hello, darling. I just called to make sure that you made it safely to your parents' house."

Tyler sounded so sexy that a shiver ran down her spine.

Desiree walked into the study with the cordless phone to escape her mother's interest as she pretended to busy herself cleaning the kitchen counters.

"That was thoughtful of you, Tyler. Actually, I've been here about forty-five minutes. We've already opened our presents, and everyone loved what I gave them."

"That's because you have such excellent taste."

"Especially in men, right?" Desiree whispered, teasing him.

"Right," he laughed, joining in her amusement.

"When are you and Tiffany leaving tomorrow?"

"Our plane leaves around three o'clock. We have a lay over but should get to West Virginia around eight o'clock."

"Call me from your parents to let me know that you're safe," she instructed.

"I will. I love you, Desi."

"I love you, too, Tyler." After she disconnected, Desiree sat at her father's desk thinking. She had never told Tyler her about father's pet name for her, yet one night he had called her Desi while they were making love and now often used it when he was feeling emotional. Feeling a rush of warmth, she thought, *It's kismet. Our relationship is meant to be.*

Shaking her head, she looked up to see Marcus Junior leaning against the doorjamb watching her. "I didn't mean to eavesdrop; I just got here. I wanted to warn you that Dominique and Sasha are dying to know where you got those earrings, and they're not going to let it rest."

"How do they know I didn't buy them myself?" Desiree pretended to be indignant, and Marcus Junior gave her a long look.

"And forget about your five year plan to save enough money for law school? I doubt it. If you don't want to tell them, don't. It will give them something to worry themselves to death about over the holidays. At least I know that you didn't go back to Travis. He would never spend that kind of money on earrings. Even I can look at them and see that they cost quite a bit." He hesitated. "Even though you can't measure love by money, they at least show that he appreciates you, and that's something I never felt Travis did. I just kept my mouth shut."

"Who's Travis?" Then she linked her arm in her brother's and they rejoined the others.

Dominique and Sasha continued to barrage Desiree with questions. Marcus Junior sat on the couch next to his father, and they listened to the banter between the girls. Several times Marcus Junior shook his head chidingly at Dominique and Sasha as they interrogated Desiree. Her father said nothing; he just sat back with his arms folded across his chest and listened. Desiree followed her brother's advice and refused to give her sisters any real information about the earrings. She came up with all kind of flip answers, such as, "I found them on the subway," or "I stole them," or "I got them as a gift for being named paralegal of the year."

Dominique and Sasha refused to accept the possibility that she had purchased them and demanded to know who gave them to her. Sasha declared that she knew that a man had to have given them to Desiree and that she had to be putting out because no one would spend that kind of money on someone who wasn't. Upon hearing this, Desiree's father sharply admonished Sasha for her off-color remarks and she fell silent. Then Dominique picked up the gauntlet and demanded to know what man had given them to her, how long she had been dating him, and why had she had never brought him over and introduced him to the family.

Before Desiree had to think up an answer, Marcus Junior answered the question for her. He gave Desiree a conspiratorial wink and told Dominique, "Desiree was afraid that you would scare him off."

Finally tired of the third degree, Desiree said in exasperation, "You two may as well give up! I'm not telling."

Never one to let someone else have the last word, Sasha said, "He must be really ugly. You're so intent on hiding him."

Then Dominique jumped on that before Desiree could answer. "He can't be as ugly as Abdul." And everyone burst into laughter, including Sasha.

After her laughter had subsided, Sasha continued her musings. "Well then, he must be some rich oil sheik from a foreign country or something. They're the only ones with money nowadays. I know that it's not a black man because even if he did have that kind of money he wouldn't spend it on a girlfriend. Even a wife would be lucky to get it. Black men like a sure thing before digging that deep in their pockets. Only the wives of athletes can figure on getting some real nice jewelry, and then only when their husbands mess up."

Desiree was taken aback by Sasha's off-the-cuff remarks. She knew that she was only running her mouth the way she always did, but her comments hit too close to home. Wanting to end her sisters' interrogation, she settled on a dumb silence in answer to their questions. Dominique finally gave up, infuriated, and Sasha teased that she was going to hire a private detective to investigate and find out who gave Desiree the earrings. Once she found out his identity, she was going to try to get a pair of earrings out of him for herself, she claimed.

At this everyone in the room broke into laughter except their father. Desiree became aware of his uncharacteristic silence and gave a start of surprise when she spied his intense gaze on her.

"Hello, Nancy, this is Tyler. I'm on my way to pick up Tiffany." His voice was brisk and businesslike.

"You can't," Nancy responded crisply.

"What do you mean, I can't?" he demanded, his hackles rising.

"Tiffany has the flu. The doctor said that she needs complete bed rest for at least three days, which means that she can't spend the holidays with you."

"Don't play games with me, Nancy. The child just got over a bout with the chicken pox at Thanksgiving, and now you expect me to believe she has the flu?" Anger dripped from his words.

Nancy's reply was sharp. "Tyler, do you really think that I would make up something like this? I'm not any happier about this than you are. Chad left on Wednesday with the Van Horns and Tiffany was supposed to be with you. I had plans of my own that I had to cancel."

"Why didn't you call me and tell me?" he demanded.

"I just found out yesterday myself. I tried to call you at home, but you didn't answer. You must have been out all night with that woman. Honestly, Tyler, you should leave a number with your answering service in case of emergencies."

He ignored her reference to Desiree. "You're right, Nancy. I will in the future. May I speak to Tiffany?

"Hold on, I'll get her, but you can't talk to her too long. She's pretty doped up from medication."

Tyler heard the phone extension pick up.

"Daddy?"

Tiffany sounded weak, and Tyler felt sympathy for her and wished he could trade places with her and make her well again.

"Yes, pumpkin. I hear you're sick."

"I don't feel well. The doctor said that I have the flu."

"I know, honey, but you'll feel better in a week or two. I know that this is probably the worst thing in the world to you right now, especially because you were sick at Thanksgiving. Think about it like this. In twenty years you'll have a story to tell your children about how you survived the year of the plague," he said, trying to get her to find some kind of humor in the situation.

"But I so wanted to see grandmother and grandfather."

Tyler tried to soothe Tiffany's feelings. "I'll take you this summer when you're on vacation."

"Promise?" Tiffany said.

"I promise. Our flight was this afternoon, but I'll change my ticket for tomorrow and bring your Christmas presents to you."

"You can if you want to, Daddy, but I'm awfully tired. I want you to come when we can have some fun."

A lump rose in Tyler's throat. "Okay, honey. I'm going to hang up now, and I'll be up when I get back from West Virginia."

"Okay, Daddy," Tiffany agreed before she hung up.

Once Tyler arrived in Wheeling he rented a truck. It was the most sensible vehicle to drive in the hills with the snow. His parents were expecting him, but he hadn't given an exact arrival time because he knew his mother would constantly worry and stare out the kitchen window all day long.

As he drove up the driveway to his parents' house, he felt nostalgic. His life hadn't been perfect, but he had some good memories of times gone by. Taking long strides up the steps, Tyler unlocked the front door and walked down the hallway to the kitchen.

Rosalind Banks stood over the kitchen sink. Her back was to the door and he took in the familiar scene. The aroma of apple pie and sweet potato pie wafted through the air to him as he studied his mother. She was unaware of him as she stared out the window, apparently deep in thought.

Her hair was grayer than he remembered. She was dressed neatly in a denim dress with a white turtleneck beneath it and bedroom shoes. She also had a cardigan pulled on to ward off the chill.

Tyler wished his mother would let him buy her some diamond earrings, but he knew from past experience that even if she wanted a pair she would be afraid of what his father would think. And he wasn't up for a long sermon about Jezebel, coupled with quotes from scripture.

"Hello, Mom," Tyler said quietly.

His mother swung around, dropping the dishcloth into the sudsy water and exclaiming, "Tyler, I didn't see you drive up. It's so good to see you!"

"It's good to see you too, Mom." Enveloping her in his arms, he gave her a big bear hug.

"Let me look at you," he said pushing her slightly back. Though plump, his mother was a pretty woman. Tyler had inherited her piercing green eyes and facial features. Her face was totally devoid of makeup, yet she looked attractive.

"Where are the children?" Rosalind Banks inquired.

"I didn't bring them. Chad went skiing and Tiffany has the flu."

Disappointment crossed in his mother's features.

"I promise I will bring them sometime this summer."

"Promise?"

"I promise." Tyler was struck by the similarities between his mother and Tiffany. They were miles apart, yet they had used the exact same words, with the exact same inflection. The old adage that blood would tell entered his mind. His thoughts then briefly moved on to the similarities between Nancy and Chad before he focused on what his mother was saying to him.

"Your father should be home soon. He just went into town to get a part for the car. It's acting up again."

"Why won't Dad get another one? He's had that old Buick for eight years now, and cars just don't last the way they used to."

"I know." She sounded wistful. "A new car would be nice. The heater takes time to get going, and sometimes I have to run it for a full ten minutes before the car is warm enough to drive."

Tyler said gently, "You know that I can help with that. All you have to do is say the word."

"I know, son, but you have to talk that over with your father. You know that he feels too many material things undermine his image to his members," she responded quietly.

At his mother's words, his old resentment began to ignite deep inside him. He thought about his childhood and all of the things his mother had done without that she shouldn't have had to. Pushing these thoughts away, Tyler reached into the pocket of the overcoat he had shed on entering the kitchen and withdrew an envelope that contained a card with money. He always gave his parents separate checks at Christmas. It was the only time except his mother's birthday and Mother's Day that he could be certain she could splurge and buy things for herself without having to worry about the cost.

Along with money, he always gave each of them a personal item. This year it was perfume for his mother and a wool scarf for his father. "Thanks, honey. Your gift and the children's gifts are under the tree in the living room. Please take their gifts back to them for me."

"Will do," he agreed.

Tyler sat at the kitchen table and listened as his mother recounted the news of the people he had gone to school with, their parents, who'd died, and who had moved away. He nodded at the appropriate times and once again he realized that not much had changed since he had graduated from high school and left the small town. Suddenly his mother's voice changed to a whisper.

"Laurel Mackintosh has moved back from Richmond and is living here with her little girl. She and her husband got a divorce. They say that he was abusive to her."

Laurel Mackintosh was a girl he had dated casually when he lived in Wheeling.

"If you're going to stay for a couple of days, maybe we could invite her over."

"It would be nice to see her, Mom, but I don't want you to go out of your way to invite her. There's no need for you to use your matchmaking skills. I'm in a very serious relationship with someone."

His mother looked at him in surprise. "Tyler, honey, that's wonderful. What's her name?"

"Her name is Desiree Diamond, and I'm in love with her."

The softening of Tyler's voice when he spoke her name showed his mother how much in love he was. She cast her eyes towards the ceiling and silently thanked God for answering her prayers.

"How long have you been dating her? When am I going to meet her?" Tyler's mother demanded, openly curious about his newfound love.

"I've been seeing her for a few months, and I hope that you meet her soon." Tyler didn't realize how his eyes shone, or how his face revealed the love he had for Desiree.

Rosalind Banks searched her son's face and breathed a sigh of relief, content that he had found happiness.

Later that afternoon, Tyler sat watching his father from a tire that hung from a tree limb. The snow had hardened to make a crackling sound under their footsteps. Finally, in response to his father's continued grunts from under the hood, he said, "Why don't we go into town tomorrow and buy you another car? We should be able to get a good deal because it's the end of the year and dealers always push to sell cars before the year closes."

Jackson Banks yelled from under the hood, "No thanks, Tyler, I've almost got this one fixed."

Earlier, when Jackson Banks entered the kitchen, Tyler had caught a rare glimpse of the love his father had for him before he masked his expression. They had hugged briefly before sitting down over a steaming cup of coffee. In the wide scheme of things Tyler and his father got along fairly well as long as they didn't discuss the Bible, equality of the sexes, or politics.

"There you go, as good as new," said Jackson, straightening his body slowly as he closed the hood of the car. The two men walked slowly around the back door and stomped the snow off their feet before entering the kitchen.

Dinner was an exact replica of Tyler's childhood memories. They all bowed heads and held hands as Jackson said grace. Then Mother loaded their plates with the country fried steak, mashed potatoes, and corn. Seated across from his father, Tyler watched him carefully as he shoveled in fork after fork of the savory meal. He noticed that his father breathed heavily a few times in order to swallow a mouthful of food.

"Dad," Tyler said half jokingly, "maybe you should slow up a little. This is some heavy food we're eating."

"Your father always eats as if there's no tomorrow," Rosalind Banks chimed in. "And he's not been sick a day in his life."

Tyler studied his father as he bent his head over his plate. He had less gray hair than his mother did and his skin had a ruddy, healthy complexion. Though he had a potbelly, it seemed to go okay with his thickset shoulders and big frame. "I guess if you're used to something there's no need to change your habits." Tyler shrugged his shoulders and then tackled a second helping of food with gusto.

Tyler lay in his bed the morning of his departure and thought about the days he had spent at his parents' house. Never had he felt so close to his father as he did now. They had spent quality time together, and his father had graciously accepted his Christmas gifts from Tyler. He had asked about the kids and Nancy, but the questions had lacked the admonishment about the failure of his marriage they usually contained. *Maybe Dad's mellowing in his old age.*

Tyler had called Desiree the evening of his arrival, but her conversation had been somewhat stilted. He had guessed she wasn't alone in the room, and he understood her behavior because he understood her.

Desiree had come a long way since the beginning of their relationship and was now able to discuss her feelings for him. However, he knew that family was important to her and for this reason he had not pressed her to introduce him during the holidays.

In light of the newfound companionship he shared with his father, he had decided before he left to talk to him about his relationship with Desiree.

After putting his luggage in the truck, Tyler walked to the side of the house where his father was fiddling with some tools on a workbench. When Tyler cleared his throat to indicate his presence, his father turned around and smiled at him. "All ready to go, son?"

"Pretty soon," he grimaced. "Mom's packing me a lunch to take on the plane with me. I didn't have the heart to refuse and tell her that the food on the plane would be more than adequate."

"Your mother never changes. Leave her be. That's her way of showing her love for you."

"I know," Tyler responded quietly. "There's something I want to talk to you about before I leave." His father eyed him questioningly. "I'm in love with someone. Very soon I plan on asking her to marry me."

His father became suddenly still. "Well," he said after a long pause, "I'm not going to say that in the eyes of God you're still married to Nancy because we've already been over that time and time again. However, I do want to say this. I hope that you're sure this time. You were once in love with Nancy."

Tyler pushed his hands in his pockets as he rocked back and forth on his heels. "I know, Dad, but I never felt for Nancy what I feel for Desiree. I now know that I had to experience true love in order to recognize what it is. Desiree and I click." He snapped his fingers. "And we have a lot in common. She's a paralegal, but has aspirations of becoming a lawyer. She's smart, beautiful, and fun to be with. I've never met any other woman like her."

"Well, she sounds like a paragon of virtue, Tyler, and you have my blessing."

"I've been searching my whole life for someone like her," Tyler continued. He reached into his back pocket, pulled out his wallet and opened it. He withdrew a picture of him and Desiree which a street vendor had taken the weekend they went Christmas shopping together. In the picture, Tyler had his arm around Desiree's shoulders and her face was upturned smiling at him. Tyler took a deep breath and handed the picture to his father.

A stunned look stole over his face. He swallowed and handed the picture back to Tyler. "You've got to be kidding!"

Tyler responded in a serious tone, "I've never been more serious about anything in my whole life. I'm going to marry her, if she'll have me."

Rosalind Banks walked over to where they stood at the side of the house. She had her arms wrapped around herself in order to ward off the cold. Looking at their faces she nervously asked, "What's wrong?"

"Ask him," Jackson Banks retorted harshly, pointing at Tyler.

"I showed Dad a picture of the woman I plan to marry and surprise, surprise, he doesn't approve." His voice was riddled with sarcasm. Tyler then handed the picture to his mother. She looked surprised as she stared at the picture.

Tyler's father broke in before his mother could say anything. "She's colored. Tyler's gone and gotten himself into another ridiculous situation."

Tyler turned sharply and looked his father squarely in the face and corrected him. "She's black, or if you prefer, African-American. Please don't embarrass yourself again by referring to her as colored. And you may as well accept it, if you want to be a part of my life in the future."

Tyler's tone brought a look of outrage to Jackson Banks's face. "Have you thought this through? What if you have children? What's going to happen to them? They'll be ostracized. How about Tiffany and Chad? People will laugh at them. People will talk. They'll talk about them and they'll talk about you."

Tyler's rage was as apparent as his father's was. "Yes, I've thought this through. If Desiree and I have children, they will be secure in the knowledge that they have two parents who are deeply in love, love them, and will do everything in their power to make them feel secure and have a happy childhood. I have no qualms about marrying Desiree. Tiffany and Chad will accept it, and in time they will come to love Desiree as much as I do. My kids will be fine. Desiree's a wonderful person."

Jackson Banks gave a snort of derision. "You once felt this way about Nancy. And look how that turned out."

Tyler's response to that was quiet. "I was a boy then. Now I'm a man."

"If you were truly a man, you would take into account people's feelings other than your own," Jackson Banks said.

Tyler gave his father a derisive look. "Now if that isn't the pot calling the kettle black." He added sarcastically, "And believe me, that pun was intended."

Rosalind Banks had been completely silent during the argument between her husband and son. She slowly handed the picture of Desiree back to Tyler and she gave her son a long look. "Son, are you sure that this is right for you?"

"Absolutely," Tyler responded.

"Then you have my blessing," she said with sincerity.

"No, he doesn't. We will not sanction this marriage." Jackson pointed his finger at his son. "If you do marry this woman, your mother and I want nothing else to do with you."

"Speak for yourself!" His mother's voice rose sharply. "Tyler is my son, and he will always be my son."

"You know, Dad, you were right when you said earlier that Mom never changes. But then neither do you. My God, man, you're a minister. Have you forgotten that? God doesn't see color. He only looks in a person's heart," he continued as he stared at his father's stony face. "So much for your Christian rhetoric and all of your words about all men being the same in the eyes of God. You're a phony."

His father's face was red and mottled with rage.

"I'll call you to let you know when the wedding is going to take place." He gave his mother a quick kiss on her cheek before he strode off in the direction of the car.

Rosalind Banks turned fiercely to her husband and glared at him. "Never have I been as ashamed of you as I am now. I want my son to be happy and I wouldn't give a hoot if it took a green woman to do it. Didn't you notice how happy Tyler was this Christmas in comparison to last? That's what is important to me, Jackson Banks." She sucked in a deep breath. "I have watched you make many mistakes over the years in your treatment of me and the raising of Tyler with your self-righteous ways. But this time I will not stand idly by and keep quiet." She pointed her finger in his face. "You will accept this marriage and support Tyler in his decision or you will find yourself a lonely, divorced old man." And with this she turned her back on him and stomped back into the house.

Jackson Banks stood there looking as if he were having an apoplectic fit.

Odd One Out

CHAPTER ELEVEN

Christmas Day at the Diamond house had been a warm, loving affair. Marcus Junior had left early the day after Christmas to work overtime at the post office and, as usual, Desiree, Sasha, and Dominique had traveled to the largest mall in Brewster in order to hunt for after-Christmas bargains. Their parents never went with them, content to remain at home and baby-sit the twins. Even Dominique had refrained from making a smart remark when Sasha said if they went shopping in the city they could go to Times Square and visit Abdul, who was handing out pamphlets about the Nation of Islam. Catching the unenthusiastic expression that crossed Dominique's face, Desiree had tactfully replied, "If you don't mind. I prefer not to drive into New York City the day after Christmas."

The only incident to mar the day was their shopping experience in the J C Penney store. They were laden with bargains and were standing in line to purchase more items when their attention was drawn to a little boy standing at a different register, screaming at the top of his lungs. Looking to be about four, he was fair complexioned with light brown, curly hair. His face was beet red from his temper tantrum and his eyes were wet from crying. His facial features were an exact replica of the woman by his side, who held one of his hands. She was a tall, dark-complexioned woman with bold African features. She was obviously embarrassed by her son's behavior and swung her head around as if she were searching for someone to rescue her.

Suddenly a tall white man emerged from the men's room with a look of consternation on his face. Muttering excuses, he threaded his way through the queue of people at the register, reached the woman's side, and grabbed the little boy out of her arms.

Immediately the boy stopped screaming and said plaintively, "Mommy won't let me play with my toy." He pointed to a wind-up stuffed animal the woman had placed on the edge of the counter.

"She has to pay for it first, son." The man's tone was mild in comparison to his expression.

"I already told him that, and he wouldn't listen." Aggravation was evident in the woman's voice and the look on her face. "We're not buying it for him now. He's old enough to know how to behave in public," she said in a British accent. She suddenly plopped the stuffed animal on the counter and stomped off. Immediately the boy began yelling again, and the husband hurried after his wife with his screaming son in his arms.

"Talk about a bad seed," Dominique muttered to Desiree and Sasha. The people around them heard her remark. Some began snickering, and others breathed a sigh of relief that there was a modicum of peace now that the trio had left.

Once they had paid for their purchases the Diamond sisters sat at a table at Starbucks. After each ordered a cappuccino, Sasha broached the subject of the screaming child. "I love shopping the day after Christmas. But honestly, why won't people get a baby-sitter? They bring their kids to the mall and then spoil the whole shopping trip for everyone around because they can't control them."

"I'm with you, Sasha. That's why I leave the twins at home every year. They can amuse themselves with the stuff they got yesterday. Why would parents buy their children more toys the day after Christmas anyhow? That's just silly." Dominique shook her head in mild disgust.

"Maybe they couldn't afford to buy some of the things that they wanted before Christmas. We have to overlook that child's behavior. That little boy was really too young to know the difference," Desiree guessed.

"Well, I don't know about that. He was old enough to know that he wanted that stuffed animal, and his screams got worse when she took it away from him," Sasha said.

Dominique whispered so that the people at nearby tables couldn't hear her, "You see that he was mixed." Her tone was snide.

"I know. I was surprised to see what her husband looked like. It's more common to see a black man with a white woman than the other way around. I notice every time people see the opposite they do a double take. She is indeed brave," Sasha replied with a slight chuckle.

"Brave or stupid? It's the kids that suffer, and children should not pay for their parents' mistakes. People are looking through rose-tinted glasses if they think society has changed that much. There's still a lot of racism in the world. It may not be as obvious, but it's still there nonetheless."

"Well, I have to agree he did behave badly," Sasha said in a mild voice.

Desiree had lapsed into silence as she listened to the discourse between Dominique and Sasha, but she felt she couldn't keep quiet any longer, and when she spoke her words showed her exasperation. "He's not bad because he's mixed. He misbehaves because of their parenting skills."

"You're right," Dominique agreed. "But because the parents are of different races, they probably have different parenting skills. They probably confuse the child by a lack of consistency. Everyone knows that black people and white people differ about how you should discipline children. Every white person I know thinks spanking a child is abuse. I say a good whack on the behind never hurt anyone. I certainly got one, and I'm a better person for it."

"That's a matter of opinion." Desiree's tone was curt, and her words were laced with sarcasm.

Leaning forward so as not to be overheard, Sasha said, "Did you notice that the mother had a British accent? I work with a woman from England, and she said that there isn't as much racism in England as there is in the United States. Because England never had slavery, black people don't have the resentment for whites that African Americans do."

"That's all well and good then. Maybe then all inter-racial couples should live in England. Also, think about the kids. When you have children, you never really know what you're going to get. I guess that little boy got the worst traits of each race. A lot of mixed children have identity problems. What we saw today is the result of fooling around with nature," Dominique whispered, making sure the people sitting at the other tables didn't overhear her.

Dominique's racist remark only made Desiree angrier. "That's a nasty thing to say, Dominique. And you have absolutely no facts to support a statement like that."

At this time Sasha joined in. "I might have to agree with Dominique on this one. Abdul says that's it's a big mistake to marry a person from another race. He also says that interracial children have to suffer for their parents' selfishness. Abdul says that by mixing with other races, we're weakening our own. He says that if Allah wanted us to be the same he would have made us all the same color, that we were all made different colors for a reason and we shouldn't mess with it."

Desiree's tone became acidic and her words dripped with sarcasm. "And of course if Abdul said it, that means it's gospel. You never used to be so narrow minded, Sasha, and I must say I don't like these racist ideas of his. I tried to give him a chance on Labor Day, but the more I hear what Abdul says, the more I'm starting to dislike him. Also, if Abdul is a true Muslim he would know that when Malcolm X went to Mecca he met Muslims of all races. Some had white skin, blue eyes, and blond hair. Islam is a religion, not a skin color. Maybe instead of preaching bigotry, Abdul should read *The Autobiography of Malcolm X*. He might learn a thing or two."

Sasha started in surprise at the sharpness of Desiree's response and her caustic remarks about Abdul.

Dominique quickly intervened. "Good heavens, Desiree. What's the matter with you? One would think you had a personal stake in this conversation."

Before Desiree could respond Sasha chimed in, trying to lighten the conversation. "I know what's going on here. The man who gave you those earrings is a white man." At her joke she and Dominique began laughing and slapped each other a high five while Desiree sat quietly sipping her cappuccino and inwardly fuming.

No more mention of their differences of opinion was made for the rest of the afternoon, but it felt as if there was a dark cloud over the rest of their shopping expedition. Desiree was unaccustomed to being the odd one out when there was a disagreement among the Diamond sisters. She was usually the peacemaker, and for Dominique and Sasha to be on the same side was a unique situation by itself. Desiree knew that it was unfair for her to become so angry with her sisters. They didn't know how personal that conversation was to her, or how they'd offended her with their callous remarks. But their points of view worried her because she knew that was how they really felt.

As they continued shopping, Desiree noticed she got several sidelong looks from her sisters, as if they wanted to ask what was wrong with her, but she pretended not to notice, feeling it was best to let the matter drop.

Desiree opened her apartment door with a sigh of relief. After a few days with family, she was ready to return to her own space and to a world that included Tyler. She had missed him terribly during the holidays, and hadn't spoken to him except for his brief phone call to let her know he had arrived at his parents' home.

Their initial plans had been to meet at her apartment a couple of days after Christmas. But when Tyler spoke to her from West Virginia he'd filled her in on his change of plans because of Tiffany's illness. When he returned to Danbury he was immediately going to visit Tiffany and rent a nearby hotel room for a couple of days.

Desiree understood and readily agreed with Tyler's change of plans. She hoped Chad would have returned from his skiing trip by then so that Tyler could spend some time with him also. He needed to spend time with his children, but she secretly hoped Tyler would make it back by New Year's Eve so she could celebrate the beginning of the new year with him.

After she finished unpacking, she cleaned her apartment and set up the telephone and answering machine Marcus Junior had given her. After several tries she got the message on the answering machine recorded the way she wanted and silently hoped that she wouldn't have to figure out how to do that again.

⟢⟡

Desiree dialed Natalie's phone number. "Merry belated Christmas!"

"Merry Christmas to you also, Desiree. I tried to reach you at your parents' several times during the holidays, but the line was always busy."

"Same here. How was your Christmas?"

"Well, the one thing I really wanted I didn't get."

"What was that?" Desiree asked.

"I wanted to unwrap this present in my belly." At this the two of them laughed uproariously. "That's why I'm lying down at six o'clock in the evening. Iman is putting a hurting on my back."

"So you know that it's a girl?"

"Yes, and we're going to name her Iman. It means faith and belief."

"Once you have her everything you're going through will be worth it." She paused. "Guess what?"

"What?"

"I saw Travis." There was silence on the phone line and Desiree hurriedly reassured her. "Don't worry. I'm not back with him."

"Thank God! You almost made me lose the baby. You've been doing so well without him I would hate for you to get mixed up with him again."

Desiree chuckled. "I went Christmas shopping in the city and he was in Central Park taking pictures of models. He's going with one of them. I saw her kiss him, and I didn't feel one bit of jealousy." She added almost as an afterthought, "Her name is Chanel, and she's mixed."

"That figures. That's why he got so angry with you the night that the two of you broke up. Your wisecrack was a little too close for comfort. Dark-skinned men always seem as if they're trying to prove something by dating outside of our race."

At Natalie's words Desiree felt uncomfortable. Natalie was her best friend, and she hadn't yet told her about Tyler. It wasn't that she was ashamed of him, but Natalie's opinion was important to her and she didn't want to feel her disapproval.

"I have something to tell you."

Natalie became quiet at Desiree's words because she could tell by the tone of her voice that there was something weighing heavily on her mind. "What is it?" At Desiree's continued silence Natalie became concerned, and her next words were louder than the last. "What is it, what's wrong?"

"Remember the last time we talked I told you that I'd met a man, and that I liked him."

"Yes, and then we had to go because Michael broke a glass in the kitchen."

"Yes. Well, I've been seeing him for some time, and I've kept it from you. I'm in love with him, truly, truly in love with him, and you're the first person I've told this to."

Natalie sounded excited for her. "Are you kidding? Why are you keeping it a secret? I think that's great."

Desiree's words were slow. "Not really. It's not exactly a good situation for me."

"What's the problem now?" Then jokingly, "Is he married or something?"

"No, he's divorced and has two kids, but it's almost as bad as if he were married. My family won't approve."

"Why not?" Natalie demanded.

Desiree hesitated.

When no answer was forthcoming, Natalie continued, "How does he treat you?"

Desiree absently fingered the diamond studs she wore. "He's wonderful. We do things together, he takes me to nice places, and he respects my feelings about things. We can talk about everything. Tyler is the most passionate and caring lover I've ever been with. I was with him in New York when I saw Travis. Travis was very disapproving."

"Of course he was disapproving. No man ever wants to see his ex with someone else. Even if he didn't do the right thing, he certainly doesn't want someone else doing it. That serves Travis right. He blew it. I'll bet he's just jealous."

"One of the reasons that Travis disapproved is the same reason I haven't told my family about Tyler. Tyler's white." Suddenly there was complete silence. It was as if a nuclear bomb had been dropped and cut off communication between the two of them.

Desiree whispered, "Did you hear what I said? Tyler is a white man. He's a lawyer at Buchanan & Buchanan."

"I heard you," Natalie responded slowly. "I'm just trying to digest this information."

Tears began to form in Desiree's eyes and she fought them back. "I knew you would disapprove. That's why I waited so long to tell you."

"Don't go putting words in my mouth," Natalie instructed sharply. "I'm just surprised, that's all. You've never even felt attracted to light-skinned black men, and now you say that you're in love with a white man?" Natalie sounded incredulous.

Desiree's voice became almost inaudible. "Yes. It's strange and it's totally unexpected. This thing with Tyler, it caught me off guard. It didn't even begin as a sexual attraction. I mean, I see attractive men all of the time and I don't want to sleep with them. But the more time I spent in his company the stronger the sexual desire got. Tyler and I click in and out of bed." Desiree added almost as an afterthought, "He kisses me. I mean he really, really, kisses me. Tyler makes it a work of art. He pulls me to him. And then he holds me close, and I feel an intimacy I never felt with Travis. While making love, Travis didn't kiss me. Of course when he came over he would kiss me, and he would sometimes kiss me when he was leaving. But the long melting kiss that gets a woman in the mood, I never got that from Travis. I never said anything before because there were other things that Travis did well, but in our relationship I always felt a lack of intimacy. I felt that Travis was holding back because he was afraid of being vulnerable. I accepted that because I thought that's the way he was, and I loved him, or felt that I was in love with him. But this is different; the relationship I have with Tyler is unique. I've never felt this way before."

"How does Tyler feel about you?" Natalie asked.

"He says that he loves me, and I believe him. Not necessarily because of what he says, but because of what he does." And now Desiree gave Natalie the details of her relationship with Tyler from her first meeting him until they had last seen each other on Christmas morning.

When she finished all Natalie could say was, "Wow! No wonder you fell in love with him. You would have had to be an android not to have. When are you going to tell your family?"

"I don't know. I know that Tyler wants to meet them, and he's getting impatient. But I want to make sure that our relationship is solid enough to withstand anything before I bring any family into it."

"I understand. But the sooner you tell them the sooner they can get used to it. Have you two talked about marriage?"

"Not specifically. He always talks about us as if we will be growing old together, but I honestly haven't thought that far ahead."

"Well, you had better start thinking about it," Natalie warned. "You're not the kind of woman to sleep with a man, especially a white man, forever and a day without a commitment. That's how I knew that Travis wasn't right for you. Deep down inside you knew that also. Otherwise you would have put your foot down a long time ago about the two of you setting a marriage date. You know it and I know it."

Suddenly Natalie burst into laughter. "No wonder Travis was so pissed. Black men cross over to the other side all of the time, but whenever they see a black woman with a white man they have a coronary. As far as I'm concerned, you won."

"It's not about winning or losing. I'm not having a contest with Travis or trying to get back at him. I'm just trying to find love, peace, and happiness."

"And that's what makes it so good." Natalie continued to laugh. "The best revenge for someone who did you wrong is to find true happiness with another. It just blows them away."

"You're right," Desiree agreed. She then recounted how Travis had insulted her before Tyler returned with her hot chocolate.

Natalie's laughter finally subsided. "Have you heard from him since then?"

"No, and I must say that I'm surprised. I know that I told him not to call me, but I thought he might if only to say something derogatory."

"I doubt if that's the last you'll hear from him. Beware; men can be really nasty when they feel they've been snubbed. And for a white man! Oh, my God!"

Desiree had to laugh in spite of herself. And then she just had to ask, "Well?"

"Well what?" Natalie countered.

"Well, tell me what you think. Do you disapprove? Do you think that I'm betraying our race?"

"If I did think that I wouldn't tell you. I would just talk about you behind your back to Martin."

Desiree breathed a sigh of relief when she realized Natalie was teasing her.

"I'm just kidding, honey. I love you and I want you to be happy. If it takes a white man to give you the happiness that I have with Martin, then I want you to be with that white man."

"I'm glad that you feel that way. But everyone won't. Things would be so much easier if he were a black man. Things wouldn't be so difficult. If I had fallen for a garbage man or janitor people might consider it inappropriate because of his education. But if he treated me the way that Tyler does, I wouldn't care."

"They're respectable jobs, and it beats selling drugs, but what makes a relationship is not the job, it's having similar goals and respect for the same things. The only things that you and Travis had in common are the fact that you're both single and black. That isn't the blueprint for happiness. The Bible teaches us not to be unevenly yoked. From what you told me, you and Tyler connected through work and the rest came later. If you want him, have him, and bump what every one else thinks." Natalie chose her next words carefully. "And that includes your family. Life is too short to waste time with someone you don't love. Things could be a lot worse. You loving a white man is a whole lot better than you loving a married one. At least Tyler is available; he wants you and you want him."

"You're right!" Desiree looked up at the clock and realized that they had been on the telephone for quite some time. "I need to get off of the telephone. I'll never be able to pay this phone bill."

Natalie teased her. "Yes, you will. You have a rich lawyer in your pocket, and from what I hear about him he'll be more than happy to help out with your phone bill. But I'll let you go because I have to go to the bathroom. Before we hang up there's something I would like to say to you," she said seriously.

"What is it?" Desiree held her breath waiting to hear Natalie's words.

"This man appears to be good to you and for you. You need to take care of you. Live your own life, make your own decisions. You are the one who has to live with him; you and no one else."

"What about your comments about Travis dating outside our race?"

"That's a different situation. I wasn't talking about you and Tyler," she laughed. "You did not purposefully seek out a white man. I've known you for a long time, and no one loves our men more than you do. You fell in love with this man because of the circumstances of your life, and I shouldn't be surprised. We're at work more hours than any other place so it shouldn't be such a big surprise when a black woman ends up with a white man she met at work. Do whatever you need to in order to find love, peace, and happiness. Everyone else does. I got your back."

At these words Desiree felt almost overwhelmed with love for Natalie. Gulping back tears, she said, "Thank you, Natalie. You don't know how much that means to me."

To this Natalie simply replied, "Well, I'm reserving my final judgment until I meet him. But from what I've heard, I'm sure I'll like him. And If I don't, I just won't tell you," she added jokingly.

Desiree laughed. *Natalie can make me see the humor in every situation. I guess that's why she's my best friend.*

～✑

Later that night, Desiree woke to the sound of the shower in the bathroom. She knew that Tyler must have let himself in with the key she had given him at Christmas and a feeling of happiness surged through her body.

Sliding out of bed, she quickly stepped out of the boxer shorts and tee shirt she had been wearing and softly cracked open the door to the bathroom. Reaching her hand inside the bathroom, she slid her hand along the wall and cut off the light before she went inside and crept into the shower behind Tyler. Desiree let the night light guide her to stand only an inch from him.

Desiree slid her arms around his middle and kissed him softly on his back. "Hey, lover." Her voice was barely audible over the noise of the shower and she ran her hands down the length of his back. His body was slick with water.

Tyler turned around to face her and she had to step back. His shaft was fully erect, and it closed the distance between their bodies.

"Hey you." His voice was sensuous, and his tone was laced with desire. He pulled her towards him. Their bodies melted together under the spray of water and

Tyler ran his hands down the length of Desiree's body as if he were a blind man using Braille.

She wound her body around his before stepping back. "Let me bathe you." Her voice was husky with desire.

Tyler turned his back to her, and she reached for a loofah. Desiree generously lathered it and she began to wash him. Starting at the back of his neck she methodically washed him. Then she turned him around to let the water rinse him off before she turned him to wash his front.

Tyler stood quite still, unabashed by his obvious desire for her. She washed him gently, mindful to caress and explore every inch of him. Desiree carefully sponged him from head to toe before turning him so that he could rinse off.

Tyler's expression was unfathomable in the darkness of the room, but the rigidity of his body showed his response. Taking the loofah from her he began to repeat every movement Desiree had subjected his body to. As he did so, he fondled her breasts, kissed her stomach, and the inside of her thighs. Then he encircled her waist with his hands and parted her legs by wedging one foot between hers and sliding her legs apart.

Tyler gently massaged between her legs and the inside of her thighs with the loofah before dropping it to the shower floor. In the dimness, he found her center and inserted one and then two of his fingers, probing, feeling, and exploring her until she cried out. Then lingeringly, his mouth followed the path his fingers had taken.

Desiree writhed and suddenly broke free of his touch. Moving closer she began planting small kisses on his chest and upper torso, then followed the line of silky hair to his penis which throbbed, alert and wanting to be relieved. Desiree dropped to her knees and gently pulled him towards her. Taking the palm of her hand she cupped him from underneath and held him before she slid the tip of him into her mouth.

Tyler braced himself by planting his hands on the tiled walls. She gently held his tip in her mouth and she began to suck, pulling more of him into her mouth. Desiree continued to pleasure Tyler and he moaned and threw his head back, letting the water pummel his head.

Desiree worshipped him, not letting go, even when she felt him instinctively try to pull back from her. She held on to him until she felt him tremble; she sucked him until he went soft, his satisfaction complete.

Tyler drew Desiree to her feet and pulling her out of the shower he gently toweled her body before he carried her into the bedroom.

Briefly he left her, and when he returned to bed he was dry and held a bottle of sensual oil in his hand. He began to smooth it into her skin, kissing every inch of her body that he oiled.

Turning her gently on her stomach, Tyler ran his hand over her buttocks, kneading her, readying her for him, making sure she was moist and would welcome the intrusion of his body. He probed and entered her, pausing a moment in order to let her adjust to the position. Tyler then began to move in long rhythmic strokes, holding his climax, kissing her neck, her shoulders, and calling out her name before their bodies reached their peaks in unison.

Tyler lay atop Desiree planting soft kisses on her back and shoulders before he maneuvered them so that they were lying on their sides. They lay still in the aftermath, waiting for their heavy breathing and accelerated heartbeats to subside.

"Honey?" she said softly.

"Huh?" Desiree smiled in the darkness at the short but complete sound of satisfaction Tyler had grunted at her.

"How are Chad and Tiffany doing?"

"That's like a cold shower."

"Well, I'm concerned. Your relationship with them will ultimately affect your relationship with me."

He sleepily ran a hand over his face before answering. "Tiffany is on the mend, and by the way, she loved the doll and accessories you chose for her. Chad was in a really good mood. He had a great time skiing, and if I go to Wheeling this summer he has agreed to go without a fight."

She turned his face upward and looked into his eyes. "What do you mean, if you go? When I spoke to you when you were in West Virginia you said that it was a definite trip because the kids didn't make it for Christmas. Nothing went wrong down there, did it?"

Desiree's intuition and ability to read between the lines sometimes amazed Tyler. He felt sorry for any future witness who might try to hide something from her once she became a lawyer. "I can honestly say that I have never enjoyed my parents' company more than I did this Christmas, and that I think my father finally understands me and I understand him." Adroitly changing the subject, he said, "I have a surprise for you."

Eagerly Desiree asked, "What is it?" She knew from previous experiences that Tyler's surprises were always a lot of fun.

"I made reservations for us at a bed and breakfast at Sturbridge Village for New Year's," he said.

"You're kidding! I've always wanted to go there. Dominique, Benjamin, and the twins go once a year and they love it."

"I thought that it might be a nice way to begin the new year; our first of many years together."

Desiree said softly in the darkness as she cradled Tyler's head, "You don't know how much I want that, too."

"Good." He playfully slapped her behind. "Now go to sleep. We have a three hour drive ahead of us tomorrow."

Their ride to Sturbridge Village was entertaining as they sang along with popular songs playing on the car radio. They teased each other unmercifully when one of them messed up or grew silent at certain parts because they didn't know the words.

Desiree knew that she and Tyler shared a liking for the same kind of rhythm and blues music, but she was surprised to hear Tyler sing lyrics to some of the older songs from the soul groups of the '60s.

When she asked him how a preacher's son from West Virginia had learned them, he explained, "My dad didn't allow us to have a record player or listen to secular music in the house. So at night I would sneak out of my bedroom window after he and my mother went to sleep and meet some of my friends at a speakeasy that stayed open until five o'clock in the morning."

"You never got in trouble?"

"Nope." Tyler sounded smug. "It never crossed my father's mind that someone would disobey his orders. My best friend's father owned the bar, and the people that saw me there couldn't say anything to my dad because most of them were married and were carrying on with girls from the wrong side of town that were half their age. Others kept quiet because they disliked my father's holier-than-thou attitude and loved the idea that his son was pulling the wool over his eyes."

Sturbridge Village was located in Sturbridge, Massachusetts at the intersection of I-90 and I-84. The largest outdoor museum in the northeast, it made Desiree feel as if she had been transported back to the 1830s once they crossed the covered bridge at the entrance. Desiree looked around in delight at the employees dressed in period clothes. The women had on long dresses with aprons and the men wore knee breeches, hats, and pointy-toed shoes with silver buckles.

Everywhere she looked a costumed villager was going about his daily chores, such as the cobbler hammering a leather sole to a shoe. Antique shops were filled with china and knickknacks. Candy stores sold saltwater taffy and homemade licorice made while visitors watched.

Tyler drove the half-mile from the Old Sturbridge Village shops to the Sturbridge Country Inn where they had reservations. It was a renovated mansion that was a combination of old amenities and new ones.

Once inside the lobby, Desiree walked over to a rack which held brochures of what entertainment Sturbridge Village had to offer while Tyler checked them in at the front desk.

She was flipping through the brochure, folding back the pages of things they might want to do, when she became aware that their entrance had been a source of interest to an elderly couple.

Desiree could tell that they were tourists and she guessed their ages to be in the early eighties. The wife was trying to quiet her husband, but Desiree heard him say in a plaintive voice, "In my day it was unheard of. What's this world coming to? If God didn't care if we mixed the races he would have made us all the same color. He made us different shades for a reason."

His wife's face was beet red and she bent her head in embarrassment when she realized Desiree had overheard her husband's remarks.

Desiree stomped over to the man and faced him squarely. Her voice was cutting and her words were clear. "Ever since slavery, white men have always wanted and had relationships with black women. There was a time we didn't have a choice, but thank God now we do because I'm sure that none of my fellow sisters would choose to go with someone like you." The old man began to sputter and Desiree turned up her nose, gave him a haughty look, and walked away.

Sidling up next to Tyler at the front desk, she linked her arm with his and smiled when he turned towards her and handed her keys to their room. Desiree stood on her tiptoes and planted a kiss square on his lips. Tyler grinned as he bent down to retrieve their luggage.

Their room, the Loft Suite, consisted of a king-sized bed, skylights, sitting room, and wet bar.

"It's beautiful," Desiree exclaimed. "Thank you so much for bringing me here, Tyler."

"Thank you for being a part of my life, Desiree. I've never been happier."

"Neither have I." She sat down on the bed and Tyler did likewise. Tyler lay back with his hands folded behind his head and stared at the ceiling. Desiree laid her head on his chest. "I have a confession to make."

"Oh no, a woman and secrets. That's a dangerous combination," he teased.

Desiree drew little circles on his chest with her fingers and Tyler felt a curl of desire begin to mount inside him at her touch. "I was a little upset to think that I wasn't going to get to spend New Year's Eve with you. I knew that things changed and that you needed to go and see your kids, and I felt that you should. But you know what they say about New Year's and all, and I didn't want us to be separated."

Tyler looked at her curiously. "No, I don't know. What do they say about New Year's?"

Desiree looked a little embarrassed. "There is an old wive's tale that states whatever you do on New Year's Eve is what you're going to do all year long."

Tyler looked devilish and moved his eyebrows up and down in an excellent imitation of Groucho Marx before he began pulling back the covers on the bed. "That cinches it. It's time to go to bed, because I know what I want to do to you all year long."

Hours later, they walked through town visiting shop after shop. The weather was unusually mild, and as they shrugged out of their winter coats, he looked up at the sky and said, "Global warming."

Tyler held their coats draped over one arm and held Desiree's with the other as they walked from shop to shop. He tried to buy Desiree everything she admired, and after awhile she wouldn't show too much interest in any one item or look at anything too long for fear that Tyler would load her down with more presents. Her favorite gift was a crystal elephant posed with its trunk up. When Tyler handed it to her he said, "An elephant with its trunk up means good luck. I haven't had anything else since you came into my life."

Deeply moved by his words, Desiree blinked back tears before she moved into the circle of his arms.

Earlier they had eaten a meal of shepherd's pie and peach cobbler dessert in one of the small restaurants in the heart of town. The last thing they wanted to do before they returned to their room was to go on the Quinnebaug River tour.

The boat ride was wonderful. They were able to see the entire town from the wooden boat as it headed up the Quinnebaug River. The guide was interesting and recited information about the waterway as well as all kinds of historical facts.

Once inside their suite Desiree had run to the bathroom, determined to be the first in the tub.

Tyler laughed good-naturedly at her babyishness. Picking up a bottle off of the table, he shouted through the door, "I'm going to open the champagne while you're in there. I hope there's some left by the time you get out." At this he heard an increased splashing of water as Desiree tried to hurry to get finished.

When she walked into the sitting room she saw he sat with an unopened bottle of champagne in front of him. "I waited for you."

"I'm also going to wait for you," she smiled at him as he headed towards the bathroom.

Tyler reappeared wearing the bottom of the silk pajamas she had bought him for Christmas. Without saying a word, he opened the bottle and filled their glasses and they clinked them together. "Happy New Year's, darling."

"Happy New Year's to you too. Do you think that we can stay awake for another two hours?" Desiree sounded hopeful.

"I don't know. We've had a busy day."

"If I fall asleep, wake me right before midnight so that we can count down until twelve o'clock," she begged.

Tyler laughed his warm throaty laugh. "I can't wake you if I'm asleep myself."

Hours later, it was midnight and Tyler watched Desiree's sleeping form. Instead of disturbing her sleep, he took that time to thank God with a silent prayer. *I don't know what I did to deserve her, but I thank you for bringing her into my life.*

Coming Clean

CHAPTER TWELVE

Desiree and Tyler were exhausted as they drove back to Danbury, and conversation seemed unnecessary. When his voice broke the silence, Desiree gave a small start of surprise.

"After I see you upstairs, I have to go to my place. I have paperwork to do before I go in to work tomorrow, and I also need to get my mail."

"Can you believe that we have to go to work tomorrow? It seems as if we just left."

Tyler chuckled, "We've been off work for two weeks. I wonder why days don't seem to pass as quickly when we're on the job."

Desiree humorously added, "They do seem to pass quickly enough when I have a typing or research deadline to meet."

"I have a new client to meet with first thing in the morning. I think that Arthur Buchanan has assigned your friend Jillian as the paralegal on the case."

"And I'll be working with Ralph Benson. Jillian's a good person and a wonderful paralegal. You should enjoy working with her." Desiree looked at Tyler out of the corner of her eye. "Don't you go falling in love with her now that you'll be working with her instead of me."

Tyler covered her hand with his free one as he expertly parked his car in a parking space outside of her apartment building. Looking deeply into her eyes he said, "I don't think that lightning can strike a person twice in a lifetime, do you?"

That night, as Desiree lay in bed, it felt strange for Tyler not to be by her side. It seemed as if they had been a couple forever; she had grown used to his constant presence. Not having him around was not a situation she intended to get used to.

She had barely arrived at work the next morning when she heard her name being paged over the intercom system to come to the front lobby because she had a visitor.

She swiftly walked down the corridor to the reception area. Once there she walked over to the desk where Blanche Harding was sitting. "Did you say that I have a visitor?"

Blanche's face was bland. "Actually the woman sitting over there is looking for Mr. Banks, but he's not in yet. Then she asked to speak to anyone connected to the Worthy case. That's still your case, isn't it?"

"Yes, it is." Desiree's tone was cool as she remembered how Blanche had gossiped about her and shown an interest in Tyler. As far as Desiree was concerned, Blanche Harding had two strikes against her.

Desiree walked over to the woman sitting on the leather sofa in the reception area. With a smile and outstretched hand she said, "My name is Desiree Diamond. I understand that you would like to speak to someone working on the Worthy case."

The woman shook Desiree's hand. "Yes. My name is Shannon Cavanaugh."

Shannon Cavanaugh was a stunningly attractive woman with russet colored hair. Her gray, slanted eyes were beautifully shadowed with gold and brown eye shadow. Her forest green dress and four-inch black pumps showed off her long legs. Her body language oozed sexuality, and Desiree felt unsophisticated in comparison.

"Is there somewhere we can talk privately?" the woman asked.

"There's a conference room where I sometimes work. We'll go there." As she turned to leave, she paused at Blanche Harding's desk. "If Mr. Banks comes in will you please ask him to join us in the conference room?" Desiree received a curt nod by way of reply.

Desiree motioned for Ms. Cavanaugh to take one of the chairs at the conference table and then poured her a cup of coffee. "I'm just the paralegal who did background work on the Worthy case. Mr. Banks is the attorney. Actually, all of the work is complete. Everyone is just waiting for their day in court."

To this Shannon Cavanaugh replied, "After you hear what I have to say there may not be a need to go to court."

Her voice was husky and Desiree could barely catch her words. Desiree raised her eyebrows. "What do you mean?"

Shannon Cavanaugh expelled a long breath. "Two years ago my name was Anthony Miles Cavanaugh. I recently had a sex change operation."

Desiree's jaw dropped, and then she felt her face get hot from embarrassment. "I'm sorry for my reaction. You just caught me off guard."

"I expected that." She showed no resentment at Desiree's reaction. "For many years I lived a lie. Although I lived my life as a man, I knew from puberty that I was meant to be a woman. After years of agonizing I went to Europe and had a sex change. The person you see sitting before you has finally come to terms with herself."

Just then the conference room door opened and Tyler strode in. He looked surprised to see that Desiree was not alone, and giving a polite nod to Shannon Cavanaugh he said, "Did you need to see me about something?"

"Yes, this is Ms. Shannon Cavanaugh and she has some information that might be pertinent to the Worthy case."

"Really?" Tyler then gave her his full attention. "What kind of information is this?"

Shannon Cavanaugh then repeated the exact words she had just told Desiree. Tyler's eyes widened with surprise, but he managed to recover quickly. Sitting down in one of the empty chairs at the conference table, he asked, "What does this have to do with the Worthy case?"

"While I was Anthony Miles Cavanaugh I worked as a clerk under CEO Bernard Slaughter, and we were lovers. He fired me because I ended our sexual relationship."

For a full minute, the only sound in the room was that of the clock on the wall ticking. Then Tyler calmly said, "Do I have your permission to tape record this conversation?"

Ms. Cavanaugh nodded her head in agreement. He turned to Desiree and said, "Ms. Diamond, would you please get a tape recorder?"

Once Desiree returned Tyler began. "Ms. Cavanaugh, why did it take you so long to come forward with this information?"

"I've been in Europe. My father died when I was a child, and my mother and I were very close. I moved away because I wanted to save her the embarrassment of her friends knowing that she had a transsexual for a son. I only came back to the States because she was deathly ill. My mother died on Christmas Eve."

Shannon Cavanaugh wiped away a tear. "When I got back to the states I heard about Bernard Slaughter being sued for sexual harassment. I couldn't get involved while my mother was alive, but now I can live for myself."

With her next words Shannon Cavanaugh's voice got stronger. "I want to pay that bastard back for what he did to me. He fired me because I wouldn't sleep with him again, and at the time I couldn't do anything about it because I didn't want to make public the fact I preferred to sleep with men."

For the next hour, Shannon Cavanaugh was forthright with her answers to Tyler's questions. Apparently she had had a secret sexual relationship with Bernard Slaughter for over a year. She had begun seeing a therapist and had been urged her to announce her true gender preference. She had fallen in love with Bernard Slaughter and wanted to have an open relationship with him. When she suggested this to him he had become incensed at the suggestion and had beaten her up, which had warranted a trip to the emergency room.

Ms. Cavanaugh produced pictures that the police took when she visited the emergency room. At the time, however, she had refused to divulge the name of the person who had attacked her. According to her, when she went into work later that day, Bernard Slaughter apologized to her for losing his temper. He said that he would come over that night and make it up to her. When she told him their affair was over, he fired her on the spot.

"Is there anyone who can attest to the fact that there was an intimate relationship between the two of you?" Tyler probed.

"Mrs. Adams lives in the apartment across the hall from me. She takes her dog out every morning between five and five-thirty. I know that she sometimes saw Bernard leave. I also have a video of us making love. I felt guilty at the time for secretly taping us, but now I'm glad that I did. A close friend persuaded me to do it just in case things didn't turn out the way I hoped."

She wiped another tear from the corner of her eye. "My friend received harsh treatment from his lover when he came out of the closet, and he was giving me the benefit of his experience."

After Shannon Cavanaugh left, Desiree and Tyler stared at each other across the table. Simultaneously, slow smiles spread across their faces before they reached over and gave each other a high five.

That night they lay in bed talking over the day's events. Tyler had a meeting scheduled with Bernard Slaughter and the other top executives of his corporation later in the week. He knew that getting Claire Worthy a fair out-of-court settlement would come easily.

"What about Shannon Cavanaugh? She also deserves compensation for what Bernard Slaughter did to her." Desiree was drowsy from sleep as she cuddled in Tyler's embrace.

"We can't add her to the Worthy lawsuit because our case isn't a class action one, but we can threaten to sue later on her behalf. They'll probably offer her monetary compensation. I'm sure that Reynolds and Smythe will be more than happy to close the book on all of this stuff. The longer they drag their feet, the more it will cost them in the long run with lawyer fees and all."

"Why do you think that they've continued to support Bernard Slaughter? He's an embarrassment to the firm, to say the least."

"They'll probably get rid of him now." Tyler's satisfaction was evident.

"Good, I like to see people get what they deserve." Though her words were slurred with sleep, she heard him answer her softly.

"So do I."

A few days later, she was roused from a deep sleep by the ringing of her telephone. "Hello," she whispered quietly, not wanting to wake Tyler.

"Hey, sis!" Sasha's bubbly greeting nearly knocked Desiree off her side of the bed. "I know you're not still in bed this time of morning!" Sasha sounded as if she had been awake for hours and had drunk three large cups of coffee.

"What time is it?" Desiree was wide-awake now and tried to peer around the breadth of Tyler's shoulders to look at the alarm clock on the nightstand.

"It's ten-thirty in the morning. I know it's Saturday, dear, but give me a break. What are you still doing in bed? You never used to be such a late sleeper."

"I didn't go to bed until late last night." It was true. She and Tyler had developed the habit of staying up as late as they pleased Friday night, and sleeping in the next morning before they went downtown and had brunch.

"Oh. Well, get plenty of rest today, girl, because tonight you're going to a party."

"Tonight I'm going to a party?" Desiree repeated dumbly, still trying to gather her wits. She was acutely aware that Tyler's eyes were open and he was watching her. "My sister Sasha," she mouthed at him.

"Yeah, I want you to come into the city and go to the party with me. It's guaranteed to be a hoot."

"Why are you inviting me, and not Abdul? Aren't you still seeing him?"

"Yeah, we're still seeing each other off and on, but we're not exclusive," Sasha replied. "Besides, he would be offended if I suggested that he go to this party with me. This ain't his kind of party."

"Why, because he's Muslim?"

"No, not because he's Muslim." Her voice was droll. "Because he would be offended. This party is a I'm-Just-Not-That-Into-Him party."

"What!" Desiree exclaimed.

"Yeah. All of the women are supposed to bring a guy, whether it's your current boyfriend or just a really good guy friend who you know needs a girlfriend. It gives all of the other women the opportunity to check him out for themselves. They can flirt with him, give out their phone numbers, and everything. The woman who brought him can't or won't get mad because that's his reason for being there."

"That's crazy, Sasha. I would be mad if someone did that to me." Desiree was shocked, and her voice showed it.

"How would you know? Who would tell you? If the situation were reversed, you don't think the guy that brought you would tell, do you? They say what you don't know can't hurt you."

"It still seems kind of mean, don't you think?"

"Actually, I don't. All of the guys there think that they're just going to a party, but really it's a stress-free episode of *The Dating Game*. The reality of it is, the girlfriend thinks that he's a really nice guy, but she's just not that into him for whatever reason. At the party, that same guy may find his soul mate, and then later on he'll be grateful."

"Are you kidding?" Her feelings of doubt were mingled with concern for the men who didn't know the real deal when they were asked to attend the get-together. "I still think that's a terrible thing to do."

"Why? I think it's the best way to meet a bunch of eligible men that have already been screened. It sure as hell beats going to a bar. At least the next girlfriend has a little background information on him."

"Whoever came up with this farce?"

"A girl in my office got the idea from a *Sex and the City* episode and all of the women think that it's a great idea."

"Well, you're supposed to be bringing a man. How are you going to pass me off?" Desiree was aghast. "Please don't tell me that you expect me to pretend to be your man."

"Of course not, silly. Tiara's the hostess, and she said that I could bring you because everyone knows that I go with Abdul and he's a Muslim. They don't expect me to bring him because of that. Sometimes people are so dumb. Muslims socialize, too. But I wouldn't dare suggest this sort of thing to Abdul. He can be sort of intense, you know. And besides, I'm not quite ready to give him up. He has certain attributes that I enjoy, if you know what I mean."

"All too much." She looked at Tyler watching her. He seemed extremely interested in her end of the conversation, and made no attempt to pretend that he wasn't.

"I don't know about this, Sasha. I don't feel like going to some party to meet a lot of losers."

"Losers? Don't call them that! And I wouldn't use that term to anyone at the party. Some girls are actually bringing their brothers. And you never know who you're talking to." Sasha laughed.

Desiree searched for a way out. "Besides, I kind of have plans for tonight."

"Doing what?"

Desiree was at a loss for words. She and Tyler had nothing specific planned for that evening, but they always did something together on a Saturday night. Because of that, she couldn't immediately come up with anything definite to tell Sasha and get out of the party gracefully without hurting her feelings.

"Are your plans with Diamond Jim Brady?"

"Sort of," Desiree replied lamely.

"If he's not giving away any more diamonds, maybe you're ready to bring him to the party and trade him in for another model."

"I don't think so." Desiree's response was quick and to the point. "I think that I'll keep what I have."

"When am I going to meet him?" Sasha teased. "You're keeping him such a secret; again I have to ask, he's not married is he?"

Desiree looked at Tyler. "No, he's definitely not married." In a hurry to detract Sasha from the current topic of conversation, she said, "Okay, I'll come."

The train ride to Penn Station was uneventful. Tyler hadn't been exactly ecstatic at the thought of her traveling into New York City to go to a get-a-man party, and even though she explained that she was simply accompanying her sister Sasha and didn't really want to go herself, she had seen the uncertainty in his eyes. It bothered her when he dropped her off at the train station looking forlorn. He had stood and watched her train pull away. *I'll call him the minute I get back. I'll take him out to dinner and a movie. He always insists on paying, but this time I'll insist.*

As the train ground to a halt around nine-thirty that evening, Desiree saw her sister standing on the platform swiveling her head around, trying to figure out which car she was seated on. Standing up, Desiree bent down and picked up her weekender case. Her case was light because she had only packed a nightgown, underwear, and an outfit to wear home the next day. Desiree gingerly descended steps. In spite of all of the bright lights, some areas weren't well lit. However, Desiree spotted Sasha moving towards her with a bright light. Her smile was bright, and her appearance was stunning. Sasha's makeup, as usual, was dramatic, and her hair was pulled back from her face. Sasha's coat was unbuttoned, and to Desiree's dismay she saw that her dress was the exact replica of the one Desiree was wearing.

Taking in Desiree's appearance Sasha grinned widely from ear to ear. "Well, well, well, look at us. We have on the same dress. What are the chances of that happening?"

"Not very good." Desiree loved her sister but didn't want to go to a party dressed like her. Between the fishnet stockings that really jazzed Sasha's outfit up and Sasha's bubbly personality, she would feel like a retired store mannequin. Desiree's heart sank. "I don't have anything to change into. I only brought this one dress. You'll have to be the one to change."

"Why should I change? I think it's funny. Two sisters, living miles away from each other, each buy the same dress without the other knowing and wear it to the same party. I'm sure some psychologist could make a lot of money providing some elaborate psychological explanation for what is surely just a coincidence. But it does go to show that we're more alike than people like to think."

"But I don't want to wear the same dress as you, Sasha," Desiree whined. "I feel like Cinderella."

"Why on earth would you say that?" Sasha looked genuinely confused.

"You're so—" She didn't finish her sentence because Sasha interrupted.

"So what? Flamboyant? That's not always a compliment. And don't forget that Cinderella was the one who ended up with Prince Charming." She looped her arm within Desiree's and propelled her to the subway station, barely giving Desiree time to grab her overnight bag. "Come on, we don't have time for me to go home and change. The party's already started, and besides, this will be a good conversation piece at the party, or at least something to amuse our family with the next time we're together. I think that they might enjoy hearing about this."

The apartment building where the party was being held was on the Upper West Side. It was not a far walk from the train station, and Sasha good-naturedly carried

Desiree's bag the short distance. "I told Tiara that you would be coming straight to the party from the train station, and she said that you could stash it in her room for the duration of the party."

"Great! That means that I won't have to keep an eye on my stuff while I'm there."

"You shouldn't have to do that anyhow. The caliber of men attending is supposed to be pretty good. In fact, all of these people are supposed to be high class. They shouldn't have to steal."

"Those are the people who do. I saw an exposé on television that said that the people who don't need to steal are the ones that do."

Sasha laughed. "I saw that, too. Can you imagine? Stealing for kicks. I can think of better ways to get my adrenaline rush than that."

"So can I." Briefly the image of Tyler's face popped in her mind.

Her thoughts were interrupted by Sasha's words. "We're here."

Once they entered the building there was a flight of stairs. Once they finished the first set of stairs, there was a landing before the second set began. In the corner of the landing they almost collided with a couple who seemed engrossed in each other. The man gave them a small smile as he surreptitiously wrote down the woman's name and slid the piece of paper into the pocket of his pants. The smile the woman gave Sasha and Desiree was at the same time secretive and satisfied. Sasha was leading the way, and once they had passed the couple she looked over her shoulder and gave Desiree a knowing wink. Desiree simply shook her head in response.

Once they reached the second landing Sasha veered to the right and went into a small alcove and knocked on the door. They could hear the sound of music. Immediately the door was opened. The woman standing in the doorway was breathtaking. She had smooth cocoa brown skin, pearly white teeth, full lips, and slanted eyes that needed no makeup. Desiree was stunned by her beauty as she enthusiastically hugged Sasha before she beckoned them in. "I've been waiting for you."

"Desiree just got in." She turned to Desiree and introduced them. "Tiara, this is my sister Desiree. Desiree, this is Tiara, our hostess."

Tiara smiled warmly at Desiree. "How cute." She pointed a finger at their dresses. "It's so nice of you to come," she said, reaching forward and shaking Desiree's hand. Then she said in a conspiratorial whisper, "We have about eighteen couples here and believe me, there seem to be some pretty good prospects."

"I'm not looking for real, girl, I'm just window-shopping," Sasha laughed. "Just in case."

Then Tiara turned her attention to Desiree. "How about you, Desiree? Are you game?"

Desiree was at a loss of words. True, it seemed as if everyone was having a good time, but she still didn't like the whole idea that the men there didn't know the real deal. Besides, she was in love with Tyler, so she wasn't even window-shopping. Her response was noncommittal, and between the sound of the music and people's conversation she doubted that either Tiara or Desiree heard her lack of enthusiasm.

Tiara continued, "Let me take care of this for you. I'll put it in my guest bedroom closet. You can take your coats off and put them on the bed in there." She pointed to a room on the right.

Desiree was standing in the corner taking in the atmosphere of the party when she noticed that she was being watched. About her height, the man had a completely bald head and seemed to exude confidence. She saw couples seated on the couch, on the loveseat, and leaning on walls, and in the room people were sipping wine and laughing and talking.

Just then Sasha reappeared and said, "There's a buffet set up in the kitchen. Let's go and get something."

"Okay." Desiree followed her sister, aware that several people stared at them as they passed in their identical dresses. They were in the process of putting food on their plates when a tall, good-looking man approached them. "Haven't we met before?" he asked Sasha. Sasha rolled her eyes and looked at Desiree before she answered him. "Come on now, buddy. You can do better than that, can't you?"

He grinned and held out his hand. "I'm Sexton Johnson."

"Hello, I'm Sasha, and this is my sister Desiree."

His smile was encompassed them both. "I know that it seems like a line, but I do know that I've seen you before."

"Really, where?" Sasha's look was challenging.

Then he hit his palm to his forehead. "Are you a nurse?"

Now it was Sasha's turn to look surprised, but then she recovered.

"Yes, I am. I guess that Tiara told you." She looked around, searching the room for Tiara to see if she was standing in the area that Sexton had come from.

"Actually, no, I saw you at the hospital over a year ago. I was in there for knee surgery. You weren't my nurse, but I saw you right before they gave me the anesthesia. I can remember thinking, 'If I die on the table, at least I had a glimpse of an angel beforehand.' " Sasha and Desiree both laughed at his obvious flattery. He added, "I never saw you after that."

"I'm head nurse, and sometimes I work swing shift and cover for people when they're out."

He stared at her. "I asked about you, but the other nurses couldn't seem to figure out who I was talking about. You're truly beautiful. I can't believe that you're here."

"What do you mean by that?" Sasha asked.

"Never mind." He looked around and beckoned over the man that Desiree had seen eyeing her earlier. Her heart sank. *Oh, no.* Mentally she kicked herself. *It's wrong for me to be here. This really is false advertising to the utmost. I'm not looking for a man. This guy should not waste his time on me.*

Sexton turned as the man approached them. "Calvin, this is Desiree and her sister Sasha."

"How are you doing?" He smiled and offered his hand. Desiree shook it and felt the warmth of his hand as it encircled hers. They were large and surprisingly moist. "Hello, nice to meet you."

"Likewise. Are you enjoying yourself?"

Sexton whispered something in Sasha's ear and they walked off in the direction of the wet bar, placed strategically between the den and living room.

"I haven't been here long, but so far, so good."

"I should have told you before I asked you that. I'm Tiara's brother." Desiree was surprised. "Are you really?" She gave him a long look and noticed the family resemblance. "I take it that you're not exactly thrilled to be here."

"No, I'm not. Tiara made me come. She's hoping to hook me up with the love of my life. As a matter of fact, she mentioned a lady named Sasha, and I'm betting that's the Sasha who's your sister. I guess I moved too slowly. Sexton has her."

Desiree corrected him. "He's talking to her, but believe me, he doesn't have her." Then she changed the subject. "So I take it that you're a personal friend of his."

"Yes, I'm his athletic trainer. I told Sexton about my sister's little get-together and he wanted to come. He thought that it was one of the funniest things that he'd ever heard of."

Desiree grew still. "What do you mean?"

Calvin stared her straight in the eye. "I know the purpose of the party. And so does Sexton. He wanted to come and see the show."

"Oh my goodness. Do any of the other guys know?"

"I can't answer that. The only thing that I do know is that I love my sister, but she needs to stop being in denial."

"Denial about what?" Desiree's tone was quizzical.

"About the fact that I'm gay."

Desiree gave a start of surprise. "I would have never guessed."

"I hope not. I don't hang a sign around my neck. My family knows. But their attitude is that they don't want to know any of the details." He nodded his head in the direction of his sister. She was watching them and seemed pleased with what she saw. "I told her over a year ago, but she hopes that I'm just going through a phase. As if there is such a thing. I'm thirty years old, and way too young to be going through a midlife crisis."

"Oh, I'm sorry."

"Sorry about what? The fact that I'm gay? Every person has things in life that they can't change, and this is it for me. I've made my peace with the fact that I'm a double minority. It's been hard. Being black and gay is no fun, trust me, it's like a double hit."

Desiree gave him a look. "Does Sexton know?"

"I haven't told him, and I don't think that I ever will. I can't believe that I told you. I don't usually divulge such personal information to a complete stranger." He silently assessed her for a moment. "There's just something about you. It makes people want to confide in you."

Desiree knew from work that many times people felt comfortable talking to strangers. That way they could get things of their chest and not have to see that person over and over again and relive the painful conversation.

"I usually keep my professional life and my private life separate. Until this day, I've never mixed the two. He's a pro basketball player and I'm his athletic trainer. I don't think that it would be good for business or his career. People have a tendency to think gay people only hang with gays, and Sexton is certainly all about the ladies."

They looked again at Sasha and Sexton. They appeared to be in a personal discussion and were not talking to any of the other couples in their midst. Calvin watched them, and he looked wistful. "Believe me, if there was any way I could change my sexuality, I would. Life would be so much easier. But sometimes you have to play the deck of cards you're dealt and live with it."

"Do you have to deal with a lot of prejudice?" Desiree liked Calvin. He seemed like a nice guy and she wished happiness for him.

"I have from former friends who somehow found out or suspected the truth. But as long as my family can accept me the way I am, to hell with how anyone else feels. Everyone in my family, though they don't approve, has tried to accept it. Tiara is different."

"I must admit I'm surprised to hear that. I only just met your sister, but I liked her immediately. The minute she opened the door she made me feel welcome."

"That's Tiara. She got very close to my college sweetheart, who later became my wife." At Desiree's look of surprise he said, "Yes, I was married. And after five years of marriage I came clean because I got tired of being on the down low. I loved Leslie, but I always felt something was missing. I know that she loved me very much and I disappointed her when I asked for a divorce, but in the long run she'll be better off. Evidently she shared some intimate details about our relationship with my sister, so that's why Tiara still has hope for me and thinks all that I need is the right woman and that will fix all of this for me. I love Tiara to death; we're only a year apart in a family of five kids, so we've always been very close. She only wants the best for me. That's why I agreed to come, but this is it. I can't see myself doing this again."

"I came only because my sister insisted." She nodded her head towards Sasha, who was still seated sipping wine and conversing with Sexton.

There was silence for a minute, and then Calvin spoke. "I noticed you the minute you walked in."

"Why?" Desiree was curious to know why.

"It was your body language. You seemed different from some of the other women here. I said to myself, 'Now that's a lady I can talk to.'" He dropped his voice to an amused whisper. "I don't smell desperation around you. It's very attractive to a man. If it weren't gay, I might hit on you myself."

Desiree laughed and then admitted, "I do have a boyfriend, so I'm not looking."

Calvin pretended to be horrified. "And he let you come to this?"

"It's not about letting. Sasha didn't want to come to this alone, so I agreed."

"It must be nice to have an understanding mate and family that you can hang out with whenever you want." His voice was sad.

"Being heterosexual doesn't always guarantee you an easy way to go in life, Calvin."

"I don't mean to sound like a whiney cry baby, but I'm pretty sure my problem is bigger than any problem that you might have. You're beautiful and you have a relationship that you're obviously very happy in. That's the real American dream."

"You know it's true that the grass always seems greener on the other side. It's true that I'm happy, but my relationship has drawbacks, too. My family would also have a problem accepting my choice of mate."

"Why?"

"He's white."

"Oh." And then he shrugged his shoulders. "So what? I find it a little hard to believe that in this day and time that would be such an issue. I think my family would be overjoyed if my problem was your problem. Is your family that uptight?"

Desiree was silent for a moment. "I wouldn't call them uptight. Let's just say we're traditional. Blue collar, middle class, white picket fence, the whole nine yards."

"What did they say when you broke the news?"

"Nothing. I haven't told them yet," she replied slowly. "And my man is getting impatient." It was true. Tyler hadn't pushed her into meeting them, but she knew that it hurt his feelings that she hadn't tried to make it known to them that she was in a committed relationship with him.

"Desiree, take it from me. Do the right thing. Tell them. Hiding this important part of your life from them will make them feel as if you're ashamed, and it will taint their whole perception of the relationship when they do find out. The way people find things out helps out a lot when it comes to their acceptance."

Desiree and Calvin spent the rest of the night talking. She and Calvin had discussed plays, books, and what the stars were doing, and she was surprised when Sasha tapped her on the shoulder and asked her if she was ready to go. Desiree turned to look at the grandfather clock against the wall and saw that it was almost midnight. They had exchanged phone numbers earlier in the evening and he'd promised that he would get in touch with her soon, that maybe they could do lunch.

"Well, well, well, look at you all hooking up with a guy. So you see it wasn't a bad night after all, was it?"

"Actually no, Sasha. Talking to Calvin was quite pleasant. It's always nice to meet new people."

"It appeared that it was more than pleasant. I know that Tiara seemed pleased that the two of you hit it off so well. She told me when she went to get your overnight bag that he hasn't had a decent girlfriend in years. I don't know why she's so worried about him. He's probably just playing the field and not ready to settle down. He's not that old, and he's good looking with a good job. It should be easy for him to find someone."

"It should be," Desiree replied in a noncommittal voice.

"I would have left earlier, but Sexton and I didn't want to interrupt."

Desiree had promised Calvin that she wouldn't tell Sasha that he was gay because of his connection to Sexton, and she knew that he wouldn't tell Tiara that her boyfriend was white. "So what did you think of Sexton? Not too bad, huh?"

"Yeah, too bad he's a pro basketball player. That knocks him right out of the dating pool for me, and that name of his is outrageous. What were his parents thinking? It was all I could do not to choke on my drink the minute the words were out of his mouth. I took his telephone number, but I probably won't call him."

"Why not?"

"Girl, please. Basketball players are notoriously promiscuous, and I'm not interested in competing with a whole lot of groupies who are a whole lot younger and firmer than I am."

"He might be bored with that. Maybe he thinks that it's time for a change. You're an interesting person, Sasha, and Sexton seemed very nice and very much taken with you. I don't think that it's right that you completely rule him out just because of what he does."

"Get real. They travel all of the time. What kind of boyfriend would that be? One thing I can say about Abdul, I can count on him to give me a tune up whenever I need one, if you know what I mean." Sasha gave Desiree the look.

Desiree replied in a resigned tone. "Darling, I always know what you mean."

Out of the Closet

CHAPTER THIRTEEN

Desiree let herself into her apartment the next afternoon and was surprised to see Tyler asleep in the recliner in her living room. The television was playing, the remote was in his hand, but his eyes were closed and the rhythmic rise and fall of his chest told the story. Desiree gingerly placed her bag on the floor and noiselessly tiptoed over to him. She leaned over and kissed him on his cheek. Tyler's eyes opened and his expression was completely unguarded.

Desiree slid onto his lap and he folded her into his embrace. "Hey," she said softly.

"Hey to you, too."

"What are you doing here? I thought that you were going to go and play golf today."

"I wasn't in the mood. I didn't sleep well last night, so I did some grocery shopping this morning and then came to see if you were home yet."

"Sasha and I had a late breakfast before I caught the train. Are you okay?" She leaned back in order to get a good look at his face.

"It's nothing." He gave a self-deprecating smile. "'I'm just used to you lying next to me, that's all." He looked vulnerable as his eyes searched hers. "Did you have a good time?"

"I sure did. I spent the whole night talking to one man."

Tyler looked at her questioningly. "Am I to be traded in for a newer model?"

"Absolutely not! Calvin," she explained, "the guy that I spent the evening socializing with, said he noticed me from the moment that I arrived at the party. It suited his purpose to spend the night talking to me, and it suited my purpose to spend the night talking to him." She paused. "He said that I appeared safe, and I liked that."

"Safe? That's an odd way to describe someone who looks like you. I would describe you in other ways."

"I'm not his type. He's gay. He, too, was there at the request of a sibling." She felt Tyler's body beneath her relax a little, but she still felt the need to make him feel more secure. She spoke quietly with her face in his chest. "I'm glad that I went. At first it was only because Sasha asked me to and I don't like to disappoint her. But as the evening went on I can remember thinking to myself, 'I'm so glad that I don't have to do this anymore. I'm so glad that I'm not looking.' Everyone appeared to be enjoying themselves, but it's hard. It's hard to find someone that you love to be with in and out of bed. I have that with you and wouldn't want to give it up for anything." Tyler's answer was to simply draw her closer within the circle of his arms.

The following weeks at Buchanan & Buchanan were extremely hectic for both Tyler and Desiree. He had started a new case where he was suing a company on behalf of a woman who alleged she was kept from promotions because she was a woman.

He also had several other cases in the fire, and he was in and out the office a lot of the time. The days that he was on hand they had lunch together, and when he wasn't around she usually ate with Jillian in the lunchroom.

Desiree was glad to be seeing so much of her. They had a lot in common and usually spent their hour lunch talking about their favorite television shows, or Jillian's new baby. She was obviously curious about Desiree and Tyler's romance, but she never pried.

Desiree had grown accustomed to the coldness of many of the other women at the firm, and she ignored it because she knew that any one of them would have jumped at the chance to be in her shoes.

She was now the primary paralegal working on a case with Ralph Benson. Desiree had previously worked with him on other cases and he had always been cordial to her.

She looked up from her desk to find him smiling at her. He had a manila folder in his hand, which he unceremoniously dropped on her desk. "Those are the notes that you took from last week's meeting with our client. I've made some notations in the margins, and would like you to find as many precedents as you can to support our case."

"Okay." Desiree automatically looked at the clock on her desk. It was already four-thirty, and it would take hours to do a thorough job. "Do you need it today?"

"Yes, if you don't mind. I'll authorize the overtime. I'm going to take whatever you dig up home and review it. Marie and the children are out of town visiting her mother, so it's a good opportunity to get a lot of work done. I'll be in my office, and since you will probably be staying late, I would like to treat you out to dinner as a thank you before you go home."

"Thank you, but that's unnecessary," she declined. "I already have dinner plans."

Ralph Benson immediately slapped one hand to his forehead. "What an idiot I am. Of course you already have plans. It's Valentine's Day. That's what happens when you've been married so long; days like this completely slip your mind." He hesitated and then said, "Just go ahead and work on that until five o'clock. I can wait until tomorrow for the rest of the information."

"Thank you for understanding, Mr. Benson," she said to his retreating back.

From the foyer of her apartment, Desiree caught the scent of Chinese food. She smiled because they had a deal that on the nights that they didn't eat out the first one home had to begin preparing dinner. Obviously Tyler had taken the easy way out and ordered take-out.

Desiree kicked off her shoes in the hallway and soundlessly walked into the kitchen, sliding her arms around his waist. She lay her forehead on his back, loving his fresh shower smell. "I guess that we're staying in tonight." Cartons of sweet and sour pork, shrimp fried rice, sesame chicken, and egg rolls were on the kitchen counter.

"If you don't mind. It's just so cold outside that I didn't think you would like to venture out again tonight." For days the temperature had not risen above sixteen degrees.

"As I've said before, you're a smart man, Tyler Banks." Desiree melted against him and gave him a lingering kiss. "Do I have time for a quick shower?" she asked.

"Take your time. The food only arrived a few minutes before you did. Besides, Chinese food heats up real well in a microwave. The mail is on the table."

Desiree took a long, hot shower. Standing under the showerhead, she let the spray wash over her and, as always, her thoughts were on Tyler. He rarely spent a night at his apartment. They had drifted into a comfortable yet passionate relationship, and Desiree felt that one of the main reasons things were going so well between them was because they didn't let the outside world intrude in their lives.

When she reentered the kitchen clad only in her bathrobe and furry slippers, Tyler had lit long tapered candles and had turned on her CD player. Soft music played in the background.

"Happy Valentine's Day, darling," he said. Grabbing her hand, he led her over to the dinette table and pulled out her chair for her. Tyler had already placed their food on plates and a bottle of wine was in the center of a glass bucket with ice the room was illuminated by the glow of the candles.

"Happy Valentine's Day to you also, sweetheart." She leaned forward and her lips lingered on his before she sat down in the chair he held out for her.

"How did your day go?" Tyler asked after he swallowed a mouthful of shrimp fried rice.

"Busy," she replied. "That's why I'm running a little late."

Tyler looked at her seriously. "You know that you can quit your job anytime you like. You're wasting your talents working as a paralegal. You should be in law school full time."

"I can't quit my job anytime," Desire denied. "How do you expect me to pay my bills?"

"I can take care of that for you, Desiree."

"I can't let you do that. I would feel cheap," Desire replied slowly, obviously groping for words. "I don't like the kept woman idea. Besides, lately I've been thinking that I should apply for some loans and begin going to school part-time. I've put off law school long enough. I'm afraid if I put it off much longer I won't go at all."

Tyler was quiet. He watched her as closely as a hungry hawk watching a chicken at dinnertime.

She continued, "I was thinking about applying to attend NYU in the fall. I can take classes on the weekends. It's a relatively short train ride."

"NYU has an excellent law school and New York is a wonderful place to live." Tyler's face was inscrutable as he listened to Desiree's tentative plans for her future.

"You sound as if you wish you had never moved to Danbury," she commented.

"That's not true. If I had never moved to Danbury I would have never met you, and that would be a tragedy."

Desiree glowed at his words. It was wonderful to be in love with a man who was open about his feelings. Most men were afraid to share their hearts, but Tyler was different. Even though she had never met his mother she wanted to kiss her on both cheeks for raising such a sensitive son.

When she finished, Desiree sat back contentedly. She and Tyler had each sampled from the variety of entrees.

Tyler leaned back and patted his stomach. "That was good."

"I agree, you couldn't have cooked a better meal," she teased, wrinkling her nose at him.

Picking the candle and bottle of wine off the table he said, "Grab your wineglass, and let's relax on the loveseat." Once they entered the living room, he placed the candle on the coffee table and held his glass in the air. "I would like to make a toast."

Desiree immediately lifted her glass.

"To us," he said, "today, tomorrow, and forever. Desiree Diamond, you are the most beautiful, most sexy, most intelligent woman I've ever had the pleasure of being with. I've never enjoyed the company of one person more than yours."

Tyler got down on one knee and looked deeply into her eyes which were wet with tears. "I love you when you're happy, and I love you when you're angry. With you, I've found the love of a lifetime, and I want you to be my wife."

Ignoring Desiree's gasp of astonishment, Tyler reached in his side pocket and withdrew a velvet box. He opened it to reveal a large, square-shaped diamond engagement ring.

He took her hand in his and slid the ring on her finger. "Desiree, will you be my wife and spend the rest of your life with me?"

"Yes," she answered without hesitation.

Tyler couldn't sleep from excitement that night, and he lay in bed listening to Desiree's deep breathing next to him. They had talked for hours and had exchanged Valentine's cards they had each hidden in the apartment. Tyler was tickled pink with the card Desiree had given him. When he was opened it played the music of the song "I Will Always Love You."

They made plans knowing for breaking the news to Desiree's family. Tyler let her decide how she wanted to handle it. Desiree had briefly filled him on her sisters' comments at Christmas about interracial relationships and children. There was a time Desiree would have counted on Sasha for support, but after the episode in the mall she felt that the only ally she could count on was Marcus Junior. Desiree wanted to talk to him alone first. Through the years, he had been the one person she could talk to about serious issues, and although they hadn't always agreed, they had always agreed to disagree. After she talked to Marcus Junior she would take Tyler to

Brewster and introduce him to her family. Tyler understood. He knew that she was nervous about their reactions, and she knew he had waited to propose until he thought their love was strong enough to survive to anything.

Tyler told Desiree, to her astonishment, that at Christmas he had told his parents about her, and that he planned on marrying her. He left out his father's reaction to the news because it had no bearing on their future. After thinking out her plan of action, Desiree fell into a deep, untroubled sleep.

Hours later, Tyler was awakened by a knocking at the front door. The clock on the nightstand showed that it was past three o'clock in the morning. "Someone must have the wrong apartment." Tyler lay there for a few minutes willing the person to go away, but then he heard the knocking again. This time it was louder and more persistent. He realized with annoyance that he would have to get up and tell whoever it was that they had the wrong apartment.

Glancing at Desiree, he was relieved to see that the noise hadn't roused her. He quietly slipped from bed, and not bothering to put on a shirt, he walked down the hall barefooted in his pajama bottoms.

When Tyler opened the door, he was surprised. He immediately recognized Marcus Junior from the many family pictures Desiree had on display in her apartment. He reeked of alcohol as he half slumped against the doorjamb.

The tail of Marcus Junior's shirt hung out one side of his pants, his trousers were wrinkled, and his eyes were bloodshot. He wore no overcoat, yet he seemed unaffected by the cold air.

"Who the hell are you, and where is my sister?" His voice boomed with intoxication and outrage.

Desiree awoke when she heard her brother's voice. She hurried towards the sound of voices, tying the sash of her robe as she walked.

Marcus Junior's eyes widened at the sight of his sister when he fully realized what the situation was.

Desiree looked embarrassed, and Tyler felt sorry for her because of the predicament she found herself in. In an effort to take control of the situation he began, "My name is Tyler Banks," and he held out his hand.

Marcus Junior ignored the proffered hand and looked past him. "Desiree, what the hell is this white man doing at your place this time of morning half-dressed?" His words were slurred. Desiree was distressed to realize that and had obviously fallen off the wagon and was drunk.

Ushering him inside, she guided him to the sofa. "Tyler is a friend of mine."

As Tyler closed the front door he gave Desiree a sharp look at her casual description of him. Then he walked into the living room and studied Desiree as she sat next to her brother. He didn't see much of a family resemblance, but he knew from conversations with Desiree that her brother was very near and dear to her.

"What's wrong, Marcus Junior, and why are you drunk?" Desiree's voice was high with anxiety. She had never seen him in such a state.

"Why not?" he retaliated. "I may as well get drunk. Trying to do the right thing doesn't really make any difference in life."

Understanding dawned on her. "Does this have to do anything with the promotion at the post office?"

Her brother hiccupped, "Oh yeah, you mean the promotion I didn't get. I found out earlier today that they gave it to some twenty-three-year old white boy that they hired less than six months ago."

"But why?" Desiree wailed.

"Because they can." He answered harshly. His attention returned to Tyler, and suddenly a look of blind fury stole across his face. "This apartment has only one bedroom. Where the hell is he sleeping?"

Tyler remained silent, watching the scene. His hands were balled in his pockets, and he rocked back and forth on his heels.

Desiree knew from past experience that meant he was doing some deep thinking. "Tyler is my boyfriend," she whispered.

Her words were not very loud, and Tyler barely heard her.

Marcus Junior's temper erupted. "I can't believe that you're sleeping with a white man. Didn't my experience with Ahmad's mother teach you anything? I can't even see my son because after they use you they throw you away like you're garbage. You can't trust them. Black folks need to stick together. White people always do. No matter how much they like you, when push comes to shove they will even choose trash over you and make it your boss.

They always support each other, and it's about time we started doing the same." Marcus Junior glared at Tyler. "In the end, he'll betray you. They always do."

After Marcus's outburst, Tyler began, "I love your sister and I—"

Marcus Junior's voice cut across his words. "I was not talking to you." His words were icy and he looked at Desiree. "Alexandria loved me also until she found another serviceman to give her money."

Marcus Junior began to rise from the sofa, and Tyler held out his hand to steady him. "Let me help you." He added as an afterthought, "I hope you're not driving."

At hearing this, Marcus Junior knocked his hand away. He turned to Desiree and sneered, "Listen to your white man trying to tell me what to do. See how natural it is for them to think that they can give orders?" He took two steps forward and looked menacingly at Tyler. "I don't need your help, and stay away from my sister."

With that he began to walk towards the door, and Desiree wailed, "Marcus Junior, you can't go anywhere in this condition. Stay here."

"You, him, and me? I'm not staying here. You must be out of your mind. I'll walk to the corner and hail a cab to the train station." Marcus banged the door to Desiree's apartment against the wall, and the Diamond family portrait that hung nearby vibrated from the force.

Desiree stood there dumbly as she watched her brother stumble down the stairs. She began to cry softly, and Tyler went to her to put his arms around her for comfort. She pushed him away, avoiding his arms. "I'm exhausted. I'm going back to bed." She didn't look at him as she walked towards the bedroom.

Tyler followed her. "I'm sorry your brother didn't get the promotion," he said quietly. "He can try again. This doesn't have to be the end of the world."

"That's easy for you to say, Mr. Lawyer." Her tone was harsh and her words bitter.

A red flush of anger swept over Tyler's face. "Things haven't always been easy for me either, you know."

"No matter how hard they've been for you, they have been ten times harder for my brother," she stated resentfully.

He became very angry and his voice rose. "This is not my fault, so don't take it out on me. I'm not the enemy."

"Maybe yes, maybe no." Desiree muttered the words, but Tyler heard them and he looked hurt.

"So Marcus's words hit home. You're going to punish me because he's pissed off with white people."

"I really don't want to talk about this anymore tonight. I'll decide what I'm going to do in the morning." She ran a hand listlessly through her hair.

"Decide what you're going to do about what?" At Desiree's continued silence Tyler said harshly, "This must be the shortest engagement in the world. We should send it in to the *Guinness Book of World Records*. Maybe we can get a prize or something."

"You saw how Marcus Junior felt. He'll never accept a marriage between us, and I was counting on him to be an ally. If he won't accept us, none of my family will."

Tyler shouted, "You can't pay any attention to him! He's drunk. He's roaring, stinking, rotten drunk."

Desiree's anger nearly boiled over at his description of her brother. "Yes, he's drunk. But he's right about one thing. Black people should stick together. I should have fallen in love with a black man. I could have beautiful black babies, raise them right, and help to strengthen my race."

Tyler's temper exploded. "Forget this shit!" he said and walked over to the closet. Reaching inside, he grabbed a pair of pants and shirt and began to put them on.

Desiree watched him from her upright position in the bed. "Where are you going?" she demanded.

"Where the hell do you think? I'm leaving," he yelled. "I can tell when I'm not wanted. You're right about rethinking this engagement. I was married for years to a woman who didn't have a mind of her own about a damn thing. Nancy cared about everyone else's feelings but mine, and I refuse to put myself through that again. Marriage is work in an ideal situation, and we don't stand a snowball's chance in hell if you crumble at every bit of adversity."

He snatched up the velvet box on the nightstand which held her engagement ring. Desiree had taken it off earlier because it needed to be sized to fit her finger and she hadn't wanted to take the chance of losing it. "Good luck finding that perfect black man you're looking for," he sneered as he stormed out of the bedroom, slamming the door. Moments later, she heard the front door to her apartment door close with a bang.

After Tyler left, Desiree cried as she had never cried before, and when she was finished all of the anger that was inside her had dissipated and all she felt was alone.

She woke with a splitting headache and decided to call in to work and take a sick day. She spoke only briefly to Ralph Benson and informed him that she was ill, to which he wished her well and hoped to see her the following day.

After she hung up the telephone she walked into the bathroom and emptied three Tylenol tablets into her hand and swallowed them. Stumbling back to bed, she lay there and thought about the previous night's events. She felt sorry for Marcus Junior, but Tyler was right that it wasn't his fault.

Last night's argument had gotten completely out of hand. She had been so angry on her brother's behalf she didn't stop to think about what she was saying. In the cold light of day, she knew that she needed Tyler to be a part of her life, and if her family really loved her, they would accept Tyler.

She also knew that it was up to her to apologize to Tyler. She hoped that he would forgive her. *I can fix this. Tyler said that he was brave enough for the two of us. Once I talk to him he'll understand that I didn't mean the things that I said. I was just upset because I didn't want my family to find out about us this way.* She cringed when she thought of the things that she had said to him, and hoped that they hadn't made him stop loving her. If he did still love her, than they could work everything out and begin planning their life together. *When he calls I'll straighten it out.*

She waited for hours and then, not being able to wait any longer, she again dialed the telephone number of Buchanan & Buchanan. Desiree bristled when she recognized the voice of Blanche Harding. "Miss Harding, this is Desiree Diamond calling. Will you please connect me to Mr. Banks?"

There was a pause and then Blanche Harding responded. "He's not here." Then she jeered. "Don't tell me that you don't know."

"Know what?" Desiree demanded.

"He came in earlier today and wrapped up some paperwork. Then he left because he's taking an *indefinite* leave of absence." Blanche the stressed the word indefinite for effect, her voice crowing with triumph at the realization that Desiree had been unaware of Tyler's plans.

Desiree hung up without saying a word and then dialed Tyler's apartment. After the phone rang several minutes, she hung up.

The next number she called was his answering service. "I need to get a message to Mr. Banks."

"Is it an emergency?" The voice sounded curt.

"Yes," Desiree replied crisply. "Please have him call Desiree Diamond immediately."

She waited by the phone all evening, but Tyler didn't call. Desiree redialed the number to his answering service.

"Excuse me, but this is Desiree Diamond calling again. Did you get in touch with Mr. Banks and ask him to phone me?"

"Yes, I did." The impersonal voice sounded offended.

"Do you have a number where I can reach him?"

"Mr. Banks is out of town and I am not at liberty to give the number out to anyone." Now the voice sounded impatient.

"I didn't go to work today, and I forgot to tell you to have him call me at home. Will you please call him again and tell him that?"

"Yes, I will."

Desiree continued to sit by the telephone, but Tyler didn't call. Right before she retired for the night, she sifted through the accumulated mail. Desiree automatically separated it, putting aside all of the letters that she knew were pre-approved invitations for credit cards. When she reached the last envelope, she opened it slowly, thinking it was from a member of her family. There was no return address. It was a Valentine's card from Travis. The front showed a beautiful array of a dozen roses displayed on the outside. On the inside were several stanzas about starting over. On the blank side of the card were words written in Travis's handwriting. *I miss you, Desiree. Please call me so that we can talk. Love, Travis.* The irony of the situation was more than she could handle, and that night as she lay in bed she stared at the empty side where Tyler usually slept and wept quietly in the darkness.

Absolution

CHAPTER FOURTEEN

The next few weeks, Desiree walked around as if she were a zombie. Tyler had not returned her calls, and the office grapevine was working overtime since Blanche Harding had informed everyone that Desiree didn't even know that Tyler Banks would be out of the office for an indefinite length of time.

Even if Blanche hadn't spilled the beans, everyone could tell by looking at Desiree that she was very unhappy. She had lost weight, and the hollows under her eyes showed her lack of sleep.

She didn't dare venture into the cafeteria at lunchtime. The prying eyes of the other employees would search her face for answers to what had happened between her and Tyler. Friday morning, Jillian unceremoniously walked into Desire's office and plopped down in the chair across from her. "What going on? What happened between you and Tyler?" Desiree's eyes filled with tears and her only answer was to hang her head and stare at some imagined ink spot on her blotter.

"You don't have to worry. I won't discuss anything you tell me with those female vultures in the secretarial pool or with anyone else." At Desiree's continued silence, Jillian's voice softened. "Darling, you need to talk to someone. It's obvious that something terrible has happened and that it's eating you alive. Maybe telling someone who doesn't have a personal stake in the outcome of the relationship can help."

It was true that she needed to talk to someone. She had not bothered to call her family and tell them about her love for Tyler because it was apparent by his lack of response to her repeated phone calls that he didn't want to marry her anymore. She had also tried several times to contact Marcus Junior, but either he was never home or he was just refusing to answer the telephone.

"I destroyed my relationship with Tyler, and I don't think that it can be repaired." Desiree whispered the words and a fresh onslaught of tears began to form in her eyes.

Jillian watched her quietly for a few minutes and then handed Desiree a tissue from the Kleenex box on the desk. "What happened?"

Desiree poured out the whole story to Jillian, including the things she had said to Tyler. She was embarrassed to repeat the comments she had made, but Jillian excused her behavior with a flip of her hand.

"Honey, you were upset. When people argue anything is liable to come out. I love Marlon to death, but sometimes when the baby is cranky and I don't feel like he's pulling his own weight, I can turn into a regular little Tasmanian devil."

At this Desiree gave a half- smile. "The difference is that the two of you are married. It's worth it for you to try and work things out. I feel Tyler thinks I'm more trouble than I'm worth."

"Nonsense." Jillian pushed this explanation aside. "He's just gone somewhere to cool off. If he still wasn't in love with you he wouldn't have taken off. He could walk right past you at work and ignore you. The fact that he's bolted means that this break-up is just as hard on him as it is on you." Jillian sat quietly for a moment mulling over Desiree's situation. Thinking aloud she said, "He hasn't quit the firm, and he's going to have to call in to check and see if there are any messages. My office is just right outside the answering service department. I'll let you know when he does."

"Please don't do that, Jillian. I don't want to harass him. I've left numerous messages for to call me and he hasn't. I can't make him talk to me, and I can't make him fall in love with me again."

After Jillian left and she was once again alone, Desiree sat at her desk, crying softly with her face cupped in her hands.

For lunch Desiree decided to walk to the park. Jillian had asked her to join her and some of the other parale-gals and, although she wouldn't have minded her friend's company, she didn't want to be in a crowd. Desiree sat quietly enjoying the unusually mild day for March in Connecticut. She had her head bent down when she real-ized a part of the sun had suddenly been blocked. She looked up and saw the tall, long lines of Travis. He had a wry smile on his face and he looked somewhat uncertain. "How are you doing, Desiree?"

"Fine." She was startled and replied without thinking, "How are you doing?"

"I'm doing okay. I hope I'm not disturbing you, but I feel that we need to talk."

"How did you know where to find me?" She was stunned, and her face showed it.

"I asked the receptionist to let you know that you had a visitor, but she said that she saw you leave the building and sometimes you walk to the park at lunchtime."

Desiree was tired from too many sleepless nights, and her voice and expression showed it. "What do you want, Travis?" Without giving him a chance to answer the first question she spoke again. "And why are you here?"

Without asking her permission, Travis sat down on the bench next to her. "I'm here because I don't like the ways things ended with us, and I really feel the need to talk to you."

"Why do you feel the sudden need to talk to me? You had years to do that and you didn't."

"I know that, Desiree. And I deeply regret that." His tone was somber.

"So you felt the need to come to my job?" she queried and looked at him with one brow raised.

Travis cleared his throat and said quietly, "I tried calling you at home several times, but every time I tried a man answered the telephone or I lost my nerve when you answered and I hung up." His voice tailed off lamely.

"So you came to my job."

"Please believe me; I'm not trying to cause any trouble for you."

"I'm sorry, but I don't believe you. You saw me in New York with a white man that you know I work with." She stressed the word 'white.' "And now you have this great desire to have some kind of contact with me."

"I know that you're dating someone from work and that this might be awkward for you. That's why I was kind of relieved when I was told that you might be here in the park. Why are you here alone?"

She replied dully, "He's not here today."

"Then my timing is perfect. That enables us to spend some time talking without being interrupted and possibly fix this."

"Fix this?" She looked at him questioningly.

"Desiree, I missed you immediately after our split. I just thought that we needed to take a hiatus. I never expected . . ." He stopped.

"You never expected what, Travis? You never expected another man to want me, is that it?" She looked him squarely in the eye, and he looked away, embarrassed.

"Of course that's not it, Desiree. I know other men want you. Other men have always wanted you. When we used to go places together, I would see other men looking at you. But I always felt secure. I never felt any jealousy, because I always knew that you were a one-man woman."

"Fix what?" she again asked.

"I'm ready to make a commitment. If we work together and sort through our problems, I think that now is the time for us to get married. I love you, Desiree." He drew in a deep breath. "I miss your voice." He reached over and grabbed her hand and looked deeply in her eyes. "I miss your smile, the soft feel of your skin, the smell of you when you wake in the morning, but most of all I just miss you."

"This would be funny if it weren't so tragic. These are things I'm hearing for the first time. In all our years together, you never shared any of this with me."

"I find it hard to talk about my feelings, Desiree. I just always thought that you knew. I didn't think that I needed to tell you something that was so obvious."

"It wasn't obvious to me. I guess that I'm a whole lot more insecure than you give me credit for." Thoughts of Tyler entered her mind and her eyes welled up with tears.

"Don't cry," Travis said, wiping away the tear that trickled down her left cheek. "It's not too late, we can work things out."

"I'm not crying tears of happiness, Travis," she mumbled. "I'm crying because this is too late."

"So you're in love with the man that I saw you with?"

"Yes," Desiree replied without hesitation.

"What can I do to change your mind?"

"Nothing. You're right, Travis. I am a one-man woman, and you're not that man anymore," she replied dully. "I would like to give you a piece of advice."

"What is it?" Travis asked softly.

"When you find another woman and fall in love with her, don't mess it up. Love is more valuable than a pot of gold, and can be just as elusive if you don't take care of it."

"Desiree—" he began but she interrupted him gently. "Please leave now, Travis."

As she watched his retreating back she realized that she was happy that she and Travis had talked. Maybe the next time Travis fell in love he wouldn't take it for granted and would do whatever he could to preserve it.

Right before she left work that day, Desiree heard her name being paged over the intercom system. Hoping that it was Tyler, she felt her heart begin to beat wildly as she hurried to the extension in the law library. Breathlessly she picked up the receiver. "Desiree Diamond speaking."

"Desiree, this is your mother." Desiree couldn't breathe when she heard the emotional crack in her mother's voice. "Mom, what's wrong?" Her immediate thought was of her brother. "Is it Marcus Junior?"

"No, dear, it's your father." Nadine Diamond hesitated, groping for the right words. "There's been an accident at work. A building collapsed at his work site and he was buried underground for hours."

Desiree listened with dread for her mother's next words. "Is he okay?" Her voice shook with fear.

"No, he's not okay. It's serious." Nadine Diamond's voice was high-pitched with fear and anxiety. "Once he was rescued from the rubble he was rushed to Mercy Community Hospital, and he hasn't regained consciousness. Marcus Junior and Sasha are on their way. I called Dominique, but she wasn't at home. I was able to reach

Benjamin, and he said that Dominique had a meeting with her sorority sisters and that he was going to try and reach her on her cell phone. They're planning their spring gala ball; it's being held on April 22. It's supposed to be a big affair. Benjamin said that he would reach her and they would be here as soon as possible." Desiree knew her mother was rambling in the way people do when they're unnerved.

Desiree interrupted her. "I'm going to tell Mr. Buchanan that I'm leaving, and I'll be there as soon as possible."

"Thank you, darling." Nadine Diamond began to cry. "I'm so afraid. I don't know what I would do without your father."

"Don't talk like that. He's going to pull through this. Dad's a fighter. He always has been and always will be."

After Desiree spoke briefly to Arthur Buchanan and received his sympathy she hurriedly ran down the hall and almost collided with Jillian.

"Whoa," she said. "Where's the fire?"

Desiree briefly explained the situation to her. "My father is at Mercy Community Hospital in Brewster. I'm on my way there now."

"My prayers are with you and your family." Jillian drew Desiree to her and gave her a comforting hug. "Drive carefully," she warned. "You can't do anyone any good if you get in an accident and end up in the hospital yourself."

The drive to Brewster was a blur. Desiree silently prayed that everything would be all right. *Lord, I know that you don't give us anything we can't handle, but please*

*let my father pull through this. I don't know if I can deal
with another loss right now.*

Dominique, Mildred, Bianca, and Stephanie were
lingering over their coffee at the restaurant. The other
members had left at the close of the luncheon meeting.
The four were chatting pleasantly about how much they
had accomplished that day and how successful they
expected their spring fling to be.

"I think your idea of having an island theme is great."
Dominique complimented Bianca. "By that time, all of
the women will be so sick of cold weather, snow, and
heavy coats, they will be excited at the idea of wearing a
backless dress or spaghetti-strapped formal."

Bianca beamed at Dominique's compliment, but
before she could respond Mildred abruptly changed the
conversation. Looking pointedly at Dominique, Mildred
inquired, "How is Desiree doing?"

Dominique was surprised at Mildred's interest in her
sister. "She's doing quite well," she answered with pride.
"She'll soon be going to law school. Desiree has such a
bright mind. In the courtroom, she'll be a force to be
reckoned with."

Mildred looked at Dominique slyly. "I agree with you
there. I could never be the trailblazer that she is, and my
hat goes off to her for her guts. I saw her blow off Adam
Westlake at your party, so I understood why he brought
that other woman to the hospital Christmas party. I can't

help but wonder, though, at some of the unwise choices that Desiree is making. How your parents feel about that whole affair."

"Whatever are you talking about?" Dominique's tone was acidic because she knew that Mildred was deliberately baiting her. She obviously had some dirt on Desiree that she wanted to share. "If you have something to say, Mildred, just spit it out."

Mildred's eyes narrowed. She was angered by Dominique's tone and the superior look on her face. "I don't mean any harm, Dominique," she lied smoothly. "I just didn't think that your family would so readily accept Desiree dating a white man."

"What on earth are you talking about?" Dominique responded hotly. "My sister is not dating a white man."

Mildred attempted to look apologetic, but she failed miserably. "I'm sorry. I wish I hadn't said anything, but I thought that you knew."

"What makes you think that Desiree is dating a white man?" Dominique demanded.

Mildred wet her lips and leaned forward, saying in a conspiratorial whisper, "I saw her myself. Richard and I were having dinner at Antonio's in New Fairfield. Your sister was seated not far from where we were, but she didn't see us because she only had eyes for him. I must say, he wasn't bad looking for a white man."

"Oh, is that all?" Dominique said in relief. "I'm sure that you're mistaken. She does work for a law firm, you know. I'm sure that he was just a business associate."

Mildred leaned back in her chair and grinned like the Cheshire cat. "I don't think so, sister dear. He held her hand and kissed it. It was quite a show and quite obvious to me and the people around them that it was not a business dinner between friends, but two people very much attracted to each other. I was going to speak on my way out, but they were so engrossed with each other I didn't want to intrude." Mildred twisted the knife a little more. "I would have never said anything, but I honestly thought that you knew. I know for a fact that Benjamin knows because Richard mentioned it to him at work. He said that Benjamin made no comment when he asked him about it so he let it drop."

An uncomfortable silence descended on the group. Throughout the small scene, Bianca and Stephanie had sat quietly listening to the drama. They felt sorry for Dominique, and giving Mildred looks of chastisement, they made flimsy excuses and left. The reaction of the others to her instigating was not what Mildred had expected, and their abrupt departures forced Mildred to her feet. She left Dominique alone to recover from the shocking news.

Dominique sat absently stirring her cold cup of coffee when her cell phone rang. "Hello, Benjamin. What? When? Where? I'm on my way," she said abruptly before disconnecting.

Dominique sat alone in her car at Mercy Community Hospital. She had been upstairs in the hospital waiting room with the others but had felt as if the walls were closing in on her. That day she had been dealt one piece of bad news after the other, and she needed time alone to think. First, it was the bombshell Mildred had dropped at lunch, and then the news of her father.

When Dominique had received Benjamin's phone call, it had catapulted her out of the catatonic state she had remained in after the departure of her sorority sisters.

Her hands gripped the steering wheel so hard her knuckles hurt. Silently she prayed to the Lord to answer her prayers and let her father pull through this.

Dominique had begun praying to God when she was a child. During her whole adult life when there were things that frightened her, or things that she didn't understand, she immediately looked to Him for guidance.

The first time Dominique could remember praying for something other than toys was when she was a little girl and had been frightened at a bus station. Her mother was taking her, Marcus Junior, and Desiree to Alabama to visit their sick grandmother. The bus had stopped outside a small town in Alabama, and Dominique had been pulling on her mother's hand impatiently. Her mother walked very slowly because she was very tired, and her stomach was too big for her to hurry. Dominique knew her mother was so big because she had been told that she was soon getting another brother or sister.

It was dark outside and Dominique ran ahead, ignoring her mother's sharp command to slow down and wait for the rest of them. She knew that if she didn't hurry she would wet her pants and somebody four years old was way too old to have accidents like that. She rounded the corner and saw three white ghosts standing around a black man. Dominique stopped, transfixed by the scene. She had been reading stories about ghosts, but these ghosts didn't look like pictures of the ones in books. They had pointed hoods on their heads, and their robes fell to their feet. They stood around a black man. Two of the ghosts held him by his arms laughing while the third slapped him repeatedly in the face.

Her mother and Marcus Junior finally caught up with her, and holding two-year-old Desiree in her arms her mother bent down angrily to scold Dominique for running out of her sight. When she realized what had stopped Dominique's flight, she immediately put her fingers to her lips to warn them to be quiet and hurriedly pressed them all against a wall in the darkness. Desiree squirmed in her mother's arm from the pressure of being held too tightly. Marcus Junior had instinctively grabbed Dominique and put his arms protectively around his little sister.

They stood there, huddled together in the darkness. They were afraid to leave because they knew that the shadows hid their presence from the ghosts. The ghosts finally stopped hitting the man and one of them spoke.

"Boy, if you tell anyone about this I will come back and kill you and your family. I know where y'all live."

The other ghosts released the man's arms, and one of them dug his hands in the black man's pockets and withdrew a dollar bill and some change. "Y'all always broke. Damn, this wasn't even worth the effort." Laughing and jeering, they walked past them without a look in the direction where Dominique hid with her family in the shadows.

After they left the black man just stood there silently staring at the ground. Dominique looked at her mother. She had been silently crying, and her face was soaked with tears.

Once they were safely on the bus, Dominique asked her mother plaintively, "Mommy, why were those ghosts hitting that black man? What did he do?" Not wanting Dominique to be overheard, she motioned for her to be quiet and replied in a whisper, "Probably nothing. And they weren't ghosts. That was the Klan. They are the worst cowards in the world. They hide behind sheets and use scare tactics to hurt people because they are too cowardly to fight fairly."

"I wet my underpants," Dominique mumbled, ashamed to tell her mother.

"That's okay, honey. Before long we'll be at your grandmother's house and we'll all take a long bath. After that, we'll all feel much better."

Dominique's last thought before she could muster up the will to go back into the hospital were of the gossip that Mildred had imparted. How dare Desiree date a white man? Had she lost her mind?

Hours later, all of the Diamond family, except the twins, was gathered in the waiting room at Mercy

Community Hospital. Benjamin had left Nichelle and Nicholas with their next-door neighbors, not wanting to upset them with the news of their grandfather unless he had no choice.

Glancing at her wristwatch Sasha said, "He's been in surgery for over an hour. Someone should come out and tell us something."

"His surgeon is Dr. Khan, and he probably won't send word until he's certain of the prognosis." Nadine Diamond's face was lined with worry.

Desiree watched Dominique. Her sister was unusually quiet. She had not spoken to any one person directly since she had entering the hospital waiting room. Desiree knew that Dominique was worried about their father, everyone was, but her reaction was strange. During other crises in their lives, Dominique had been the one to step up and take charge, but this time she just sat there in mute silence. Earlier, Desiree had asked Dominique about seeking help in order to seek out their father's doctor for information, but all she had received as a reply was a quelling look and silence.

Staring at their mother's weary expression, Dominique finally spoke. Obviously as an attempt to give their mother something to do she said, "Come walk with us, Mother. Benjamin and I are going down to the cafeteria and bring coffee back for everyone."

Desiree declined the offer. "None for me, I'm wired enough as it is."

"I'll bet you are," Dominique replied crisply.

Desiree looked at her in surprise. Dominique's voice had bordered on rudeness, but again she attributed it to anxiety about their father.

Dominique gave Desiree a sharp look before she and Benjamin walked out of the hospital waiting room.

Sasha stood impatiently. "I'm going to the desk and ask someone to find out Dad's status."

Once they were alone, Marcus Junior cleared his throat. "Desiree, I know that this may not be the right time, but I want to apologize to you for what happened the last time we saw each other."

She brushed aside his apology. "It's okay, Marcus. I know that must have been a shock for you seeing Tyler, a white man, at my place, at that time of morning, dressed only in his pajamas." Her voice trailed off and her eyes avoided his. "I'm just sorry that you were in so much pain."

Marcus Junior's face expressed deep regret for his behavior. "Being in pain doesn't give me the right to try to make you miserable also. Is Tyler the man who gave you the earrings at Christmas?"

"Yes," Desiree replied quietly.

"You've been dating him all this time and didn't say anything to us?" He looked at her in confusion.

"Yes." Now she looked her brother directly in the eyes. "I was afraid that you would disapprove. And I was right." Her words ended on a bitter note and she turned away.

Her brother looked guilty. "Well, Dad's accident sort of puts things in perspective, doesn't it? Sometimes it takes a tragedy to make people think about what is really important. If you love him, and he loves you, I want the two of you to be together. I haven't said anything to the rest of the family. It's your business to tell, not mine."

"There's nothing to tell. Tyler and I aren't seeing each other anymore." Desiree could see the immediate look of remorse on her brother's face.

"Why? Because of me?" Marcus Junior asked. "Desiree, if I could change what happened that night, if I could take back the horrible things that I said, I would."

"Tyler and I didn't split because of you. It was because of me. I'm a coward." Thinking of the man in the hotel lobby she had confronted at Sturbridge Village, she continued, "I can fight small skirmishes, but I'm no good in heavy combat."

"You don't give yourself enough credit, Desiree. You have more strength than you know," Putting his arms around her comfortingly, he gave her a brief hug. "I truly believe you can withstand anything you want to. Look at Mom and Dad. They're both strong, and you are their child." Changing the subject he continued, "I want you to know that I haven't had a drink since that night. I took a few vacation days off from work and checked myself into a rehab center."

Desiree was relieved to hear that. "I guess that's where you were when I tried to call. I'm glad to know that you're back on track."

"I'm attending AA meetings again. Life is full of problems, and every time there's a crisis in my life, I turn to alcohol. I need to find other ways to deal with disappointment. Then maybe if I'm up for another promotion at work and don't get it, I'll handle myself differently."

Desiree immediately thought of her and Tyler's last conversation. "You're going to try again for another promotion?"

"Of course," he replied softly. "I'm the son of Nadine and Marcus Diamond, aren't I? I come from strong stock."

Every time the door to the waiting room opened, the Diamond family looked up expectantly. When Dr. Khan finally walked into the room, he gave them a reassuring smile. "I've finished working on your father, and he's resting comfortably."

Marcus Junior voiced the words everyone else was afraid to. "Is he going to be all right?"

Dr. Khan replied, "It wasn't as bad as we first thought. It took me so long to give you a status on him because I had to make sure that there was no internal bleeding. As it turned out, I didn't have to operate. His lungs weren't punctured; there was just bruising to his chest and ribs where the weight of a beam had pinned him. I taped his ribs in order to minimize movement so they can heal quickly. I can safely assure you that he's going to be fine."

Everyone breathed a sigh of relief and said in unison, "Thank God." Nadine Diamond wiped away tears of joy. "One other thing, he has a suffered a broken leg so I had to set it and put a cast on it." He looked at the Diamond children. "Your father has the constitution of a horse. A weaker man would have been in a lot worse condition. I hope all of you are as strong."

Marcus Junior gave Desiree an I-told-you-so look before he clasped her hand with his own and squeezed it.

"He's being moved to a private room as you requested, and then all of you can see him, one at a time. But don't any of you stay too long," Dr. Kahn warned. "And whatever you do, don't excite him."

Nadine Diamond left for the hospital room. It was the unspoken agreement that she was to go, and the rest would follow later. Feeling that she could now relax, Desiree looked at the other members of her family, and announced, "I'll be right back. I'm going to the ladies' room."

Desiree's steps faltered as her gaze was drawn to the man at the nurse's desk. He had his back to her, but she could recognize the broad shoulders and tall stature of Tyler Banks from any angle. He was giving the nurse hell as he insisted, "Your inpatient sheets need to be updated. She has to be in this hospital. Look again; her name is Desiree Diamond."

"Tyler?" she whispered, and then more strongly when he didn't turn around, "Tyler? Are you looking for me?"

Tyler slowly turned around, and his face was pale. His eyes were red from lack of sleep and he, too, had lost weight. Time seemed to halt as they stared at each other across the expanse of the room. Then Desiree ran to him as if she had wings on her feet. Throwing her arms around him, she hung on to him, holding him as if she would never let go. The nurse at the desk stared at the couple and then said loudly in Tyler's direction before she stomped off, "I told you we hadn't admitted a Desiree Diamond."

"What are you doing here? How did you know?" She had her arms wrapped around his waist and her head was buried in his chest.

Tyler held her, smoothing her long hair with his hands. "I called into work this afternoon for my messages and Jillian said that there had been an accident and you were in the hospital. I had to come."

"There was an accident. But it's not me, it's my father."

"Your father?" His voice sounded hollow as he repeated her words.

"Yes, a building collapsed and he was trapped underneath the rubble for hours, but the doctor said that he was going to be okay, with time."

Tyler pried her body away from his and looked deep into her eyes. "Jillian deliberately led me to believe it was you." He gathered her close again. Thinking aloud, he said, "She knew that I wouldn't be able to stay away."

Desiree half-smiled. "I told her what happened between us. I guess she was trying to be a matchmaker. Since her subterfuge sent you to me I'm very grateful to her, but do I have a reason to be?"

"That depends. Why all of the messages? What did you want to say to me?" Tyler loosened his hold on her and stepped back.

Desiree looked at him and said clearly, "Tyler, I was such a fool. I was so upset about what happened to

Marcus Junior, I didn't know what I was saying. I love you and want to be your wife, if you'll have me."

"Desiree, you don't know the hell I've been through. I love you, but I can't live my life with a woman who holds me responsible every time someone white does something wrong to a black person. I can't shoulder the responsibility for my whole race. I can't keep apologizing for what society has done to you, or what my ancestors did to your grandparents, or your great-grandparents. I can only account for my own actions."

"I know that, Tyler. I know that you're different from a lot of men. You're a good man. The color of your skin doesn't matter. I don't want to lose you. Let me prove to you how very much I love and want you."

Tyler saw the sincerity in Desiree's eyes, and inside he was full of jubilation, but he held his emotions in check. He had to be sure. "I can't marry a woman who is ashamed to be seen with me."

"I'm not ashamed to be seen with you." She spoke loudly enough so that anyone within earshot could hear her words. "Tyler Banks, will you marry me, and be my partner for the rest of my life?"

Tyler felt as if they had come full circle and it was time for them to celebrate.

"Yes." He reached into his pocket and pulled out the velvet box that held her engagement ring. "I was going to get a preacher and marry you today while you were in the hospital if I could." Tyler looked embarrassed. "I kind of figured I could take advantage of you while you were under sedation. Let me put this where it belongs." Tyler slid the ring on her left finger. It was still too large for her, and Desiree slid her right hand under her left palm to secure it.

Tyler leaned forward and kissed her hand, and the ring sparkled in the fluorescent lights from the ceiling. "Come," she said decisively, putting her hand in his. "My family is in the waiting room, and it's high time they met you."

The Showdown

CHAPTER FIFTEEN

When Desiree entered the lounge area holding Tyler's hand, all of the family was present except her mother. At the sight of Desiree and Tyler, shock registered on her siblings' faces. Dominique had been absently staring out of the window, but at their appearance she held out one hand and used it to brace herself against the wall for support.

Desiree said clearly, "Everyone, this is Tyler Banks, my fiancé."

There was complete silence. Then suddenly Marcus Junior stepped forward, extended his hand to Tyler, and broke the silence. "Welcome to the family."

Tyler accepted his handshake and the two men looked at each other. As their eyes connected, mutual understanding passed between them and words were unnecessary.

Sasha had been standing, but at Desiree's announcement she sat down in one of the hospital chairs. Then she quickly recovered and exclaimed, "Well, well, well. Who would have ever thought it? Go ahead, sister. When you bust out, you go all the way, don't you?" She waved her hand at Desiree.

Desiree gave her a wry smile, and Dominique rounded on Sasha. "You would think that this is okay, wouldn't you? I would have expected this from you, but not Desiree." Dominique pointed an accusing finger at Desiree. "I know that a good black man is hard to find, but this is ridiculous. Mildred Brown told me at our luncheon today that she saw you holding hands in a restaurant with a white man. Out of respect for Dad and for what our family is going through, I decided to speak my piece at a later, better time. But since you've chosen this ridiculous time to share this information with us, I may as well say it now. This relationship is unacceptable, and I will not condone your relationship with this . . ." Dominique stuttered, trying to find words to express her feelings, ". . . this person."

Tyler was amused. *She sounds exactly like my father. I wonder how they're going to get along.*

Desiree's reply was firm. "His name is Tyler, and you had better get used to saying it, Dominique, because if you want to see me, you're going to have to see him."

"Have you completely lost your mind? You, marrying a white man! That's crazy! It's hard enough to get along with your own kind!" Dominique exclaimed. With these words she shot a dark look in Benjamin's direction.

Benjamin quietly admonished his wife. "Dominique, what Desiree does with her life is her own business, and we have no right to interfere."

Dominique turned around to face him, "That's easy for you to say. She's not your sister. I bet if she was you would sing a different tune." Dominique placed her hands on her hips. "And I have a bone to pick with you anyway. Mildred said that you already knew about this. Why didn't you tell me?" Dominique demanded. She looked ready to do battle.

"Because it wasn't my business to tell. It's Desiree's. And I must say that I don't care for your attitude or tone, Dominique. You know that I love Desiree as if she were my own sister, and I feel that she has the right to live her own life as you do. Frankly I wouldn't give a rat's ass about the color of the man's skin if my sister had a glow on her face like the one Desiree has when she looks at this man." Benjamin slowly articulated his words before he strode out of the room, his back rigid with anger.

Sasha was quite amused to see Dominique and Benjamin argue. That in itself was a rarity, and she smirked from behind the hand she had in front of her mouth.

Dominique turned back to Desiree once Benjamin had left the room. She changed the tone of her voice as she tried to reason with Desiree. "Look, I know it's hard to be single out there, but you don't have to settle for . . ." Dominique hesitated before casting a quick look at Tyler. "You don't have to settle for him. Just be patient, the right man for you is out there."

"I've already met the right man, and it's Tyler," Desiree retorted firmly.

"I never thought I'd see the day when I wished Travis was a part of your life." Dominique's words were hard.

"Dominique, in order for you to come to terms with this, this is what you need to do. Think of the kind of man you want for me, think of how you would want that man to treat me, then close your eyes and picture how you would like that man to look. And then make his skin white. The man that you are envisioning is Tyler Banks."

"That is ridiculous," Dominique scoffed, "and impossible for me to do. All I can say is that Travis hurt you a lot more than you let on."

Desiree's tone was calm, but her words frosty. "The only thing Travis did was show me the difference between real love and the illusion of love. What I felt for him was shallow, and it would have never withstood the test of time."

"How could you do this to our family?" Dominique wailed. "Think of how embarrassed Mom and Dad will be. We have overlooked Marcus Junior's involvement with his white woman because we know that things are different when you're in another country fighting a war. War makes strange bedfellows. People behave differently. Life is different. You don't know how long you have on earth, so many people live as if there is no tomorrow. But this, there is no excuse for this relationship."

Now Desiree's tone changed from frosty to acidic. "I don't need an excuse. I love Tyler and he loves me, and I don't need your approval, Dominique. You're not the boss of me. This is my life, and I will live it the way I want to." She looked at Tyler and her voice softened. "He makes me happy."

Dominique turned to her brother and wailed, "Marcus Junior, say something. You can't possibly agree with this. You have already been burned by an interracial relationship. You have a child you haven't seen in years."

Marcus Junior flinched at her words. "I don't need you to remind me of that. I think about Ahmad every day. For years I tried unsuccessfully to locate him."

Surprise was mirrored in everyone's eyes at this revelation. Raw emotion showed on Marcus Junior's face as he spoke. "Maybe things would have worked out between me and Alexandria if I hadn't been shipped to another base. Her father retired from the military soon after the birth of my son. I haven't been able to find them, and Alexandria hasn't tried to find me. Maybe I should have married her when she got pregnant, but I thought she was too young because she was still in college. If I had, then maybe I could be a part of my son's life. I just don't know. Things were hard with her father being a white colonel and all. There's still a great divide in the military, and Alexandria's father was very disapproving of our relationship. I should have fought to the death for my father's rights, but I just gave up at the time. It just seemed easier to let go. All that I do know is that I have tried to come to terms with the loss of my son." He shook his head sadly from side to side. "I am not completely blameless for the loss of that relationship."

The air in the room hung heavy around them as they listened to Marcus Junior's passionate words. He had never confided in them that he had searched for his son and had failed. He had kept his pain and suffering hidden from them all.

As an obvious attempt to lighten the atmosphere, Sasha piped in, "I just have one thing to say."

"What is it, Sasha?" Desiree asked, wary of what Sasha's next words might be.

For a minute Sasha said nothing, but then she deliberately focused her eyes on Tyler's feet. "Obviously," she paused, in order to give her words the full effect, "it's not always true what they say about white men." Then she burst out laughing.

Tyler's expression never changed, he just gave a wry smile as he looked at Desiree.

"Sasha, you are disgusting. Have you no class?" Dominique shrilled.

Enraged, Sasha's voice was as shrill as Dominique's when she shouted, "Look who's talking about class. You've done nothing but make a scene since Desiree walked in here with her mystery lover. Your own husband even walked out on you from embarrassment."

Nadine Diamond walked into the room in time to hear the last of Sasha's words.

"What's the matter with all of you? Squabbling at a time like this. Your father and I can hear you clear down the hall." Mrs. Diamond was so intent on quieting her children she didn't notice Tyler or that he was holding Desiree's hand. Then suddenly she did.

"Mom," Desiree slowly enunciated her words, "this is Tyler Banks, my fiancé." Desiree held out her hand with her engagement ring.

Mrs. Diamond automatically took a step back and placed her hand on her heart.

"You're giving her a heart attack." Dominique rushed towards her mother, protectively putting her arm around her shoulder.

Nadine Diamond brushed Dominique's concern aside. "Don't be silly. It would take more than something like this to kill me." Sudden intuition dawned on Nadine Diamond. Turning towards Tyler she asked, "Are you the man who called the house for Desiree Christmas morning?"

Sasha chimed in before Tyler could answer. "Well, if he isn't, you just told Tyler that Desiree is cheating on him."

Tyler smiled at Sasha. He liked her bubbly personality. "Yes, ma'am," he responded quietly.

"And you're the man that bought her those earrings?" Her mother searched his eyes as if trying to see into his soul.

"Yes, ma'am. I am guilty of that also."

Desiree noticed with pride how all of the women's attention, even Dominique's, was arrested by the sensual quality of Tyler's voice.

He had been silent throughout the Diamond clan's bickering as they had thrashed out their opinions about his and Desiree's engagement, but now he felt it was his time to speak. "Mrs. Diamond, I love Desiree with all of my heart and I want to marry her. I would have come and met you sooner, but we needed to make sure we knew what we wanted before we involved other people. When your husband is stronger, I would like to formally ask him for Desiree's hand in marriage. I hope that you will accept this marriage, because I know how important her family is to her."

"And what if I don't give my approval?" Nadine Diamond studied Tyler quizzically. "What would you do then, Mr. Tyler Banks?"

Tyler's reply was unhesitating. "I will marry her anyhow." His eyes surveyed the people in the room. "I love my mother with the same zealousness that Desiree loves all of you. I understand the bond that mothers and children have for each other, and I don't want to come between that. But make no mistake," and with these words his eyes were unwavering as they locked with Dominique's, "Desiree and I will be married."

Nadine Diamond sized Tyler up with the same capabilities that she had used over the years on the first day of school to assess her new students. She liked what she saw. "So be it. At least you're not wishy-washy. I can't stand that in a man."

At this, Dominique dropped her hand to her sides. "Am I the only person in this family with any sense?"

She turned on her heel, and as she stormed out of the room Sasha hurled after her, "Well, if you have any sense, I'm glad I'm crazy."

Sasha looked at Desiree and Tyler. They had eyes only for each other and now spoke in whispers that no one else could hear.

Jokingly, Sasha looked at her sister and quipped, "I told you that a black man didn't buy you those earrings."

Desiree's only response to her sister's teasing was to look over at Marcus Junior. Simultaneously they shook their heads.

Desiree was the last person to visit her father. When it was her turn to see him, she went solo. She remembered Dr. Khan's warning that he was to have no undue excitement.

Benjamin was sitting in a chair by her father's side when she walked in, and he stood at once. He wrapped his arms around her, gave her a brief hug, and whispered softly in her ear so that her father couldn't hear. "I'm in your corner, honey." Then he left them alone.

Marcus Diamond lay against the impersonal white bed sheets of the hospital bed. His eyes were closed, and she bent over and kissed him softly on one cheek, being careful not to jar the bed so he that he wouldn't feel any discomfort. Immediately his eyes opened. Her smile was tremulous, and she watched him closely. "You gave us quite a scare. If it's at all possible, promise not to ever pull something like this again." Her father began to chuckle, and a look of pain swept over his face when his bandaged ribs protested against the movement.

"I'll do my best. What was all the commotion about earlier? I asked Benjamin, but you know how close-mouthed he can be."

Her father struggled to talk, and Desiree had to lean forward to catch his words.

"It's nothing for you to worry your head about," she responded soothingly. "All you need to do is rest try to get better."

"Don't treat me as if I'm a baby. There's nothing wrong with my faculties. I can't very well rest if I know that you kids are fighting about something. Is it about me?"

Desiree hurriedly reassured her father. "No, Dad, it's not about you."

"Then what is it?" Marcus Diamond watched his daughter's face.

"Daddy, the doctor doesn't want you to get excited, and I think that the best thing for you to do is rest. We'll talk later."

"Go and get your mother," he ordered. "She'll tell me what's going on."

Desiree had never known her mother to lie. Accordingly, she decided to give him some of the information rather than let him become agitated. "Dominique and Sasha got into an argument because Sasha was defending me about something," Desiree responded slowly.

"What was she defending you about?" His tone was persistent.

Desiree dropped her eyes from her father's careful study.

"Don't you know that you can tell me anything? It won't stop me from loving you."

Desiree continued to be silent, and now when her father spoke his voice had a warning inflection in it. "Desiree?"

Desiree spoke hesitatingly. "Dominique's disappointed in me."

"What is she disappointed about this time?" Her father ended his sentence with a frown.

Desiree hung her head and mumbled her words. "I don't think that this is the right time for this conversation. I would rather wait until you're feeling better."

Marcus Diamond tried to joke. "You must think that you have done something so terrible that the news might impede my recovery."

Desiree dropped her eyes. "I don't want to disappoint you."

Her father chided her gently after he heard her words. "Honey, during your whole life you have never disappointed me. What makes you think that you could do so now?"

Desiree hung her head and drew a deep breath. "I'm in love with a man, and I want to marry him. And he wants to marry me." Desiree avoided her father's perceptive eyes.

There was a long silence in the room and then her father asked, "Is it the white man you've been seeing?"

Desiree's jaw dropped in surprise. "How did you know? Oh, I guess Marcus Junior told you."

"Actually no, he didn't. He didn't say anything about it." Marcus Diamond waited a moment and then said, "Travis told me."

"Travis?" Surprise was evident in her face and voice.

"Yes, I saw him in the mall Christmas Eve buying presents for his mother and sister, and he told me that you were dating a white man. He said that he thought that I knew."

"You knew all through the holidays, and you never even said a word." Desiree was totally amazed that her father had kept quiet.

"That piece of news took some getting used to. I had to pray on it. I must admit I was stunned by the revelation. Then later, I was upset that you felt you couldn't come to your mother and me. I thought that we had raised all of our children to think that you could tell us anything, and for you to keep such an important part of your life hidden from us it was as if you were living a double life. I decided to wait you out, let your conscience be your guide. I knew that eventually you would either have to come clean and let us know what was going on with you, or you would have to leave him. You couldn't hide something like that forever."

"What was Travis's reason for telling you?" Desiree was curious.

"He asked me to talk to you when you came home for Christmas about agreeing to meet with him to talk things over. I decided when I saw how happy you were over the holidays to leave well enough alone, that I would let you know what Travis said when and if you decided to confide in me."

Father and daughter sat in the room, each of them quiet with thought.

"So I gather Dominique just found out?" Marcus Diamond looked amused, finally understanding what must have gone on earlier in the hospital waiting room.

"Yes," she grimaced. "Tyler got the wrong information and thought that I was the person in the accident, not you."

Her father inquisitively looked at her. "Does that mean that he's here?"

"Yes, he's in the lounge with the others. I had no intention of breaking this news until you were fully recovered because I didn't want to upset you." She glanced at her watch. "I should leave because I've overstayed my time, and the doctor was quite adamant about not getting you excited."

Her father's eyes focused on some obscure spot on the ceiling. "Desiree, while I was trapped under all of that pile of rubble, I thought about how I might never see my family again. I love all of you to death, but what I feared most was your mother being without me. I know that she's perfectly capable of taking care of herself financially if I'm no longer around, but the companionship and the love we share are so special. Even children cannot replace the love between a man and a woman." He gave her a long look. "Is this man good to you?"

"Always. That's why I fell in love with him." Her reply was soft.

"And does he want to do right by you?" Her father watched her face. He knew she was unaware of how her expression glowed when she thought of her man.

"Yes, he's asked me to marry him, and I have accepted." Desiree showed the ring she had concealed with one hand since entering her father's hospital room. The diamond seemed to wink at them.

"What is his religious background?" Marcus Diamond demanded, and suddenly his voice sounded loud for the first time since Desiree had entered the room.

Desiree grinned. "He's a Baptist; his father is a southern preacher."

"Thank God he has religion. Send him in alone. I want to talk to him."

Desiree hesitated and looked at her father's face. Seeing the resolution etched on his features, she went to do his bidding.

Thirty minutes later Desiree was still leaning against the wall outside her father's hospital room. She glanced anxiously at her watch for the umpteenth time. *Tyler's been in there a long time. Daddy must be giving him a thorough cross-examination.* She felt sorry for Tyler because he was probably trying to shoulder the blame for their secret relationship, but she knew that he could handle himself.

Just at that moment Tyler emerged from her father's hospital room. His hair was rumpled as if he had been running his hands through it, his shirt was out over the top, and his eyes glittered in a way she had never seen before. Seeing this, Desiree rushed to him and threw her arms around him, hugging him protectively. Her words were muffled as she buried her head in his chest. "Darling, are you okay? You were in there such a long time. I started to come inside to see what was going on, but I was afraid I would only make things worse."

Tyler expelled a long breath. "Whew! It's a good thing you didn't. That was some inquisition. Your dad can be a real bear. That's something I never want to go through again. I'm beginning to think that maybe you're not worth all this drama."

"What!" Desiree withdrew from Tyler's arms. She stood in front of him and placed her hands upon her hips. "Tyler Banks, are you trying to say after all we've been through that you're having second thoughts about marrying me?" she sputtered. Although Desiree didn't know it, she looked exactly like Dominique did at the start of one of her rampages. Desiree pointed her index finger at Tyler and said in an authoritative tone, "You're going to marry me." She then closed the space between them, and tapped him in the chest with her finger, accenting each word she spoke: "As soon as possible."

Tyler shrugged his shoulders and began to straighten his clothes. "Okay," he replied mildly.

Desiree eyed him searchingly, and then, seeing the teasing glint in his eyes, she knew that he had been playing with her.

"Honey, I'm only joking with you. Now that I've gotten your father's approval nothing in the world can keep me from marrying you."

On hearing these words Desiree clapped her hands excitedly, threw her arms around Tyler's neck and planted a loud smack on his mouth.

Tyler lifted her body to eye level with his. Respect and sincerity were etched in his eyes and words. "Your father is quite a man. I hope that the son we have one day will have the qualities your father just showed me in there."

Desiree took her hands and slowly ran them through Tyler's hair, smoothing it. He let her body slowly slide down the length of his and, when her feet touched the floor, he bent his head and gave her a long lingering kiss.

Oblivious to the outside world, they did not see Nadine Diamond emerge from the shadows of the hospital corridor from where she had watched them as Tyler laid his head on top of Desiree's and held her close; nor did they hear her expel a sigh of relief before she gave a satisfied nod at the couple and quietly tiptoed away to join the rest of her family in the hospital waiting room.

EPILOGUE

Six months later, Desiree walked down the aisle on her father's arm, radiant in her long white wedding gown. She and Tyler had decided to have the marriage ceremony at the church she had attended from the time she was in grammar school until she left for college. Throughout the years, she had continued to visit there when she was in town for the holidays. Church members, long lost relatives, and friends Desiree and Tyler had made over the years filled the small church to the brim.

The Diamond women were dressed in various shades of light blue and sat in the front pew. Nadine Diamond sat next to her baby sister, Andrea, who had flown in with her family from Maryland. Desiree's mother dabbed slightly at the corners of her eyes as she watched her daughter make her journey. Sasha grinned and gave Desiree a wink.

During Desiree's engagement, there had been a marked change in Dominique's attitude about Tyler. She had not openly stated her approval, because that wasn't her way, but she had purposefully sought out Tyler's opinion as she had helped Desiree make decisions about the wedding. Now Dominique's eyes shone with happiness for her sister.

As she held onto her father's arm, Desiree thought about the kind of man her father was and felt proud. She didn't know the exact details of the conversation between her father and Tyler in the hospital, but she knew that after they had talked her father forgave her for hiding their relationship from him and understood that they had the strength for a marriage that some people would view as crossing over to the other side.

Desiree's eyes met Marcus Junior's. She sent up a petition to God on her brother's behalf, a plea that he would one day find a love as deep as the one she had for Tyler. He looked exceedingly handsome in his black suit as he sat in the pew next to Benjamin.

Desiree continued to scan the pews. Martin sat in the second pew with Iman cradled in his arms. Then Desiree's eyes met those of her future father-in-law as he sat with his wife, and she felt a surge of satisfaction at the smiling nod he gave her.

Tyler's parents had been in town for a week, and his mother had impressed Desiree by her obvious love for her son. She knew from talking with her that she was a wonderful woman who only wanted happiness for him. Since the behavior of Tyler's father had been above approach and Desiree knew that Tyler and his father had settled their differences.

Natalie, the beautiful matron of honor, looked too young and beautiful to be the mother of two small children. As she turned at the altar and waited for Desiree to reach them, her smile was broad. She had been impressed with Tyler from their very first meeting and had been thrilled when Desiree asked her to be matron of honor. Her acceptance solved the problem of having to choose between Dominique and Sasha as an attendant. Tyler had asked Chad to be his best man, and Desiree couldn't help but notice that Chad had a slightly bored look on his face as he stood next to his father. However, she wasn't concerned because she knew that she was going to do everything she possibly could to be a stepmother that Tyler's children not only liked, but also respected.

Earlier, Nichelle and Tiffany had trotted down the aisle side by side, throwing flowers, and Nicholas and Michael had looked adorable as co-ring bearers.

Momentarily, her attention was caught by Abdul's expression as he sat directly behind Sasha. He didn't attempt to hide the disapproval in his eyes at Desiree's choice of mate. Pushing these thoughts aside, Desiree knew that she was willing to face disapproval from any and everybody to live her life with Tyler.

Jillian, Marlon, and the baby were there, along with Arthur Buchanan and his wife. Ralph Benson had come solo, but he seemed quite comfortable as he sat next to her college suitemate Sophie, who had flown in from Greensboro for the wedding. Desiree had quit working at Buchanan & Buchanan a month earlier because she needed time to set up housekeeping at the penthouse in New York. She and Tyler had decided to move there because in the fall she was to begin taking classes at NYU as a full time law student. Tyler was going to commute by train from New York to Danbury until he found a law firm closer to home.

As Desiree stood next to Tyler, who was resplendent in a black tux with tails, her love for him consumed her as his words resonated clearly throughout the church. As he promised to love, honor, and cherish her, she felt blessed to have found such a special man to share her life with. She knew with conviction that whatever lay ahead of them, they could weather it together.

The reception in the ballroom of the Peabody Hotel was a joyous affair. Guests enjoyed a lavish buffet and danced to the music of a live band that played everything from disco to rhythm and blues to easy listening. When Desiree and Tyler left the reception to go upstairs, the majority of their guests were enjoying themselves doing the electric slide. Even Desiree's father, who was not known to dance, participated. Tyler had reserved the honeymoon suite for them to change for their flight to the Bahamas for their two-week-honeymoon.

Tyler was dressed and sitting on the sofa waiting when Desiree emerged from the bedroom dressed in a pale yellow suit. As his wife walked towards him, he felt almost overwhelmed with love and emotion. He silently thanked God for the blessing He had bestowed on him. Standing, he held out his hand. At once, Desiree placed her hand in his and gazed up at him. Her love for him shone in the liquid pools of her eyes. "Are you ready to begin our life together, Mrs. Banks?"

"More than ready, Mr. Banks." They walked hand in hand out the door to begin their life as husband and wife.

ABOUT THE AUTHOR

Michele Cameron was born in Bridgeport, Connecticut. She attended and graduated from high school in Danbury, Connecticut.

Ms. Cameron is a graduate of North Carolina A&T State University in Greensboro with a B.S. degree in English education and has been an English teacher in central Florida for more than sixteen years. This is her first novel.

Coming from Genesis Press in February 2007:
Dawn's Harbor by Kymberly Hunt

CHAPTER ONE

A year later

The trash had been emptied, the furniture dusted and the bathrooms thoroughly cleaned. Jasmine gave an obligatory glance around the echoing corridors of the hospice to make sure she wasn't being observed and then slipped quietly into the stark bareness of room 23. No flowers decorated the bedside table, no cards from family members. There was no visible evidence that anyone cared about the person who occupied the room. She pulled up the orange visitor's chair that would have collected dust had it not been for her nightly visits.

"Well, Noah, here I am again," she said, and laughed ironically that she was on a first name basis with him. "What's going on with you tonight? Nothing, you say? I guess it's no surprise. It doesn't matter to people like us because we're both just breathing and little else." She rubbed her eyes wearily. "Actually I'm getting really tired of this . . . I mean it's worse for me. I still have to get up every day, work, pay bills, and pretend to live, but you,

you can just stay asleep until your heart stops beating. There isn't much pain in that, is there?"

She sighed deeply, flicked back a stray braid, and studied the Caucasian man who lay stretched out on the steel-framed bed before her. He wore a faded blue hospital-issue gown that stripped him of any dignity he might have had in his conscious life. Mercifully, the lower half of his body was concealed by blankets, which hid limbs emaciated by disuse, as well as the intravenous tubing and other necessary apparatus.

He was young, compared to the rest of the residents of the hospice/nursing home who were slowly, painfully, whiling away their final hours. Even in his sallow-skinned comatose state, he was a handsome man with finely chiseled features, raven-black hair and darkly arched eyebrows. She focused on the shadows beneath his closed eyes and the long eyelashes fanning them.

On the first day she had started working at the hospice, she'd learned from a chatty nurse's assistant that the man's name was Noah Arias and he had been in a car accident, which had left him in his present state. Initially he'd been on life support for a month, but after the doctors declared the coma to be irreversible, his family had requested the respirator be shut down. Surprisingly, he'd continued to breathe on his own, and apparently not knowing what else to do, the family had condemned him to Glendale Hospice, where he had been for the last two years. Alive but dead.

Jasmine squeezed her eyes shut and continued to talk. "Do you remember what I told you last night about the little girl in the apartment next door? Well, it's true she really does like me. Imagine that. I don't want to encourage it for obvious reasons, but she's an unusual kid. She likes to play with her dolls in the hallway just outside my door. She used to run away when I opened it, but yesterday she just stayed there."

Tears welled up in her eyes and she allowed them to fall. It amazed her that she could cry so much when she was alone with him, yet at the most tragic and poignant moments in her adult life she rarely shed tears. Maybe it was because talking to Noah was only one step up from talking to herself. He never gave the slightest indication of hearing anything and he certainly didn't see her, which was probably a good thing because her appearance—no makeup and unkempt braids emanating from her scalp like writhing snakes—would probably repel anyone.

She had been indulging in the one-sided conversations for nearly six months, long after having stopped the recommended therapy sessions, which had done little to ease the crushing guilt over her niece's death, guilt that was still devastating her own life.

"I don't know how she could come from that family," Jasmine rambled on. "She doesn't look or act anything like those other wild brats. And the mother . . . well, I've only seen her a few times but I'll bet she's an alcoholic or drug addict or something."

Her attention drifted toward the window. The drawn shades were lightening, telling her that in a short time a new day would dawn. She remembered the pleasure of watching the sun ascend over the Hudson River during early morning jogs through the nearby park when she used to live in the suburbs. She recalled the laughs she used to share with her childhood friend Valerie as they ran, talking about work and the impossible men in their lives.

Valerie wouldn't even recognize this Jasmine, who lived in self-imposed exile on the twelfth floor of a run-down Brooklyn housing project and paid for her meager existence with her earnings as a cleaning lady. During the day she spent most of her time escaping into the benign world of sleep, shutting out all the obnoxious sounds of the city and its people.

The truth was, since her termination from her position as a partner at Spherion Architecture, she didn't recognize herself anymore. Initially she had been crushed by the unfairness of the dismissal. The senior partners had been sympathetic to her grief at first, but they simply had not given her enough time to pull herself together. Now she realized that they probably had had no choice except to let her go because she had started over-medicating on prescription drugs for depression, which left her in a useless haze. To add to that, she had become so traumatized by flashbacks that she could no longer drive and had sold her SUV, forcing herself to rely on public transportation, which always made her late for crucial client meetings— when she remembered them at all. Even when she was present, her mind had been elsewhere.

Jasmine glanced down at her watch and back at Noah's emotionless face. "I guess I've bored you enough for the night," she said, starting to stand. "It's time for me to leave."

"Don't go."

Jasmine froze between sitting and standing. She dropped heavily back into the chair and stared at the man. "Did . . . did you say something?"

There was only the usual silence, punctuated by his breathing and her own heartbeat pounding in her ears.

Jasmine laughed and held her hand over her forehead. "Oh God, this is it. I really am insane."

"No, you're not."

The voice was raspy and barely audible, but his eyes were open and they seemed unnaturally illuminated in a mysterious shade of gray. The electric eyes were focused exclusively on her. Jasmine jumped up, nearly knocking the chair to the floor.

"I'm not imagining this. You really are speaking!"

"Yes."

"Oh, my . . . this is . . . this is weird. Please stay awake. I'm going to get the nur—"

"No!" he interrupted in a loud and commanding tone, which caused her to stop in her tracks. Instantly his voice dropped five decibels back to the hoarse whisper. "Please don't."

"But . . . but why?" she stammered, feeling light-headed. "You've been unconscious for a very long time. People have to know."

"Don't want to talk to anyone. Just you. Could you . . ." He struggled for the right word. "Sit. Please . . . didn't mean . . . to scare you."

"I'm not scared," Jasmine said. "I'm just shocked."

She sank back into the chair, resisting the urge to flee, because she still had the feeling she was imagining the whole bizarre scene. It was a good thing she wasn't the fainting type or she would have passed out by now.

"The little girl . . ." he said.

"Little girl?" Jasmine repeated, staring at him with dazed eyes.

"Yes. The little girl you talk about."

She swallowed hard. A man who had been in a coma for over two years was miraculously out of it and only interested in talking about some little girl who really had nothing to do with either of them.

"You *remember* what I was talking about?"

"You talk . . . a lot."

Considering the circumstances, she knew she wasn't completely justified to feel annoyed, but nevertheless the comment irked her. She tried to control her inner impulses.

"How long have you been awake?"

"Don't know." He took a deep breath before he spoke again. "I've heard . . . your voice . . . for a very long time. Do I know you?"

"Actually you don't know me at all. I'm just the cleaning woman. I do your room every night."

"You called me Noah."

She shifted uncomfortably in the chair. "Well, that's your name, isn't it? It's on your wrist tag."

His eyes shifted downward to study the plastic tag.

"You don't remember your name?" she asked.

"I remember." He took another deep breath. "What happened? Where am I?"

"I've been told that you were in a car accident, and this is Glendale Hospice in Manhattan. You've been in a coma for just about two years." She stood up again and started backing away. "I really have to go get the nurse. I'm no expert on things like this and someone else will be a lot better at answering your questions. They'll be able to call your family and . . ."

Her voice trailed off as she noticed his eyes were fixed in a glassy unfocused gaze toward the ceiling. She rushed back to his side.

"No! Please . . . please don't go back to sleep."

She gripped his shoulder and shook him desperately. There was no response. He seemed to have drifted back off into unconsciousness. Fighting against the familiar wave of despair, Jasmine tried to think. If she went and told the nurses now, what good would it do? Who would believe her? The nursing staff in general treated her as if she were invisible unless something needed cleaning.

It occurred to her that maybe if she stayed a little longer and continued to talk he would return. It was a long shot, but definitely worth a try.

She sat back in the chair. "I think the little girl's name is Morgan, at least that's what I heard the other kids call her. She's very pretty. She has long, curly black hair and the biggest brown eyes you've ever seen. She looks . . . she looks kind of the way I would imagine Dawn would look if she'd lived to be six or seven."

"Eerie," he said.

Jasmine's heart pounded with relief and exhilaration upon hearing his response, but she didn't trust it to last.

As much as she wanted to change the subject, she continued out of fear of losing him.

"It is eerie, and I'm not sure I like it," she said.

His eyes shimmered. "Signs . . . read the signs . . . may be a reason why this is happening . . . Divine inter . . . inter—"

"Divine intervention?" she interrupted his stammering. "I don't see anything divine about it. I think it's cruel. Dawn is gone and now I have to see her in some stranger's child."

Noah attempted a smile. "Maybe it's a sign that Dawn forgives you . . . wants you to move on."

"That's ridiculous."

"Is it?" His voice became stronger and clearer. "What happened to your daughter . . . a tragedy, but it was an accident. You can't bring her back . . . have to forgive yourself and go on. No point being alive if you don't."

"She wasn't my daughter. She was my niece," Jasmine replied sharply. "And if you're going to remember every detail of my whining sessions at least get the facts straight."

He chuckled. "No need to get hostile."

"I'm not hostile. I just don't enjoy talking about this and I can't imagine why you do. It's crazy for me to go on and on about myself when you obviously have your own health issues that need to be dealt with."

A silence fell over the room as Jasmine became even more aware of the intensity of his strange, mesmerizing stare. His eyes were like smoky cut glass with dazzling beams of sunlight piercing through, both unsettling and alluring at the same time.

"You're right," Noah said slowly. "Don't remember much."

Jasmine evaded his gaze and stared at the window. The shadowy residue of night had faded from the curtains. Daylight was rapidly approaching and she knew she had to leave before someone came in and questioned her awkward presence in the room. Yet she hesitated, trapped between her own desire to just walk out and never look back, and the urge to tell the nurse for his own good, whether he wanted her to or not. He didn't seem capable of preventing the latter, since he had made no attempt to sit up or even change positions.

"Need your help," Noah said.

"I hope you're going to ask me to get the nurse before I leave."

"No. Not that." His voice was barely a whisper now. "Please, just listen. Need you to call somebody for me. I remember his number . . ."

How could he remember something as specific as a telephone number and little else, she wondered, but she picked up a pen and a notepad from the nightstand, realizing for the first time that there was no telephone in the room. She almost laughed. Of course there wasn't a phone, a person in a coma would have no need for one. He gave her a number and she wrote it down.

"Know this sounds crazy," Noah whispered urgently, "but I'm . . . in danger. Call Aaron. Please. Tell him I have to see him . . . soon."

He's delirious, Jasmine thought. "Is that it? You don't want me to say anything else?"

"No."

She sighed. "Whatever you want. Goodbye, Noah, and good luck." She moved quickly to the door, still feeling the smoldering heat from his eyes.

"Jasmine," he said.

She paused without looking back.

"The kid next door . . . be friendly. Dawn might like it."

By the time Jasmine had made the tedious journey on the foul-smelling elevator to the twelfth floor and her Brooklyn apartment, she realized that the number he had given her wasn't even a local one and the charge was going to be her responsibility. She dialed anyway, half expecting it would be incorrect or that no one would even answer. It rang. She waited.

"Hello," a voice responded. It was masculine with a touch of a foreign accent she couldn't quite place.

"Am I speaking to Aaron?"

"Yes."

"My name is . . ." She hesitated. *What difference does it make what my name is?*

"Your name is . . .?" he repeated.

Irritated, she ignored the question. "I have a message from Noah. He wants you to come see him as soon as possible."

There was a slight pause. "Message received. Thank you," he said.

She heard the phone click on the other end. That was it. No questions asked . . . nothing. She shook her head and put the receiver down. What was all the mystery about? Who was Aaron anyway? Were the two involved in a same sex relationship? The thought disturbed her more than it should have. But it couldn't possibly be true, because even though Noah had seen her in a most unattractive light, there was something about the way he looked at her that conveyed with no uncertainty that he was a man who had, and always would, appreciate women.

Is any of this supposed to matter? Jasmine thought. *As soon as he reconnects with his past, he won't even remember me. Why should he?*

She glared at the clock. It was almost seven A.M. and normally she would have been showered and peacefully tucked into the cocoon of her bed. She had just started her preparations when a familiar sound made her stop. She heard the apartment door next to hers open, followed by a deafening blast of hip-hop music. The door slammed shut again, muffling the music, but it was still loud. A few minutes later she heard someone brushing against her door, then the familiar child's voice talking to her family of dolls as if she really expected them to answer back.

School was out for the summer; it was way too early for children to be up and out of the house. She had a good mind to walk next door and tell the mother that she should be taking better care of her daughter. It was something she definitely would have done in the distant past, but instead Jasmine leaned against the door listening.

"I want to stay with you, Daddy." The child's tone of voice was high-pitched, pleading. Then it quickly deepened into a mock imitation of a man's voice. "I'm sorry, princess, but you just can't go with me. There's no place for little girls up here."

Jasmine quietly slid the bolt and chain mechanism down, unlocking the door and opening it slightly. The child looked wide-eyed up at her from her cross-legged position on the floor. Her hair was in a messy ponytail and she wore a wrinkled green T-shirt that was much too big, and grimy, untied sneakers. She held a doll in each hand. One of them was a tiny naked girl and the other, a shabby-looking Ken.

"Hello," Jasmine said.

The girl studied her anxiously. "I'm not being bad."

"Of course you're not, but wouldn't it be more fun if you played in your room instead of in the hall?"

"But I don't have a room."

"Well, I'm sure your mother would like it better if you at least played inside your own apartment."

"She yells at me when I'm there. And there's too many of them."

"Too many of who?" Jasmine asked.

"Too many kids."

The answer amused Jasmine a little, even though the child didn't realize it.

"You mean you have too many brothers and sisters?"

The big dark eyes lowered as she avoided eye contact. "They're not my brothers and sisters. They're just kids.

328

The social lady said I have to stay with them because my daddy's dead and Grandma's sick."

Jasmine sighed. Another foster child case. She knew all too well what that was like. She didn't want to remember her own early years spent being shuttled back and forth from one foster family to another, and finally being placed in a state-run facility for orphans. The memory was too painful, so she didn't pursue it.

"What's your name?"

"Morgan."

"Princess Morgan, that's very pretty. I like it."

Morgan's face brightened. "My daddy named me. He called me a princess, too."

"Your daddy was right. You are a princess."

"I like you," Morgan said. Then she added anxiously, "You're not really a crazy lady, are you?"

Jasmine's eyebrows rose. "A crazy lady? What makes you think that?"

"Oh . . . I know you're not. It's Tasha and Bobby. They said that you're crazy and ugly 'cause your hair looks funny and you don't talk to people and stuff."

Jasmine flinched. So she had never been invisible to the so-called neighbors after all. She took a deep breath and swallowed her pride. She was, after all, talking to a child and children were usually tactless but sincere. "Who are Tasha and Bobby?"

"The kids," Morgan replied. "They're really mean and I hate them. Tasha looks like a gorilla and she's got bumps all over her face and ugly hair, and Bobby's lots bigger than me, but he wets the bed like a baby."

"I know how you feel, Morgan, but you shouldn't hate them. Tasha and Bobby don't know any better. They don't realize it's not right to say nasty things about people they don't even know. I'm glad you're so much smarter."

Morgan beamed. "When I lived with Grandma I was in second grade already . . . and I'm only six. But when I came here, I had to go to first with the babies again 'cause nobody thinks I'm smart."

Jasmine was seeing too much of her past in the child—a past she so desperately wanted to forget. Though part of her wanted to invite Morgan in and continue the conversation, she knew she was not ready. The logical choice was to retreat.

"It doesn't matter if other people don't think you're smart, as long as you know it yourself. Well, I have things to do. Goodbye, Morgan. Have fun playing with your dolls."

She struggled to ignore the child's disappointed look because it made her feel cold and heartless; still, it was not her problem. She was only one person and she couldn't be expected to bleed over and over again for the millions of children around the world who felt unloved and insecure.

"Bye," Morgan said.

Jasmine took a deep breath behind the closed door. However, it did not block out the mechanical sounds of Morgan's chatter, which had resumed as though never interrupted.

"I know there's not s'posed to be little girls up there, Daddy, but couldn't you just ask God for me? Maybe He might change His mind."

2008 Reprint Mass Market Titles
January

Cautious Heart
Cheris F. Hodges
ISBN-13: 978-1-58571-301-1
ISBN-10: 1-58571-301-5
$6.99

Suddenly You
Crystal Hubbard
ISBN-13: 978-1-58571-302-8
ISBN-10: 1-58571-302-3
$6.99

February

Passion
T. T. Henderson
ISBN-13: 978-1-58571-303-5
ISBN-10: 1-58571-303-1
$6.99

Whispers in the Sand
LaFlorya Gauthier
ISBN-13: 978-1-58571-304-2
ISBN-10: 1-58571-304-x
$6.99

March

Life Is Never As It Seems
J. J. Michael
ISBN-13: 978-1-58571-305-9
ISBN-10: 1-58571-305-8
$6.99

Beyond the Rapture
Beverly Clark
ISBN-13: 978-1-58571-306-6
ISBN-10: 1-58571-306-6
$6.99

April

A Heart's Awakening
Veronica Parker
ISBN-13: 978-1-58571-307-3
ISBN-10: 1-58571-307-4
$6.99

Breeze
Robin Lynette Hampton
ISBN-13: 978-1-58571-308-0
ISBN-10: 1-58571-308-2
$6.99

May

I'll Be Your Shelter
Giselle Carmichael
ISBN-13: 978-1-58571-309-7
ISBN-10: 1-58571-309-0
$6.99

Careless Whispers
Rochelle Alers
ISBN-13: 978-1-58571-310-3
ISBN-10: 1-58571-310-4
$6.99

June

Sin
Crystal Rhodes
ISBN-13: 978-1-58571-311-0
ISBN-10: 1-58571-311-2
$6.99

Dark Storm Rising
Chinelu Moore
ISBN-13: 978-1-58571-312-7
ISBN-10: 1-58571-312-0
$6.99

2008 Reprint Mass Market Titles (continued)

July

Object of His Desire
A.C. Arthur
ISBN-13: 978-1-58571-313-4
ISBN-10: 1-58571-313-9
$6.99

Angel's Paradise
Janice Angelique
ISBN-13: 978-1-58571-314-1
ISBN-10: 1-58571-314-7
$6.99

August

Unbreak My Heart
Dar Tomlinson
ISBN-13: 978-1-58571-315-8
ISBN-10: 1-58571-315-5
$6.99

All I Ask
Barbara Keaton
ISBN-13: 978-1-58571-316-5
ISBN-10: 1-58571-316-3
$6.99

September

Icie
Pamela Leigh Starr
ISBN-13: 978-1-58571-275-5
ISBN-10: 1-58571-275-2
$6.99

At Last
Lisa Riley
ISBN-13: 978-1-58571-276-2
ISBN-10: 1-58571-276-0
$6.99

October

Everlastin' Love
Gay G. Gunn
ISBN-13: 978-1-58571-277-9
ISBN-10: 1-58571-277-9
$6.99

Three Wishes
Seressia Glass
ISBN-13: 978-1-58571-278-6
ISBN-10: 1-58571-278-7
$6.99

November

Yesterday Is Gone
Beverly Clark
ISBN-13: 978-1-58571-279-3
ISBN-10: 1-58571-279-5
$6.99

Again My Love
Kayla Perrin
ISBN-13: 978-1-58571-280-9
ISBN-10: 1-58571-280-9
$6.99

December

Office Policy
A.C. Arthur
ISBN-13: 978-1-58571-281-6
ISBN-10: 1-58571-281-7
$6.99

Rendezvous With Fate
Jeanne Sumerix
ISBN-13: 978-1-58571-283-3
ISBN-10: 1-58571-283-3
$6.99

2008 New Mass Market Titles

January

Where I Want To Be
Maryam Diaab
ISBN-13: 978-1-58571-268-7
ISBN-10: 1-58571-268-X
$6.99

Never Say Never
Michele Cameron
ISBN-13: 978-1-58571-269-4
ISBN-10: 1-58571-269-8
$6.99

February

Stolen Memories
Michele Sudler
ISBN-13: 978-1-58571-270-0
ISBN-10: 1-58571-270-1
$6.99

Dawn's Harbor
Kymberly Hunt
ISBN-13: 978-1-58571-271-7
ISBN-10: 1-58571-271-X
$6.99

March

Undying Love
Renee Alexis
ISBN-13: 978-1-58571-272-4
ISBN-10: 1-58571-272-8
$6.99

Blame It On Paradise
Crystal Hubbard
ISBN-13: 978-1-58571-273-1
ISBN-10: 1-58571-273-6
$6.99

April

When A Man Loves A Woman
La Connie Taylor-Jones
ISBN-13: 978-1-58571-274-8
ISBN-10: 1-58571-274-4
$6.99

Choices
Tammy Williams
ISBN-13: 978-1-58571-300-4
ISBN-10: 1-58571-300-7
$6.99

May

Dream Runner
Gail McFarland
ISBN-13: 978-1-58571-317-2
ISBN-10: 1-58571-317-1
$6.99

Southern Fried Standards
S.R. Maddox
ISBN-13: 978-1-58571-318-9
ISBN-10: 1-58571-318-X
$6.99

June

Looking for Lily
Africa Fine
ISBN-13: 978-1-58571-319-6
ISBN-10: 1-58571-319-8
$6.99

Bliss, Inc.
Chamein Canton
ISBN-13: 978-1-58571-325-7
ISBN-10: 1-58571-325-2
$6.99

2008 New Mass Market Titles (continued)

July

Love's Secrets
Yolanda McVey
ISBN-13: 978-1-58571-321-9
ISBN-10: 1-58571-321-X
$6.99

Things Forbidden
Maryam Diaab
ISBN-13: 978-1-58571-327-1
ISBN-10: 1-58571-327-9
$6.99

August

Storm
Pamela Leigh Starr
ISBN-13: 978-1-58571-323-3
ISBN-10: 1-58571-323-6
$6.99

Passion's Furies
AlTonya Washington
ISBN-13: 978-1-58571-324-0
ISBN-10: 1-58571-324-4
$6.99

September

Three Doors Down
Michele Sudler
ISBN-13: 978-1-58571-332-5
ISBN-10: 1-58571-332-5
$6.99

Mr Fix-It
Crystal Hubbard
ISBN-13: 978-1-58571-326-4
ISBN-10: 1-58571-326-0
$6.99

October

Moments of Clarity
Michele Cameron
ISBN-13: 978-1-58571-330-1
ISBN-10: 1-58571-330-9
$6.99

Lady Preacher
K.T. Richey
ISBN-13: 978-1-58571-333-2
ISBN-10: 1-58571-333-3
$6.99

November

This Life Isn't Perfect Holla
Sandra Foy
ISBN: 978-1-58571-331-8
ISBN-10: 1-58571-331-7
$6.99

Promises Made
Bernice Layton
ISBN-13: 978-1-58571-334-9
ISBN-10: 1-58571-334-1
$6.99

December

A Voice Behind Thunder
Carrie Elizabeth Greene
ISBN-13: 978-1-58571-329-5
ISBN-10: 1-58571-329-5
$6.99

The More Things Change
Chamein Canton
ISBN-13: 978-1-58571-328-8
ISBN-10: 1-58571-328-7
$6.99

Other Genesis Press, Inc. Titles

A Dangerous Deception	J.M. Jeffries	$8.95
A Dangerous Love	J.M. Jeffries	$8.95
A Dangerous Obsession	J.M. Jeffries	$8.95
A Dangerous Woman	J.M. Jeffries	$9.95
A Dead Man Speaks	Lisa Jones Johnson	$12.95
A Drummer's Beat to Mend	Kei Swanson	$9.95
A Happy Life	Charlotte Harris	$9.95
A Heart's Awakening	Veronica Parker	$9.95
A Lark on the Wing	Phyliss Hamilton	$9.95
A Love of Her Own	Cheris F. Hodges	$9.95
A Love to Cherish	Beverly Clark	$8.95
A Lover's Legacy	Veronica Parker	$9.95
A Pefect Place to Pray	I.L. Goodwin	$12.95
A Risk of Rain	Dar Tomlinson	$8.95
A Twist of Fate	Beverly Clark	$8.95
A Will to Love	Angie Daniels	$9.95
Acquisitions	Kimberley White	$8.95
Across	Carol Payne	$12.95
After the Vows	Leslie Esdaile	$10.95
(Summer Anthology)	T.T. Henderson	
	Jacqueline Thomas	
Again My Love	Kayla Perrin	$10.95
Against the Wind	Gwynne Forster	$8.95
All I Ask	Barbara Keaton	$8.95
Ambrosia	T.T. Henderson	$8.95
An Unfinished Love Affair	Barbara Keaton	$8.95
And Then Came You	Dorothy Elizabeth Love	$8.95
Angel's Paradise	Janice Angelique	$9.95
At Last	Lisa G. Riley	$8.95
Best of Friends	Natalie Dunbar	$8.95
Between Tears	Pamela Ridley	$12.95
Beyond the Rapture	Beverly Clark	$9.95
Blaze	Barbara Keaton	$9.95

Other Genesis Press, Inc. Titles (continued)

Blood Lust	J. M. Jeffries	$9.95
Bodyguard	Andrea Jackson	$9.95
Boss of Me	Diana Nyad	$8.95
Bound by Love	Beverly Clark	$8.95
Breeze	Robin Hampton Allen	$10.95
Broken	Dar Tomlinson	$24.95
The Business of Love	Cheris Hodges	$9.95
By Design	Barbara Keaton	$8.95
Cajun Heat	Charlene Berry	$8.95
Careless Whispers	Rochelle Alers	$8.95
Cats & Other Tales	Marilyn Wagner	$8.95
Caught in a Trap	Andre Michelle	$8.95
Caught Up In the Rapture	Lisa G. Riley	$9.95
Cautious Heart	Cheris F Hodges	$8.95
Caught Up	Deatri King Bey	$12.95
Chances	Pamela Leigh Starr	$8.95
Cherish the Flame	Beverly Clark	$8.95
Class Reunion	Irma Jenkins/John Brown	$12.95
Code Name: Diva	J.M. Jeffries	$9.95
Conquering Dr. Wexler's Heart	Kimberley White	$9.95
Cricket's Serenade	Carolita Blythe	$12.95
Crossing Paths, Tempting Memories	Dorothy Elizabeth Love	$9.95
Cupid	Barbara Keaton	$9.95
Cypress Whisperings	Phyllis Hamilton	$8.95
Dark Embrace	Crystal Wilson Harris	$8.95
Dark Storm Rising	Chinelu Moore	$10.95
Daughter of the Wind	Joan Xian	$8.95
Deadly Sacrifice	Jack Kean	$22.95
Designer Passion	Dar Tomlinson	$8.95
Dreamtective	Liz Swados	$5.95
Ebony Butterfly II	Delilah Dawson	$14.95
Ebony Eyes	Kei Swanson	$9.95

Other Genesis Press, Inc. Titles (continued)

Echoes of Yesterday	Beverly Clark	$9.95
Eden's Garden	Elizabeth Rose	$8.95
Enchanted Desire	Wanda Y. Thomas	$9.95
Everlastin' Love	Gay G. Gunn	$8.95
Everlasting Moments	Dorothy Elizabeth Love	$8.95
Everything and More	Sinclair Lebeau	$8.95
Everything but Love	Natalie Dunbar	$8.95
Eve's Prescription	Edwina Martin Arnold	$8.95
Falling	Natalie Dunbar	$9.95
Fate	Pamela Leigh Starr	$8.95
Finding Isabella	A.J. Garrotto	$8.95
Forbidden Quest	Dar Tomlinson	$10.95
Forever Love	Wanda Thomas	$8.95
From the Ashes	Kathleen Suzanne	$8.95
	Jeanne Sumerix	
Gentle Yearning	Rochelle Alers	$10.95
Glory of Love	Sinclair LeBeau	$10.95
Go Gentle into that Good Night	Malcom Boyd	$12.95
Goldengroove	Mary Beth Craft	$16.95
Groove, Bang, and Jive	Steve Cannon	$8.99
Hand in Glove	Andrea Jackson	$9.95
Hard to Love	Kimberley White	$9.95
Hart & Soul	Angie Daniels	$8.95
Havana Sunrise	Kymberly Hunt	$9.95
Heartbeat	Stephanie Bedwell-Grime	$8.95
Hearts Remember	M. Loui Quezada	$8.95
Hidden Memories	Robin Allen	$10.95
Higher Ground	Leah Latimer	$19.95
Hitler, the War, and the Pope	Ronald Rychiak	$26.95
How to Write a Romance	Kathryn Falk	$18.95
I Married a Reclining Chair	Lisa M. Fuhs	$8.95
I'm Gonna Make You Love Me	Gwyneth Bolton	$9.95
Indigo After Dark Vol. I	Nia Dixon/Angelique	$10.95

Other Genesis Press, Inc. Titles (continued)

Indigo After Dark Vol. II	Dolores Bundy/Cole Riley	$10.95
Indigo After Dark Vol. III	Montana Blue/Coco Morena	$10.95
Indigo After Dark Vol. IV	Cassandra Colt/ Diana Richeaux	$14.95
Indigo After Dark Vol. V	Delilah Dawson	$14.95
Icie	Pamela Leigh Starr	$8.95
I'll Be Your Shelter	Giselle Carmichael	$8.95
I'll Paint a Sun	A.J. Garrotto	$9.95
Illusions	Pamela Leigh Starr	$8.95
Indiscretions	Donna Hill	$8.95
Intentional Mistakes	Michele Sudler	$9.95
Interlude	Donna Hill	$8.95
Intimate Intentions	Angie Daniels	$8.95
Ironic	Pamela Leigh Starr	$9.95
Jolie's Surrender	Edwina Martin-Arnold	$8.95
Kiss or Keep	Debra Phillips	$8.95
Lace	Giselle Carmichael	$9.95
Last Train to Memphis	Elsa Cook	$12.95
Lasting Valor	Ken Olsen	$24.95
Let's Get It On	Dyanne Davis	$9.95
Let Us Prey	Hunter Lundy	$25.95
Life Is Never As It Seems	J.J. Michael	$12.95
Lighter Shade of Brown	Vicki Andrews	$8.95
Love Always	Mildred E. Riley	$10.95
Love Doesn't Come Easy	Charlyne Dickerson	$8.95
Love in High Gear	Charlotte Roy	$9.95
Love Lasts Forever	Dominiqua Douglas	$9.95
Love Me Carefully	A.C. Arthur	$9.95
Love Unveiled	Gloria Greene	$10.95
Love's Deception	Charlene Berry	$10.95
Love's Destiny	M. Loui Quezada	$8.95
Mae's Promise	Melody Walcott	$8.95
Magnolia Sunset	Giselle Carmichael	$8.95

Other Genesis Press, Inc. Titles (continued)

Matters of Life and Death	Lesego Malepe, Ph.D.	$15.95
Meant to Be	Jeanne Sumerix	$8.95
Midnight Clear (Anthology)	Leslie Esdaile	$10.95
	Gwynne Forster	
	Carmen Green	
	Monica Jackson	
Midnight Magic	Gwynne Forster	$8.95
Midnight Peril	Vicki Andrews	$10.95
Misconceptions	Pamela Leigh Starr	$9.95
Misty Blue	Dyanne Davis	$9.95
Montgomery's Children	Richard Perry	$14.95
My Buffalo Soldier	Barbara B. K. Reeves	$8.95
Naked Soul	Gwynne Forster	$8.95
Next to Last Chance	Louisa Dixon	$24.95
Nights Over Egypt	Barbara Keaton	$9.95
No Apologies	Seressia Glass	$8.95
No Commitment Required	Seressia Glass	$8.95
No Ordinary Love	Angela Weaver	$9.95
No Regrets	Mildred E. Riley	$8.95
Notes When Summer Ends	Beverly Lauderdale	$12.95
Nowhere to Run	Gay G. Gunn	$10.95
O Bed! O Breakfast!	Rob Kuehnle	$14.95
Object of His Desire	A. C. Arthur	$8.95
Office Policy	A. C. Arthur	$9.95
Once in a Blue Moon	Dorianne Cole	$9.95
One Day at a Time	Bella McFarland	$8.95
Only You	Crystal Hubbard	$9.95
Outside Chance	Louisa Dixon	$24.95
Passion	T.T. Henderson	$10.95
Passion's Blood	Cherif Fortin	$22.95
Passion's Journey	Wanda Thomas	$8.95
Past Promises	Jahmel West	$8.95
Path of Fire	T.T. Henderson	$8.95

Other Genesis Press, Inc. Titles (continued)

Path of Thorns	Annetta P. Lee	$9.95
Peace Be Still	Colette Haywood	$12.95
Picture Perfect	Reon Carter	$8.95
Playing for Keeps	Stephanie Salinas	$8.95
Pride & Joi	Gay G. Gunn	$8.95
Promises to Keep	Alicia Wiggins	$8.95
Quiet Storm	Donna Hill	$10.95
Reckless Surrender	Rochelle Alers	$6.95
Red Polka Dot in a World of Plaid	Varian Johnson	$12.95
Rehoboth Road	Anita Ballard-Jones	$12.95
Reluctant Captive	Joyce Jackson	$8.95
Rendezvous with Fate	Jeanne Sumerix	$8.95
Revelations	Cheris F. Hodges	$8.95
Rise of the Phoenix	Kenneth Whetstone	$12.95
Rivers of the Soul	Leslie Esdaile	$8.95
Rock Star	Rosyln Hardy Holcomb	$9.95
Rocky Mountain Romance	Kathleen Suzanne	$8.95
Rooms of the Heart	Donna Hill	$8.95
Rough on Rats and Tough on Cats	Chris Parker	$12.95
Scent of Rain	Annetta P. Lee	$9.95
Second Chances at Love	Cheris Hodges	$9.95
Secret Library Vol. 1	Nina Sheridan	$18.95
Secret Library Vol. 2	Cassandra Colt	$8.95
Shades of Brown	Denise Becker	$8.95
Shades of Desire	Monica White	$8.95
Shadows in the Moonlight	Jeanne Sumerix	$8.95
Sin	Crystal Rhodes	$8.95
Sin and Surrender	J.M. Jeffries	$9.95
Sinful Intentions	Crystal Rhodes	$12.95
So Amazing	Sinclair LeBeau	$8.95
Somebody's Someone	Sinclair LeBeau	$8.95

Other Genesis Press, Inc. Titles (continued)

Someone to Love	Alicia Wiggins	$8.95
Song in the Park	Martin Brant	$15.95
Soul Eyes	Wayne L. Wilson	$12.95
Soul to Soul	Donna Hill	$8.95
Southern Comfort	J.M. Jeffries	$8.95
Still the Storm	Sharon Robinson	$8.95
Still Waters Run Deep	Leslie Esdaile	$8.95
Stories to Excite You	Anna Forrest/Divine	$14.95
Subtle Secrets	Wanda Y. Thomas	$8.95
Suddenly You	Crystal Hubbard	$9.95
Sweet Repercussions	Kimberley White	$9.95
Sweet Tomorrows	Kimberly White	$8.95
Taken by You	Dorothy Elizabeth Love	$9.95
Tattooed Tears	T. T. Henderson	$8.95
The Color Line	Lizzette Grayson Carter	$9.95
The Color of Trouble	Dyanne Davis	$8.95
The Disappearance of Allison Jones	Kayla Perrin	$5.95
The Honey Dipper's Legacy	Pannell-Allen	$14.95
The Joker's Love Tune	Sidney Rickman	$15.95
The Little Pretender	Barbara Cartland	$10.95
The Love We Had	Natalie Dunbar	$8.95
The Man Who Could Fly	Bob & Milana Beamon	$18.95
The Missing Link	Charlyne Dickerson	$8.95
The Price of Love	Sinclair LeBeau	$8.95
The Smoking Life	Ilene Barth	$29.95
The Words of the Pitcher	Kei Swanson	$8.95
Three Wishes	Seressia Glass	$8.95
Through the Fire	Seressia Glass	$9.95
Ties That Bind	Kathleen Suzanne	$8.95
Tiger Woods	Libby Hughes	$5.95
Time is of the Essence	Angie Daniels	$9.95
Timeless Devotion	Bella McFarland	$9.95
Tomorrow's Promise	Leslie Esdaile	$8.95

NEVER SAY NEVER

Truly Inseparable	Wanda Y. Thomas	$8.95
Unbreak My Heart	Dar Tomlinson	$8.95
Uncommon Prayer	Kenneth Swanson	$9.95
Unconditional	A.C. Arthur	$9.95
Unconditional Love	Alicia Wiggins	$8.95
Under the Cherry Moon	Christal Jordan-Mims	$12.95
Unearthing Passions	Elaine Sims	$9.95
Until Death Do Us Part	Susan Paul	$8.95
Vows of Passion	Bella McFarland	$9.95
Wedding Gown	Dyanne Davis	$8.95
What's Under Benjamin's Bed	Sandra Schaffer	$8.95
When Dreams Float	Dorothy Elizabeth Love	$8.95
Whispers in the Night	Dorothy Elizabeth Love	$8.95
Whispers in the Sand	LaFlorya Gauthier	$10.95
Wild Ravens	Altonya Washington	$9.95
Yesterday Is Gone	Beverly Clark	$10.95
Yesterday's Dreams, Tomorrow's Promises	Reon Laudat	$8.95
Your Precious Love	Sinclair LeBeau	$8.95

Order Form

Mail to: Genesis Press, Inc.
P.O. Box 101
Columbus, MS 39703

Name _____

Address _____

City/State _____ Zip _____

Telephone _____

Ship to (if different from above)

Name _____

Address _____

City/State _____ Zip _____

Telephone _____

Credit Card Information

Credit Card # _____ ☐ Visa ☐ Mastercard

Expiration Date (mm/yy) _____ ☐ AmEx ☐ Discover

Qty.	Author	Title	Price	Total

Use this order form, or call 1-888-INDIGO-1	
Total for books	_____
Shipping and handling: $5 first two books, $1 each additional book	_____
Total S & H	_____
Total amount enclosed	_____

Mississippi residents add 7% sales tax